My
Latest Grievance

ELINOR LIPMAN

First published in Great Britain in 2006
by HEADLINE REVIEW
An imprint of HEADLINE PUBLISHING GROUP

First published in paperback in 2007 by
HEADLINE REVIEW
An imprint of HEADLINE PUBLISHING GROUP

1

Cataloguing in Publication Data is available from the British Library

ISBN 978 0 7553 2942 7

Typeset in Garamond by Avon DataSet Ltd,
Bidford-on-Avon, Warwickshire

Printed and bound in Great Britain by
Clays Ltd, St Ives plc

HEADLINE PUBLISHING GROUP
A division of Hachette Livre UK Ltd
338 Euston Road
London NW1 3BH

www.reviewbooks.co.uk
www.hodderheadline.com

Elinor Lipman's sharp, funny, life-enhancing fiction is loved by readers everywhere, and by writers as varied as Anita Shreve and Nigella Lawson, Maggie O'Farrell and Carol Shields. Four of her novels are currently in development as feature films, and include *Then She Found Me*, *The Inn at Lake Devine*, *Isabel's Bed* and *The Way Men Act*. She divides her time between Massachusetts and New York City.

More praise for *My Latest Grievance*:

'Just occasionally you come across a writer whose sentences are so perfect, you want to swill them around in your mouth as you read, just to savour their deliciousness. Elinor Lipman is just such a writer. When you read a book you love, you both want to gallop through it and yet never finish it . . . Lipman has been described as a latter-day Jane Austen – I'd go along with that' Nigella Lawson

'Her writing is sophisticated, her critique of the academic world in the 1970s in which the novel is set sharp, her characters funny . . . Terrific' *Sunday Telegraph*

'Any book by Elinor Lipman is sure to be a real treat thanks to her snappy, witty dialogue and sparky observation . . . Sophisticated and stylish reading' *Daily Mail*

'A satirical but heart-warming family portrait' *Daily Express*

'No one balances seriousness and hilarity better than Elinor Lipman . . . Add *My Latest Grievance* to the list of her excellent works. It's a heartfelt story filled with people you'll be thinking about long after you turn the last page . . . *My Latest Grievance* is joyfully witty; this is not-to-be-missed reading' *Bookpage*

'Lipman has created a novel of warmth, wisdom, love and redemption that is funny and fun to read . . . Moments to cherish and characters to adore' *Booklist*

'Lipman's writing is warm, wise and often hilarious' *The Times*

'Full of pathos, wit and love' *Psychologies*

'As wise as Solomon and as funny as early Joan Rivers' Maureen Lipman, *Guardian*

'Frederica Hatch, the articulate, curious, and naïve narrator of Lipman's eighth novel, proves the perfect vehicle for this satiric yet compassionate family portrait' *Publisher's Weekly*

'Pure pleasure' *Woman & Home*

'Lipman is the kind of novelist you want to tell all your friends about' *The Times*

'A new novel from Elinor Lipman, one of America's finest writers, is always a treat' *Red*

'Winningly wry and dry-eyed . . . Funny, moving and very wise in the ways of life' *Kirkus Reviews*

To the memory of my parents

1

The Perfect Child

I WAS RAISED in a brick dormitory at Dewing College, formerly the Mary-Ruth Dewing Academy, a finishing school best known for turning out attractive secretaries who married up.

In the late 1950s, Dewing began granting baccalaureate degrees to the second-rate students it continued to attract despite its expansion into intellectual terrain beyond typing and shorthand. The social arts metamorphosed into sociology and psychology, nicely fitting the respective fields of job seekers Aviva Ginsburg Hatch, Ph.D., my mother, and David Hatch, Ph.D., my father. Twin appointments had been unavailable at the hundred more prestigious institutions they aspired and applied to. They arrived in Brookline, Massachusetts, in 1960, not thrilled with the Dewing wages or benefits, but ever hopeful and prone to negotiation – two bleeding hearts that beat as one, conjoined since their first date in 1955 upon viewing a Movietone newsreel of Rosa Parks's arrest.

Were they types, my parents-to-be? From a distance, and even to me for a long time, it appeared to be so. Over coffee in grad school they'd found that each had watched every black-and-white televised moment of the Army-McCarthy hearings, had both written passionately on *The Grapes of Wrath* in high school; both held Samuel Gompers and Pete Seeger in high esteem; both owned albums by the Weavers. Their wedding invitations, stamped with a union bug, asked that guests make donations in lieu of gifts to the presidential campaign of Adlai Stevenson.

It was my father who proposed that their stable marriage and professional sensitivities would lend themselves to the rent-free benefit known as houseparenting. The dean of residential life said she was sorry, but a married couple was out of the question: parents would *not* like a man living among their nubile daughters.

'What about a man with a baby?' my father replied coyly. It was a premature announcement. My mother's period must have been no more than a week late at the time of that spring interview, but they both felt ethically bound to share the details of her menstrual calendar. He posited further: weren't two responsible, vibrant parents with relevant Ph.D.s better than their no doubt competent but often elderly predecessors, who – with all due respect – weren't such a great help with homework and tended to die on the job? David and Aviva inaugurated their long line of labor-management imbroglios by defending my right to live and wail within the 3.5 rooms of their would-be apartment. If given the chance, they'd handle everything; they'd address potential doubts and fears head-on in a letter they'd send to parents and guardians of incoming

Mary-Ruths, as we called the students, introducing themselves, offering their phone number, their curricula vitae, their open door, and their projected vision of nuclear familyhood.

The nervous dean gave the professors Hatch a one-year trial; after all, an infant in a dorm might disrupt residential life in ways no one could even project, prepartum. And consider the mumps, measles, and chicken pox a child would spread to the still susceptible and non-immunized.

On the first day of freshman orientation, three months pregnant, my mother greeted parents wearing maternity clothes over her flat abdomen, an unspoken announcement that most greeted with pats and coos of delight. Mothers testified to their daughters' babysitting talents. My father demurred nobly. 'We'd *never* want to take any one of our girls away from their studies,' he said.

When I was born in February 1961, it was to instant campus celebrity. It didn't matter that I was bald and scaly, quite homely if the earliest Polaroids tell the story. Photo album number one opens *not* with baby Frederica in the delivery room or in the arms of a relative, but with me – age ten days – in a group photo of the entire 1960–61 population of Griggs Hall. A competent girl with a dark flip and a wide headband, most likely a senior, is holding me up to the camera. My eyes are closed and I seem to be in the wind-up for a howl. My mother stands in the back row, a little apart from the girls, but smiling so fondly at the camera that I know my father was behind it.

David Hatch would be a role model before the phrase was on the tip of every talk show hostess's tongue. He paraded me in the big English perambulator, a joint gift from the psych. and soc. departments, along the ribbons of sidewalk that crisscrossed the smallish residential campus, or carried me against his chest in a homemade sling, which my mother modeled on cloths observed during her fieldwork in a primitive agrarian society. In public, at the dining hall, he spooned me baby food from jars, alternating with my mother – she nursed, he fed – causing quite the stir those many decades ago. He was a man ahead of his time, and the adolescents – his grad school concentration – noticed. My mother predicted that Dewing grads, especially Griggs alums, would blame us when their future husbands didn't stack up to Professor-Housefather Hatch, the most equal of partners.

We lived our fishbowl lives in three and a half wallpapered rooms furnished with overstuffed chairs and antique Persian rugs, the legacy of a predecessor who had died intestate. We had a beige half kitchen with a two-burner stove, a pink-tiled bathroom, a fake fireplace, and a baby grand piano, which the college tuned annually at its own expense, presumably in the name of sing-alongs and caroling. The nursery was a converted utility closet with a crib, later a cot. When I was seven, my parents petitioned the college to enlarge our quarters by incorporating a portion of Griggs Hall's living room into our apartment. Noting my birth date, they asked the college to consider fashioning Miss Frederica Hatch, the unofficial mascot of Griggs Hall, a real bedroom; it was, after all, her sabbatical year.

The board of trustees said yes to the renovation. Griggs Hall had become the most popular dorm on campus, despite its architectural blandness and its broken dryers. The Hatch family had worked out beautifully; more married couples had become dorm parents. Some had babies, surely for their own reasons, but also after I was a proven draw. When I went to college in the late 1970s, to a bucolic campus where dogs attended classes with their professor-masters, I noted that these chocolate labs and golden retrievers were the objects of great student affection, supplying something that was missing for the homesick and the lovesick. The dogs reminded me of me.

I was a reasonable and polite child, if not one thoroughly conscious of her own model-childness. Because I needed to be the center of attention – the only state I'd ever known – I developed modest tricks that put me in the spotlight without having to sing or tap-dance or raise my voice: I ate beets, Brussels sprouts, and calf's liver. I drank white milk, spurning the chocolate that was offered. I carried a book at all times, usually something recognized by these C-plus students as hard, literary, advanced for my years. I drew quietly with colored pencils during dorm meetings. I mastered the poker face when it came to tasting oddball salad-bar combinations (cottage cheese and ketchup, peanut butter on romaine) favored by adolescent girls so that I'd appear worldly and adventurous.

Over the years, certain objects and rituals became synonymous with me: the wicker basket with its gingham lining in which the infant me attended classes; a ragged blanket that my psychologically astute parents let me drag everywhere until it dissolved; the lone swing that my father hung from the sturdiest red maple on campus; first a pink tricycle, then a pink two-wheeler, its handlebars sprouting streamers, which I garaged on the porch of Griggs Hall, no lock needed.

I didn't exactly raise myself, especially with five floors of honorary sisters living above me at all times. But there was the omnipresent ID card around my neck granting me entrance to all buildings and all meals, with or without a parent. Aviva and David were busy with their classes, their advisees, and increasingly their causes. Assassinations at home and wars abroad necessitated their boarding buses for marches in capital cities, but babysitters were plentiful. I was safe at Dewing, always, and good with strangers. Tall, spiked wrought-iron fencing surrounded our sixteen acres, a relic from the days of curfews and virginity.

Between seventh and eighth grade, I grew tall; incoming freshmen took me for a baby-faced classmate, which was to me a distressing development. I had no intention of blending in. I wanted to be who I'd become, the Eloise of Dewing College, an institution that others, transients, occupied only fleetingly.

Looking back today from adulthood, it's too easy to idealize my childhood in an exurban Brigadoon, Boston skyline in the distance and, for the most part, kind girls in every chair. We hoped Dewing could get better, its standards higher, its students brighter, its admission competitive, but it wasn't to be. Smart candidates would soon attend schools that accepted men and boasted hockey rinks. Housemothers came and went throughout my Dewing years. There was less intra-houseparent socializing than one would expect, given the geography of our lives. The older ladies, some carryovers from the secretarial training days, wore – or so it seemed to me – perpetual scowls. They couldn't hide their disapproval of modern Mary-Ruths in blue jeans, of their unstockinged legs, their gentlemen callers, their birth control prescriptions. Where were the debutantes of old? The girls who wore fraternity pins on their pastel sweaters and foundation garments beneath them?

My outside friends saw my home as the whole of Griggs Hall and beyond, its acres of campus lawn and flowering trees, vending machines on every floor, cool and pretty girls whose perfumed copies of *Glamour*, *Mademoiselle*, and *Vogue* beckoned from open mailboxes for hours before they were retrieved. They envied my long reign as the charter mascot. Often I came to school with my hair braided and adorned in intricate ways, courtesy of a team of boarders who preferred hairdressing to homework.

Eventually everyone, even my unconventional and high-profile mother (union grievance chairperson, agitator, perennial professor of the year, and public breast-feeder), faded to gray in the archives of Dewing houseparenting. When I was sixteen, the college hired the enthralling and once glamorous Laura Lee French, most recently of Manhattan, maybe forty, maybe more, to pilot Ada Tibbets Hall, the artistic and wayward girls' dorm next to Griggs. The timing was excellent: I was growing invisible by then, a teenager rather than a pet, despite the darling Halloween photos of me in every yearbook printed since my birth. Just as I was craving more attention, along came Laura Lee, dorm mother without a day job, single, childless, and ultimately famous within our gates.

We overlapped for two years. It was awkward even for my parents, unembarrassable progressives though they were. Fearing scandal and campus glee, we four kept our secret: that Laura Lee French, in the distant past, had been married to my father.

2

The Pearls

TO FILL YOU IN: a year before Laura Lee arrived to disturb the peace at Dewing, I found out that my mild-mannered and not especially good-looking father had been married before. I shouldn't have found out the way I did – snooping around my grandmother's house – or at the advanced age of fifteen, especially since my parents were famous for telling me more than I wanted to know. Suddenly, the huge presence that was my mother was demoted to the status of second wife. The evidence I unearthed in a bottom drawer of what had been my father's childhood bedroom and shrine (still displaying his Erector-set projects, his stamp collection, and a map of the forty-eight United States) was a framed wedding photo of a young, bow-tied David Hatch and a stranger-bride. I waited for an opportunity to detonate this connubial bomb at home, perhaps to trade it for something tangible – a sweet-sixteen party or a ten-speed bike – to offset my indignation at being kept in the dark.

I calculated too long: the truth trumped me at Christmas, in the form of a note from a Laura Lee French, saying she hoped I would think of her as my pre-stepmother and further hoped I would accept the enclosed in anticipation of – if she'd gotten her year right – a very important birthday. Swathed in lavender tissue paper was a rope of pearls, flapper-length and aged to ivory. The note read, 'A family heirloom (genuine, not cultured) with sincere best wishes for a sweet sixteen.'

My unbejeweled mother insisted I return the necklace to its sender. When I did, with a regretful note, hinting that the rebuff was not altogether my idea, the present bounced back. This time Laura Lee wrote that she had read between the lines and determined that I did want these pearls, which would undoubtedly come into fashion again. If she was wrong, and I truly did not want to accept the gift, I should save them for the daughter I might have someday. She wrote a separate note to my father, which I begged to see in the name of full disclosure and family frankness. Laura Lee wrote that she had never had children and never would, had finally forgiven him, and, though it was an illogical and, according to my mother, pathologically altruistic position, she considered me the daughter she never had.

My parents were reasonable people, proud of their up-to-the-minute and public practice of child-rearing. At a remote table in the dining hall, in a rare assembly of all three busy Hatches, and, still rarer, displaying a ballpointed sign on lined paper that said, 'Privacy, please,' we discussed Laura Lee's note. Did I think it was right to accept an expensive present from a total stranger?

9

'She's not a stranger to you,' I said. 'And certainly not to Dad.'

'Are you angry that you haven't known about her all along?' my father asked.

I said, 'I've known for longer than you think.'

'How long?' asked my mother.

I picked up my last cookie and nibbled it in a circular and dilatory fashion before answering. 'Last time I was at Grandma's I saw a photo of Dad wearing a tuxedo and looking about twenty-five, dancing with a woman wearing a wedding dress.'

'And inferred what from that?' asked my father.

'Well, first I inferred that Mom looked much better with blond hair, makeup, and contact lenses. And then I inferred that it wasn't Mom at all.'

'Did you discuss this photograph with your grandmother?' my mother asked.

'She saw me staring at it, and said, "That's your father with Laura Lee." So I had to ask who Laura Lee was, and Grandma said, "A friend." I said, "It's a wedding picture, isn't it?" and she said, "Sort of. Half a wedding picture. All the guests got their photo taken with the bride."'

'But you knew otherwise?' asked my father.

'You didn't look like friends,' I said.

My mother asked how I felt about my grandmother's fabrication.

'I hate that she lied,' my father murmured.

'She could have come to us,' said my mother. 'She could have said, "I'm not comfortable keeping this fact from your daughter. I'd like you to tell her before her next visit."'

'She's always been the queen of unilateral actions,' said my father.

I shrugged. 'Maybe she just liked the photograph. As art. Even if she had to hide it in a bottom drawer when company came.'

'Why do you say that?' asked my mother. 'Why did you call it "art"?'

I said, not as kindly as I could have, 'Because Laura Lee was so pretty.'

'All brides are,' said my father.

'Getting back to the present . . .' said my mother.

'The necklace, she means,' said my father.

'Maybe Laura Lee has a terminal illness,' I said. 'Maybe she wants to give away all of her possessions before she dies so other people don't have to clean out her house.'

My father asked if I knew something they didn't know, perhaps gleaned from my grandmother.

'Are they still in touch?' I asked.

'We wouldn't be surprised,' said my mother.

I said I didn't know anything. Could I be excused for a minute to get another snickerdoodle? Why didn't they call Grandma and ask her what's new with Laura Lee?

My parents exchanged glances that meant, Should I handle this one, or should you? My mother said, 'Your grandmother doesn't believe in divorce.' She stood up, took her cup with her, and walked to the industrial coffee machine.

'Ever?' I asked my father. 'Even if the husband murders the kids? Or has an operation to make him a woman?'

David didn't answer. He watched Aviva en route and smiled

when she returned with a refill for her and a cookie for me. She sat down and asked, 'Where were we?'

'Grandma doesn't believe in divorce,' I said.

'Additionally, she always thought that Laura Lee was a more suitable wife for her son than I.'

'Because . . . ?'

My father volunteered that Laura Lee had certain interests in common with my grandmother, certain values that a woman of Grandma's generation appreciated above intellectual and professional accomplishments.

'Such as?' I asked.

'Clothes, houses . . . things,' said my mother.

I said I was sixteen now, not much younger than Joan of Arc had been when she led the French into battle, and I ought to be able to keep the pearls. I added, 'You ended up with Dad. Maybe Laura Lee has nobody. It's not like she sent me a ticket to a play, and when I get there I'd find out that she's in the next seat, and it was all a plot to kidnap me.'

We then had to parse the emotional nuances of my mother's original reaction. We all agreed that something like jealousy might have motivated my mother. Yes, I did see that jealousy was wrong and petty and beneath her. A string of pearls was only a possession. The most valuable things in life are the intangibles, aren't they? The necklace decision would, accordingly, be mine.

I said that Laura Lee had been wearing pearls in her wedding portrait, so it was totally logical that she'd want to give them away, seeing as how they probably had a bad association.

'She probably has quite a collection of baubles by now,' my mother murmured.

'Aviva,' my father scolded.

'From men?' I asked. 'Is that what you meant? That she's popular?'

Neither answered. Instead, my mother asked my father if the pearls in my possession were the ones Laura Lee had worn at their wedding.

'Dad doesn't notice stuff like that,' I said. 'Dad wouldn't notice if I went to school with a potted plant on my head.'

'I don't remember any pearls,' he said.

Before we adjourned, we decided that each of us would write a note to Laura Lee, stating our respective positions. My father would ask if she needed assistance of any kind. My mother would apologize for the rash return of the family heirloom and enclose a family snapshot of the three of us taken by an obliging waiter on my actual birthday, at the Chinese restaurant closest to campus. Mine would be another thank-you note, polite but brief so as not to build any bridges.

'What's so bad about Laura Lee that I can't even write her a friendly letter?'

'Nothing,' said my father.

'I would think you'd feel sorry for someone who has to pass her jewelry down to a total stranger.'

'Of course we do,' said my father.

'Who divorced who?'

'Whom,' my mother corrected.

'Technically, she divorced me,' my father said.

'Why?'

'Sometimes people marry for the wrong reasons,' said my mother. 'But if they're very lucky, they correct the mistake early, before they have children.'

'There must have been *something* weird,' I said.

My father looked at my mother, a glance I knew well: *Is this the appropriate juncture to speak the truth in that frank and candid way in which we have mutually pledged to raise her?*

She nodded.

'Laura Lee is, in fact, a distant cousin,' my father said quietly.

I found this announcement first startling, then thrilling, with its whiff of incest and elopement. 'Is that legal?' I asked.

My mother said, 'They were several times removed.'

'Distant,' my father repeated. 'Our grandmothers were cousins.'

'Grandmothers?' asked my mother. 'Or was it two great-aunts on different sides of the family? It's so vague.'

I said, 'That makes no sense.'

'That generation wasn't close,' said my father. 'There was a family grudge that had to do with property or placement of a fence. This was well before people started tracing their roots and commissioning family trees.'

'Did you have Thanksgiving dinners together growing up?' I asked.

My father said no. He and Laura Lee didn't meet until after college. In graduate school.

'*Daddy* was in grad school. She was taking dance lessons.'

'What kind?'

'Expensive ones,' said my father. 'Five days a week.'

'Ballet?' I asked. 'Or tap?'

'You're not a baby,' my mother said. 'We've explained everything to you as honestly as we know how. It's not any more complicated than this: your father was married before, briefly. It's worth mentioning that he's been married to me seven times longer than he was married to Laura Lee. Your grandmother was very fond of her, which means absolutely nothing because we all know that your grandmother and I don't always see eye to eye. And, again, there is the mildly embarrassing fact that her son divorced her cousin Bibi's daughter.'

'I was just thinking,' said my father. 'Does this string of pearls have a small blue stone on the whaddyacallit?'

My mother said, 'I didn't notice,' as I answered, 'A sapphire.'

'Now that I think about it, I may have given them to Laura Lee as a wedding present.'

'Whereas I have very little use for that kind of thing,' said my mother.

'I wish you did,' I said. 'You must be the only woman in the world who doesn't even own a jewelry box.'

As soon as I said that, I braced for a condensed lecture from her seminar Private Troubles and Public Issues. Instead she held out her left wrist with a demonstrative jiggle. 'Your father gave me this watch as a wedding gift,' she said. 'I never take it off except when I bathe.'

'It's engraved with our initials and our wedding date on the back,' said my father.

'Are you sure you never had a kid with her?' I asked him.

'Do you really think that your father would have had a child that he didn't see or support?' my mother scolded. 'And are we the kind of people who would hide a half sibling from you?'

'Maybe she had a baby after the divorce and never told you.'

'Now you're being ridiculous and melodramatic,' said my

father. 'Which is exactly why we object to your watching television.'

'You saw her note to David,' said my mother. 'Her point being that she never had children and never would—'

'And I was the daughter she never had?'

'Do you find that romantic?' my mother asked. 'Because I think you're idealizing a total stranger—'

'Did you know her?' I asked.

After a pause, my mother said, 'Not well. Not at all, really. I guess you could say I knew her as a face on campus.'

I said, 'I thought NYU didn't have a campus.'

My mother turned to my father. 'She's resentful because we waited this long to tell her.'

'You never told me. I found out on my own.'

My father said, 'We were waiting for the appropriate juncture, when you could process this without being confused or upset.'

'Like you're the only guy in the world who ever married twice? Like I don't know a million people whose parents got divorced, then married other people? Teena Samuels's parents got divorced and then her mother married the guy from next door, and her father married that guy's ex-wife. Teena was the junior bridesmaid at both of the second weddings.'

'We miscalculated,' said my father. 'We should have said something earlier. You have a perfect right to be angry.'

'I'm not *angry*,' I said. 'I'm curious. What if this necklace arrived, and I didn't ask any questions? You'd worry that I was keeping it all inside, and you'd also be worried that I was lacking in intellectual curiosity.'

That was me speaking directly to their child-rearing

insecurities. I knew they were worried that they had gone amiss somewhere – that I was preoccupied with clothes, houses, frills, and things more than the textbook norm, and definitely more than a National Honor Society hopeful should be.

They asked why I hadn't come to them immediately after my grandmother effectively spilled the beans. Had my feelings been simmering and festering for eight whole weeks?

'You're the experts,' I said. 'What do you think?'

'We think,' said my mother, 'that you know we always do what's best for you. If you didn't demand an explanation eight weeks ago, it was because you trusted us. You thought, Daddy made a mistake a long time ago. Everyone makes mistakes. Some are simply not worth revisiting.'

And although I did need an explanation of the astonishing fact that not one but two women had agreed to marry the unappetizing specimen that was my father, I had a French test to study for and a sitcom to watch. I said yes, sure, I must have trusted them.

3

Room and Bored

MY FATHER, WHO COMMUTED by bike the three-tenths of a mile across campus to his classes, was one of those daft-looking professors who cinched his trouser legs and kept his helmet on until he reached his second-floor office. My mother walked to class, rain or shine, under a wool or plastic poncho, taught in sneakers, eschewed the elevator for the stairs.

It was all fine when I was little. Either or both would walk me to school, singing duets, arms swinging unselfconsciously. I was too young and too secure, walking between them, to notice that they were more peculiar than anyone else's parents.

In sixth grade I started to see the differences. Not everyone's mother painted nipples on her daughter's Barbie doll for the sake of anatomical correctness. And only Aviva had to borrow the rouge and lipstick prescribed for my role as the mayor's wife in *Bye Bye Birdie* because she owned no makeup herself. We had no car, which I had to explain almost daily (subway and buses as needed; every other destination walkable; for vacations, rent a car or borrow one from a relative). It wasn't as easy as having straightforward hippies for parents. Several of my schoolmates had longhaired mothers and fathers in sandals with corduroy feedbags over their shoulders in lieu of briefcases. Mine were a special case: intellectuals who didn't care what people thought about hairstyles, pant lengths, eyeglass fashions, furniture, possessions – with the exception of books – or any other appurtenances that I felt were critical to the outward show of near normality.

I wanted to be cool. I wanted my father to drive a car and wear a suit to work. I wanted my mother to read *Vogue*, color and straighten her gray hair, wear high heels, cut the crusts off my sandwiches. I knew from television that families were supposed to live in houses, to sleep uninterrupted by fire drills or homesick freshmen, and eat by themselves in dining rooms that didn't seat a thousand. Mothers cooked and fathers carved, except when the real-life mother was a sociologist worried about gender stereotyping, and the father agreed with the mother about everything.

And there was the basic yet awful matter of my name, Frederica Hatch, due to the unfortunate coincidence of a maternal grandmother named Frieda, who died six weeks before I was born, and a favorite paternal great-uncle Frederic, who'd been a Freedom Rider at eighty. I asked my parents if they had wanted a boy, and they scoffed at that paternalistic notion. When asked if an accidental boy child would have been Frederic, they said no. It was *Frederica* that they loved. The unlucky boy would have been Julius Frederic after Julius Rosenberg. I was always Frederica inside our house. Did I want to be burdened with a common name? Be the third Lisa and fourth Susan in my classroom? Darlene or Doreen or Maureen?

I did.

Matters were made worse because my best friend, Patsy Leonard, lived in the bosom of my ideal family – a well-balanced lineup of two boys and two girls, miraculously alternating in birth order: Peter, then Patricia, then Paul, then Pammy. Mrs Leonard cooked, baked, volunteered. Mr Leonard managed a men's clothing store, dressed stylishly, played golf. There was a cookie jar on their kitchen counter in the shape of a gingerbread house, and a big glass pitcher, round and perfect, exactly like the one used on television to spell out 'Kool-Aid' in its own condensation. Mrs Leonard wore half aprons and – to the scorn of my mother, who once witnessed the act – applied lipstick and combed her hair just before Mr Leonard came home from work.

I could hear the thinly veiled condescension in my mother's voice when she asked, 'I know they're smart people because you wouldn't spend so much time at the Leonards' if they weren't . . . but do you ever see any member of that family reading a *book*?'

I said of course I did. Mrs Leonard went to the library once a week, like clockwork.

'That's right,' said my mother. 'She's home during the day. She probably has ample time to go to the library.'

'Maybe she's home during the day because they have four times as many kids as we do.'

I wanted a sister. I wanted two brothers, one younger, one older. When I requested a sibling, my mother was succinct and scientific: 'I think you remember that I had a hysterectomy because of fibroids. You were five or six at the time – you stayed with Grandma while I was in the hospital.'

I noted that she might have obliged me before that, in the five or six years between my birth and the operation.

'You're being silly,' she said. 'First, where would we put them? Second, would Daddy and I have been able to read you every single volume of the *Golden Book Encyclopedia* if we had more children to put to bed? And how would your siblings squeeze in practicing the piano within the constraints of the dorm's quiet hours? You're also forgetting how much you dislike babysitting.'

'So?'

'There's a negative correlation between hating babysitting and living with siblings. And let me point out that you seem to have carte blanche, anyway, to run over to enjoy the company of their baby . . . Penny?'

'Pammy. Pamela Christine.'

I reminded her, as I did frequently and defensively, that Mrs Leonard had been the valedictorian of her high school graduating class.

'You think I'm a snob,' my mother said. 'But I can assure you that I don't care one iota where someone's from or what kind of house they live in or what kind of automobile they drive.'

That part was true, as long as the houses and cars weren't too grand, too status-conscious. I'd heard disparaging remarks about the Leonards updating their station wagon every two years and – worse – Mrs Leonard's silver fox-trimmed overcoat.

'Mary-Pat Leonard is a very nice, very earnest woman,' my mother said, 'and a breath of fresh air compared to some of my colleagues. I've never said one word against her. And why in the world would I? They're very hospitable, and I think it's broadening for you to spend time with all kinds of people.'

What I liked best about the Leonards was the very quality that made my mother question the family's collective brains: their ability to find happiness in an excess of Christmas decorations and marathon games of Monopoly. All that it took to gain their friendship was good manners and relative cheerfulness. While I spent a good deal of my own time cultivating a prematurely sardonic view of life, I secretly longed to be what my parents scorned the most – conventional.

What did I truly have to complain about? Nothing that growing up and appreciating my parents' particular brand of quirkiness didn't cure. I wouldn't have lasted long in a noisy Leonard house, two children per bedroom and grace at every meal. Still, at sixteen, the grass was infinitely greener. Mrs Leonard was pretty, young, fun. She, too, had a wedding photograph on her dresser that promised everything I thought a glittering white dress, a lace mantilla, and a smiling groom could deliver.

I had seen in the photograph of Laura Lee French, arm entwined and leaning toward my father in nuptial joy, the suggestion that I'd been born on the wrong side of the divorce, that this was a woman who would be best friends with Mrs Leonard. Together they'd plan the annual block party, exchange recipes, measure each other's hems against yardsticks as coffee perked on the stove.

And even though I knew, logically and genetically, that a child born to my father and Laura Lee would be someone other than me, I couldn't stop imagining the maternal road not taken. My second thank-you note to Laura Lee took on the tone of an autobiography. I filled out a form of my own making, the kind of questionnaire I liked to study in teen magazines: favorite color, favorite TV show, favorite flavor ice cream, favorite poet, favorite Beatle, last book read, dream job, most embarrassing moment, astrological sign, pets, nicknames. I hoped she would take my letter for what it was, an invitation to become my pen pal.

To my great delight and that of Patsy, she sent back an interview with herself, a Q and A, with lots of typos, yet impressing me with the special effects of a black-and-red typewriter ribbon. Her favorite food was something called Chateaubriand. Her favorite non-alcoholic beverage was a root beer float with (when available) French vanilla ice cream. Favorite team: none. Best feature: hair, waist, complexion, bone structure, posture, neck, calves, ankles. Her favorite item of clothing was a pair of black, high-heeled Rockette shoes ('Long story!' she wrote). Favorite proverb: Let bygones be bygones. Goal in life: none, other than happiness. Event or occasion she looked forward to most: meeting Frederica Rebecca Hatch.

4

The First Family

I HAD SOMETHING like a friend on campus, fellow teenager Marietta Woodbury, the rude and fast daughter of our new college president. Each visit to the executive manse was an exercise in my best behavior, self-imposed, because I enjoyed confusing the First Family, forcing them – or so I hoped – to wonder how the rabble-rousing Hatches had fared so well in the daughter department.

We'd met at Dr Woodbury's induction, a grand affair with presidents of most area colleges or their designees marching in academic regalia. The outgoing president was an elderly man, once a professor of theater at Yale, considered benign though increasingly dotty. He never could make the semantic adjustment from 'girls' or 'coeds' to 'women', which was becoming necessary in the 1970s. His chestnut brown toupee was a source of embarrassment to the board of trustees and the butt of campus-wide jokes. His vagueness needed addressing when luncheon condiments began dotting his chin, and pee often spotted his fly after trips to the men's room.

My parents had loved him, mostly because the softest part of his brain was the lobe that processed labor relations. One minute after the National Labor Relations Board declared that faculty were covered by the National Labor Relations Act – forever after celebrated by the Hatch family as a holiday with cake – the Dewing Society of Professors rose from the ashes of an impotent faculty council. Daycare center? Personal days? Eyeglass coverage? Almost everything the newly certified union put on the table sounded reasonable to ex-professor President Mayhew.

Before the next round of negotiations, the college's chief financial officer had replaced his boss with his own management-minded self. Soon the quiet phase of a presidential search began, resulting in H. Eric Woodbury, who came from a small, inferior school in Maryland, just the training ground for Dewing. He passed the wining, dining, and courting of trustees with flying colors. Mrs Woodbury promised to provide what had been absent for a dozen years during the Mayhew term: a First Lady, a hostess, a wifely presence.

Except for my parents, who saw a chill ahead at the bargaining table, all of Dewing was hopeful: Dr Woodbury had degrees from Penn and Columbia, and a slight un-explained limp that gave him the air of an injured soldier returning to civilian life on *Masterpiece Theatre*. I attended his induction in a flame-colored dress of a shiny, man-made material, bought for the occasion after negotiating hotly with my mother over its appropriateness, length, and future wearability.

My first sight of Marietta told me that she was okay: outfitted in a suit that said 'mother's taste', with a hemline that said 'mind of my own'. She had pinned her corsage on top of her shoulder, which struck me as original and rakish.

Spotting a teenage girl, me, at the punch bowl, Mrs Woodbury rushed over. She shook my hand with her gloved one and asked what grade I was in. Would I like to come over to the house once they were settled? That girl over there in navy blue – tall for her age but also in tenth grade – was her baby, Marietta. She didn't make friends very easily but was an interesting and talented young lady. Did I ride?

'Ride what?' I asked.

'Horses?' she asked hopefully.

'Not so far.'

'Perhaps when you go to college,' she murmured. 'Many schools have stables and equestrian programs.'

Before I could say that I'd hate those schools and the girls who came with them, she yoo-hooed, 'Marietta! I have someone who wants to meet you!' The girl's response was slow, defiant, but she did make her way over to us. She was one of those daunting teenage girls who could pass for twenty-five and smoked Virginia Slims. Later I would learn that I'd seen Marietta's best behavior on display, negotiated in advance for a payment equal to a mohair sweater in a color she didn't yet own.

'You at the high school?' Marietta asked.

I said yes, sophomore.

'Boyfriend?'

'Kind of.'

Mrs Woodbury chirped that she'd heard Brookline public schools were excellent. She and Dr Woodbury had decided to give Brookline High School a trial, then evaluate the situation mid-year. 'Marietta's an unconventional learner,' she offered. 'And a little more social than we'd like.'

'You can talk to my parents about it,' I offered. 'They go to every PTO meeting. Well, they alternate so someone's always on dorm duty. You could also talk to the Dewing seniors who student-teach there.'

'That must be creepy,' said Marietta.

I said no, it wasn't. Maybe that was because I'd lived my whole life in a dorm, surrounded—

'Do you meet their boyfriends, too? When they pick the girls up for dates?'

I smiled a smile that I hoped suggested chronic residential social prospecting.

Marietta said, 'My father could have had a job at an all-boys' school, but he took this job instead. Do you believe it?'

'It was a secondary school!' her mother scolded. 'No one accepts the job of headmaster if he can be a college president.'

I knew this was my chance to reel in Mrs Woodbury. Marietta could wait. I was popular at Brookline High, which she'd grasp as soon as she set foot in the cafeteria. I said to Marietta, 'I think you'll change your mind. The whole world is coed.' Then – quoting the catalogue – 'But a woman's college offers a unique environment of support while fostering independence and higher career goals.' I signaled to Marietta that this was public relations, so please bear with me. Her mother put her arm around my waist and squeezed.

'I think we've discovered a treasure,' she cooed. 'Marietta was dreading the move for all kinds of reasons, but here's one we can cross off her list: a new friend.'

Marietta asked, 'Wanna leave?'

'Can't. I have to mingle. Want to come with me? I'll introduce you to a couple of deans over by the hors d'oeuvres.'

'Men deans or women?' Marietta asked.

My parents found it distasteful that Dewing failed to promote from within its own ranks. My mother had wanted the job, had made the first cut – a courtesy extended to all faculty who had applied – but fell off when the list went from long to short. Aviva and David discussed filing a suit based on several brands of discrimination: gender, religious, or union activity.

Counsel for the union dissuaded her after a cursory evaluation of the finalists, all of whom had been presidents or deans somewhere. Aviva's administrative experience had been tested only in the Hatch parlor, where the faculty union executive committee cooked up its various strategies, and her one-semester stint as acting department head in Sociology. Still, it was her nature to feel downtrodden, to bite the hand that fed her, to grieve, protest, picket, sue.

I was slipping, philosophically speaking. Not that I didn't want wrongs to be righted, but I also wanted the freedom to voice my admiration for things material and foolish, and to wear clothes not stitched by the International Ladies Garment Workers Union.

My friendship with the Woodburys worried my parents. Wasn't the president's daughter spoiled? Rides to school and enough footwear to shoe an entire Third World village? 'If her parents spoiled her,' I answered, 'it's their fault, not hers.'

'But don't you find her shallow?' my mother persisted. 'I

don't get any sense from her that she cares about what's happening in the wider world. Do you ever discuss politics? Do you know how her family votes?'

'We're teenagers,' I said. 'Aren't we allowed to be shallow? I'm surrounded by girls' – I gestured to the floors above us – 'who spend more time on the phone than on their homework. Do I have to be a little socialist before I'm even old enough to vote?'

'Who called us socialists?' my mother asked sharply.

'No one.'

'It's not a dirty word,' she said.

'Is it something you heard over at the Woodburys'? Or at the Leonards'?' asked my father.

I said, 'Marietta doesn't know what a socialist is.'

'I meant her parents.'

'Like Dr Woodbury is going to say, "Hi, Frederica. How are your parents the commies?"'

My mother turned to my father. 'See! These associations are coming from somewhere, because she certainly didn't make those leaps from anything she heard in this house.'

'What leaps?' I asked. 'And what house? This is barely an apartment.'

'The leap,' said my father calmly, 'from protected union activity to "commie".'

I said I was exaggerating, trying to get their goat. Okay? We're even. They called Marietta spoiled and shallow, so I called them Reds.

My mother's expression turned tragic. 'But that's our very point: that you would invoke political movements when you need to insult us. It makes me extremely sad.'

29

The colloquialism 'lighten up' had not yet entered common usage, but it would have been exactly the right prescription for Aviva G. Hatch, Ph.D. I said, 'You're *extremely sad*? Some parents have children who shoplift and flunk every test. I consider myself a pretty satisfactory daughter, and you should, too.'

Hugs ensued, as I knew they would. My parents were utterly predictable in all matters emotional. They loved when I lectured them, as long as I sounded psychologically astute and came to a kind conclusion: *Dad, sometimes you agree with Mom just to present a united front, but I don't think your heart's really in it . . . Mom, you think you're being cool when you say 'Hola!' every time you pass a Hispanic student, but it's really dorky. They're Americans. Just say hi.*

I was raising them. The outer Hatches – the professors, union leaders, dorm parents, and non-fashion plates – were famous for their nonconformity and their lefty leadership. Only I knew where the cracks and seams were.

The Woodburys' united front was just as scripted and even more annoying. They were charming in a way I'd been raised to distrust – they called each other 'darling' in public – yet I found myself adopting some of the Woodbury manners just the same. My parents pronounced the Woodburys phonies, a word that sprang to their lips easily and often. Mrs Woodbury's clothes, my mother claimed, broke the rules of anti-vanity and respect for the poor and underdressed: designer, expensive, seasonally fur-trimmed, rarely repeated. 'She must be a very insecure woman if she needs to dress herself up in dollar signs,' my mother said regularly.

'What does that mean?' I asked.

'You haven't noticed that big rock on her finger. She never takes it off.'

I asked, 'Is that how you want me to judge people? By their jewelry and clothes? Isn't that a little superficial?'

She said absolutely not. Well, yes, if you belonged to a teenage clique excluding someone who couldn't afford so-called fashion. But did I not see the difference: money slavishly spent on clothes and jewelry and leather accessories when people were going hungry?

'Where?'

'Right here in Boston!'

I asked, 'Ma? Do you think people would stop starving if Mrs Woodbury stopped shopping?'

'In the big picture, globally speaking, yes.'

It's not that my mother was stupid. Far from it. I'm sure her IQ was in the genius range, although she would dismiss such categorizing as discriminatory, a scam by the testing establishment. Somewhere along the way, she'd narrowed her sympathies to the ideals I was deeply sick of. She had no compassion for the rich, the well-dressed and well-born, the socially glib and the managerial.

Perhaps I was the true egalitarian, or perhaps I was rebelling. Either way, I sensed early in my life that a tolerance for things grander than myself would come in handy later.

5

Cahoots

NOT ENTIRELY UNSELFISHLY, I proposed that my grandmother visit during my school vacation so that I – an only child with working parents, as I liked to remind them – would have company on my upcoming visits to museums and matinees. 'She won't live forever,' I said. 'I'd really like to dedicate this vacation to her just in case she dies soon.' My parents agreed, enfolding me in a group hug as reward for my outreach. Public school vacation didn't overlap with the college's spring break, and they were worried that I would sleep till noon and do nothing constructive. Several months had elapsed since the receipt of the necklace, and, because they were easily distracted by the social sciences and faculty disgruntlements, neither parent suspected that I was playing detective.

My grandmother drove from the Berkshires in what she called 'the truck', actually an ancient Hudson Hornet station wagon with bags of potting soil and bone meal in the back. I took her suitcase while she carried a pie plate holding the same apple-cranberry-raisin concoction I'd made the mistake of complimenting too effusively on my last visit.

'Where are your parents?' she asked as soon as she crossed the threshold.

'At school. We're going to meet them over at Curran for lunch.'

'I've always meant to sit in on one of David's classes,' she said.

'His classes are Tuesday and Thursday. Mom teaches today, though.'

She hesitated. 'Would I enjoy one of hers?'

'Mom would say *absolutely*.'

She raised her eyebrows, which I took as an excellent sign that we'd soon be discussing the relative merits of my father's wives. I crossed the kitchen to the bulletin board, where each parent's schedule was thumbtacked. 'Monday is Social Stratification. Ninety minutes. Starts at one p.m.'

She joined me at the bulletin board. 'I might just have lunch over at the faculty dining room today and go to one of David's classes tomorrow. Methods of Testing and Assessment sounds interesting.'

'*He* thinks so,' I said.

'I wouldn't want to breeze into your mother's seminar unannounced.'

I said I understood completely. Alternatively, we could go to the Museum of Fine Arts, the Isabella Stewart Gardner, the Museum of Science, the glass flowers at Harvard, or the Freedom Trail. But first to settle the all-important question of where she'd sleep.

'Not the guest suite?' she asked, referring to a bed and bath down the hall occasionally used to house a visiting dignitary or generous alumna.

I explained that my room had two brand-new mattresses, whereas the small, north-facing guest room had a mattress that sagged in the middle. How did she feel about that?

'I'm told I snore.'

I said, 'I'm told I sleep like the dead.'

My room was immaculate. I had turned down the corners of each quilt in what I hoped was an inviting and professional-chambermaid fashion. The stuffed animals of my youth had been banished to my closet, except for the pair that had been gifts from her. The centerpiece, though, was my dresser. On its waist-high surface was an artistic arrangement of my colognes, my two lipsticks, my hairbrush and comb, my leatherette manicure set, and – as if that's where one kept one's precious jewels – my pearls, coiled concentrically, their clasp and its sapphire ready for inspection.

'How pretty,' she said, looking everywhere but the bureau. 'Is this yellow a new paint job?'

'Relatively new.'

'What was here before?'

'Beige.' My gaze wandered, helpfully, meaningfully, to the bureau and my precise arrangement of pearls.

'What are you looking at?' my grandmother asked.

She wasn't focusing, which meant I had to abandon subtlety. 'This necklace? Does it look familiar?' I asked.

She finally put her suitcase down and came closer. Before she could answer, I confided, 'Daddy's first wife sent them to me as a birthday present, completely out of the blue.'

She answered rather casually, 'Did she say why?'

I explained that I was the daughter that Laura Lee never had due to the untimely divorce, which apparently was not her idea. 'But you know a lot more about her than I do,' I prompted.

My grandmother picked up the necklace and did what seemed an astonishing thing to me – she put her mouth around a pearl and nibbled it.

'Hey!'

'They're real,' she said. 'I was wondering if she sent you a knock-off.'

'You know they're real from biting into one?'

'Here,' she said. 'Real pearls have a gritty quality. Try it. Picture the grain of sand that started it all.'

'No, thanks,' I said. 'Besides, even if they were a fake, it would have been incredibly nice of her to go to the trouble to make a copy, don't you think?'

'It's got me worried,' said my grandmother. 'I don't think she'd give them away to the daughter of . . . let's just say "her successor".'

'The other woman,' I added.

'How much have they told you?'

I said I knew the big picture but not the small.

My grandmother said, 'I hope you don't keep your valuables lying on the bureau collecting dust.'

I said no, absolutely not.

'And never wear perfume with pearls. The alcohol isn't good for them.'

I swore that I would never wear perfume with pearls. What about toilet water? What about hairspray?

'You're too young for hairspray,' she said.

I needed to steer the conversation away from the care and storage of my necklace to its former owner and to my mother the homewrecker. 'Mom made me mail it back, but then Laura Lee sent it all over again. She wouldn't take no for an answer.'

'It's odd,' said my grandmother. 'But then again, Laura Lee was always something of a free spirit. I'm just a little worried that something's wrong and she's bequeathing these to you.'

'Dad was worried, too . . .' I stopped there, sparing her the theory that Patsy Leonard and I had embraced – that Laura Lee was forever young and immortal in her ex-husband's wistful heart.

'They were my mother's,' she said. 'Your great-grandmother Paulette's. I gave them to David to give to Laura Lee as a wedding present. She must have passed them on to you because she felt they should stay within our family. I find that very honorable. Some people might have sold them under the same circumstances.'

I asked if she and Laura Lee had been in touch lately.

'Christmas cards,' said my grandmother. 'And birthday cards, one-sided, from her to me. She's surprisingly good at remembering dates.'

'But you don't send her a birthday card back?'

My grandmother pursed, then unpursed, her lips. 'Your father asked me not to.'

'Even though she's your relative?'

'It has to do with everyone getting along,' she said. 'Unfortunately, when divorces happen, a mother's loyalty has to remain with her own child. Or at least she should keep up the appearance of loyalty.' She looked toward the door, assessing our privacy. 'Laura Lee was a dear child, very sweet. Something of a naïf, if you know what that means.'

I said I did, of course.

'Someone who doesn't find her way easily through the world. Unworldly. Childlike,' she explained.

'Naïf,' I repeated.

My grandmother said softly, 'I was very fond of her.'

I said, 'I know. Or you wouldn't have kept her picture all these years.'

My grandmother said, 'Maybe I *will* sleep in here. Which bed is yours?'

I thought it was obvious – Raggedy Ann on mine versus Raggedy Andy on the unused twin. 'This one,' I said.

'I get up several times during the night,' she said. 'It might be better if I sleep next to the door.' She turned back toward the bed and her overnight bag.

I said, 'I'm putting the pearls away. I never leave them out for the dust or the kleptomaniacs.'

'I assume you're joking,' said my grandmother. 'And while we're on the subject, I wouldn't wear them to school, where all your friends could see them and later ask to borrow them.'

'I wouldn't wear them now, except for a really special occasion. Like a prom. If someone invited me.'

'Or your wedding,' she said. 'Something old and something blue, if you're familiar with that aphorism.'

'Mom might find that a little creepy,' I said.

'You won't be getting married anytime soon. Maybe your mother will get used to them by then.'

I was about to retire the pearls to their hiding place, but I put them around my neck instead. I thought my grandmother would scold me, misunderstanding the gesture – you're *not* wearing those to the faculty dining room, are you? – but she stared without expressing reservations.

'You're quite taken with the whole idea, aren't you?' she asked.

'They're beautiful,' I said.

'I meant Laura Lee. And your father's other life.'

I sat down on the bed and fiddled with Raggedy Ann's yarny hair. After a long pause I asked, 'How could they not tell me he was married before?'

'I'm sure they had very good, very sound reasons.'

I asked if she'd hung on to their wedding photo all these years, so I'd find it someday.

'Not consciously.'

I posed the daring question I'd been saving up: 'Did you and Laura Lee talk on the phone and decide I was an adult, and that it was high time I knew about my father's secret past?'

'Nonsense,' said my grandmother.

When she didn't bring up Laura Lee or the pearls at lunch, I knew she and I were formally in cahoots. As ever, my parents were distracted by a union problem, which they promised to forget about for at least the next hour.

My grandmother chewed a bite neatly from her egg salad sandwich before asking, 'What are you two protesting these days?'

'Not protesting,' my father said. 'Aviva is our grievance chairperson. We're discussing a complaint that was filed this morning.'

My mother caught me rolling my eyes and gave an abridged version of her why-we-fight speech.

My grandmother asked, 'Doesn't this interfere with your teaching?'

My father said, 'Mother! It's inseparable from our teaching. I know you think it's getting our hands dirty, but we are just as committed to the association as we are to the students. It's in our blood now. We couldn't stop if we wanted to.'

'I didn't raise you to be a rabble-rouser,' she said.

My mother laughed.

'I don't see that it helps your careers any,' added my grandmother.

'Neither one wants to be a department chair,' I volunteered. 'Too much paperwork and not enough time in the classroom.'

'I see,' said my grandmother, which seemed to mean, You've brainwashed my only grandchild.

'Frederica has been planning every minute of your week together,' said my father. 'It's a side of her we don't see very often – the detail person – but we love knowing she has the fundamental tools.'

'What have you two done so far this morning?' asked my mother.

My grandmother said, 'I settled in. Frederica found a spot in the refrigerator for my pie. And we decided it would be nice if I stayed in her other twin.'

'You're sharing Frederica's room with her?'

Since I had made rather large fusses in the past about the sanctity of my private quarters, I rushed to explain. 'I'm practicing for when I have a college roommate.'

'Your grandmother's not being polite, is she?' asked my father.

'A little,' said my grandmother, 'but that's okay. I can always move to those guest quarters if we step on each other's toes.'

'A generation or two ago – and certainly in many cultures today – we'd be living under one roof, and it would be the most natural thing in the world for a grandmother and grand-daughter to share a room,' my mother observed happily.

'I've read Margaret Mead,' said my grandmother. She parted her lips as if to embellish the sentence but offered nothing more.

'*Coming of Age in Samoa*?' asked my mother.

My grandmother murmured, 'I heard her speak once. Afterwards I bought her memoir.'

I knew from the sudden death of expression that this event was somehow linked to Laura Lee. 'Where was this?' I asked.

She said, 'I was visiting your father in New York City.'

My mother looked at me: *See. Exactly as we discussed. She's never accepted me. Note how she embraces the past and its ex-wives.*

'I'm getting back in line,' said my father. 'Can I get anyone coffee? A bag of chips? A slice of Boston cream pie? That's what I'm having.'

'He bikes everywhere,' I told my grandmother, 'specifically so he can have dessert for lunch.'

'That's not the only reason,' my mother said, looking pained. I knew she was weighing how receptive we'd be to a sermon on clean air.

'Is that safe?' my grandmother asked.

'How many years without an accident?' my father said. 'Not even a flat tire. Going on seventeen.'

My mother made a hand motion to my father: *Go get the pie now. We don't have all day.*

'Nothing for you, Grandma?' I asked.

My mother smiled weakly at my uncharacteristic thoughtfulness. 'So what have you two been chatting about all morning?' she asked.

My grandmother turned to me. 'Frederica? Remind me what we chatted about all morning.'

'The usual,' I said.

'A lot of time devoted to accommodations,' added my grandmother.

We must have looked and sounded unconvincing because my mother said without a cue, 'Your granddaughter is quite interested in the subject of Laura Lee. The fact that you still have her wedding portrait gave Frederica the sense that you're nostalgic for that phase of David's life.'

'A tempest in a teapot,' said my grandmother. 'The photo happened to be in an old frame that was on its way to a silversmith in Pittsfield.'

My mother waited, employing her disappointed-professor's stare.

My grandmother added, 'To see if he could touch up the frame, which is silver-plated. I was going to put my own wedding portrait in it.'

My father was walking toward us, whistling. 'Look at him,' murmured my grandmother. 'That's all it takes: dessert. He's been the same his whole life.'

My mother said, as my father took his seat, 'Your mother

was observing that you're an uncomplicated man. It takes nothing more than a piece of pie to put a smile on your face.'

'Not every piece of pie. This is one of my favorites – this and their banana cream and their strawberry-rhubarb.'

'I think it's a compliment,' I offered. 'Here's Dad, a full professor with a full teaching load worrying about grievances and poor people, yet he can forget all his troubles for a few minutes when the cafeteria puts out his favorite dessert. I hope I inherited that.'

'*He* inherited that from his father,' said my grandmother. 'Which is why I have a whole repertoire of pies. I could write a cookbook.'

The cafeteria clock made its audible click to the next minute, signaling time for Social Stratification. My father settled a new paper napkin against his chest and picked up his fork. My mother gathered her tray and her book bag.

I said, 'Leave the tray. I'll put it on the belt.'

'Thank you, sweetie,' she said. Then, 'Have a nice afternoon, Jane . . . David.'

She didn't linger to hear the reminiscence that any mention of trays always prompted. 'When Frederica was little,' my father enthused, 'she'd stand by the conveyor belt for as long as we let her, watching the dirty dishes pass by. She had an amazing attention span for that; any student babysitter could sit at a nearby table and do her homework because Frederica would stand there, transfixed, until the lunch period was over and the last tray was dispatched. In fact' – and here his smile became a chuckle – 'we used to say, "Shall we take Frederica to the hypnotist now?"'

'He's not telling you that I'd kick and scream if they tried to take me home before the belt stopped.'

'Slight exaggeration,' said my father. 'You were, for the most part, a very reasonable child.'

'So were you,' said my grandmother.

This was my opening. I said, 'What was Dad like as a teenager?'

She studied my father for a few long seconds before prompting, 'David, do you remember?'

He stirred his coffee with the handle of his dirty fork. 'I'd say I was like most teenage boys: romantic, studious, dreamy.'

I said, swallowing my distaste for such appalling adjectives, 'That's not typical of the boys I know. But I guess you were your own person.'

'He wasn't any trouble,' said my grandmother. 'He was a bit of a loner, but that might have been because he spent a lot of time in his room studying.'

'When did you get your driver's license?' I asked.

'I think . . . I'm not exactly sure. It was before I went to college. Maybe the summer after I graduated.'

'What about the senior prom?' I asked. 'You must've gotten it in time for that.'

'I believe I went,' he said.

'You certainly did,' said my grandmother.

'With Laura Lee?' I asked.

He moved his pie plate a quarter turn. 'I think you know the answer to that, Frederica.' And then to my grandmother: 'She's been fixated on the topic of my divorce since those damn pearls arrived.'

'*Did* you?' I asked.

'No, I did *not* take Laura Lee to the prom. We hadn't met yet. I took a girl from my Algebra II class who, in fact, issued the invitation to me rather than vice versa.' He paused. 'Maybe it was Calculus.'

'What was her name?'

'Betty?' offered my grandmother. 'Beth?'

When neither could confirm the date's identity, I asked what she looked like.

'A big girl, I think. With red hair done up on top of her head so she was taller than I. And freckled.'

'I've drawn a complete blank,' said my grandmother.

'Didn't anyone take a picture?'

'I seem to remember her parents taking a photo when I picked her up.'

'So if you picked her up, you must have had your license,' I reasoned.

'It's coming back to me. Her name was Betsy, and after graduation she went to Carnegie Mellon.'

My grandmother asked my father, 'Don't you tell her these things? Teenage girls are very interested in details like this.'

'Overly interested,' said my father.

'Did you tell Dad about your love life when you were young?' I asked my grandmother.

'He never asked. I'd have told him anything he wanted to know.'

I asked how many times she'd been married.

My father said, 'I doubt whether that was a sincere question, Mother.'

I protested that I certainly was sincere. I had good reasons, didn't I, to wonder about the previous marriages of people I thought I knew?

'She's punishing us for not telling her about Laura Lee earlier,' he said calmly.

'Are you familiar with the expression, "It's like pulling teeth"?' I asked.

'What do you want to know?' asked my grandmother.

'Everything. Like how did they fall in love? How did he propose? How many bridesmaids did she have?'

'Frederica knows the important things,' said my father. 'I was married. It didn't work out. I met Aviva. We fell in love. We wrote our dissertations. We were lucky enough to get jobs outside Boston, in a town with an excellent school system, even before we conceived her.' He smiled. 'And now, as much as I'd like to linger, duty calls: office hours.' He leaned over and kissed me on the forehead, an act that struck me as purposefully, paternally picturesque for the benefit of anyone watching and trying to evaluate what kind of relationship a professor of psychology had with the adolescent specimen who was his daughter.

When he was out of sight my grandmother said, 'He was in grad school at NYU. She was at Sarah Lawrence, later subletting in the city, trying to be a dancer. Her maiden name was French. First date was just a favor to me – Staten Island Ferry and an ice cream sundae – because Laura Lee was the little cousin in the big city, jobless and friendless, according to her mother. He'd spotted her at a family funeral, and I did the rest. I don't know how he proposed, but it was probably not one for the books. I remember two bridesmaids and a matron of honor. They honeymooned in Bermuda, but didn't get one beach day.' She reached for her purse and pushed her chair back. 'I think this lunch has lasted long enough, don't you? Shall we set out for an adventure?'

I knew what 'adventure' meant in the lexicon of grandmotherly outings: Filene's Basement, by subway, trying on clothes without the benefit of a fitting room.

I was relieved. My mother didn't believe in recreational shopping, and I'd been to every useless museum a dozen times.

6

A Situation

I HOPED AND MAINTAINED that I was an innocent bystander in the drama that brought Laura Lee French to Dewing College. Grandma, on the other hand, got full credit – a sin of commission according to some; of omission according to her and her faction. My own accidental input was a need to pee after our April lunch, visiting a bathroom next to a bulletin board labeled DO NOT REMOVE. OFFICIAL JOB POSTINGS AS SET FORTH IN THE DSP COLLECTIVE BARGAINING AGREEMENT.

Maybe I took a little too long at the mirror probing an incipient pimple on my chin, because as my grandmother waited outside, she perused the listings, eventually helping herself to an eye-catching magenta flyer.

Later, on the subway, I asked what she was studying so intently.

'Just a situation,' she said. 'For the right person it could be a wonderful opportunity.'

I leaned over, read the description, then asked, 'Would you really want to be a dorm mother? With a hundred girls under your wing?'

'It's not for me. I was thinking of an acquaintance who's out of work right now . . . Room and board plus salary,' she murmured. 'A nine-month position with full benefits.'

I wasn't interested enough in her circle of friends to inquire as to which dowdy gardening buddy was looking for work. I agreed that it was a good deal considering you get an apartment on campus and probably not more than a couple of crises per week.

'My friend would have a very nice way with this age group,' she said. 'She's weathered a few crises herself and could really identify with students worrying about breaking up or flunking out.'

'How old is she?' I asked.

'Let me do the math . . . about five years younger than your father. But very young at heart.'

Still, I didn't catch on. I said, 'Your friend could call Mom or Dad if she wanted to know more about the school. They do that a lot – meet with people.'

'Perhaps,' she said. 'Down the road.'

I stated politely that any friend of Grandma's would be a friend of mine. Surely my parents would invite her candidate to dinner when she came to interview. She could come, too. We loved her pies.

Grandma folded the flyer and put it in her purse. 'Is Ada Tibbets Hall a nice dormitory?' she asked.

I said, 'It's famous for its weirdoes.'

'Meaning what?'

'Some are just arty, always stretching canvases in the living room. The rest are a little freaky. A lot of them don't shave their armpits or their legs.'

'So far, I don't hear anything that would discourage my friend.'

I added, not wanting to appear intolerant, 'Some people think they're the smartest dorm on campus. They've retained the bowl for the highest collective GPA as long as I can remember.'

'Is it a nice building? I meant. Not too old and not a fire-trap?'

'It looks fine. I'll ask Aviva and David tonight,' I said. 'They would know if anyone filed a grievance about working conditions there.'

She frowned. 'That's right, their second career. They always know who's complaining about what.'

Her anti-union animus distracted me from the topic at hand. I said, 'If it weren't for the labor movement, we wouldn't have weekends. Or Monday holidays. I think you're forgetting that.'

'I'm worried about their jobs! It seems to me that they've been championing their causes forever when they could have been publishing articles in journals.'

I said automatically – me the veteran of stenciling many a picket sign – 'Their only causes are hours, wages, and working conditions.'

'But they're scholars! They aren't downtrodden textile workers slaving away in some hot Carolina factory. The administration looks at the two of them and all they see is *union*. And you know what? I think they're proud of that; they

49

think they're Norma Rae and her Jewish boyfriend from up north, the agitator, from the movie.'

Loyalty to the Dewing Society of Professors and to Jewish agitators everywhere made me drop the subject of which friend she'd be recruiting for the job of Ada Tibbets housemother.

It was just as well. If I had heard the truth, I might have become complicit in her plot, out of some perverse parental backlash. Four months later, when successful candidate Laura Lee French arrived to begin resident-head orientation, I was as astonished as anyone else.

Grandma continued to hold her head up high despite occupancy in the doghouse. Her conscience was clear, she informed my father. Yes, she *had* borrowed the job posting with Laura Lee in mind, but common sense had prevailed. She was not a fool or a foe. She had asked herself how both wives of David Hatch could reside in the same community, especially within the sights of an impressionable daughter – a daughter who spent a lot of time unsupervised – and had very quickly relegated the flyer to her recycling bin.

She conceded that it was a mistake to confide her near-folly to the Schenectady cousin who happened to be Laura Lee's mother: *I'd had an idea – passing on to Laura Lee a job listing at the small women's college where David teaches – but quickly thought better of it. How is she doing? Has she found anything yet?*

It wasn't her fault that the elder Mrs French was prone to the wishful thinking of a child from a broken home: *Maybe they'll get back together. Maybe the second wife will die or decide it was all a regrettable mistake.*

Later, after we'd met, Laura Lee called it coincidence,

attributable to the small world of human resources: she could swear it all started with an appealing blind ad in the Sunday *Times*, which, by definition, did not name the college, and certainly did not footnote its faculty. She had had no idea, or perhaps had forgotten, that Dewing College employed her ex and his wife. If only the cousins had stayed in closer touch. If only Cousin Jane had added a few newsy, occupational lines to her Christmas card, Laura Lee might have known which opportunities to avoid. She had been looking for work for ages, and this position seemed so easy, practically like no job at all: sleep, eat in the dining hall, learn CPR, set a good moral example, answer knocks on the door day or night, be nice to parents and trustees, make cookies before dorm council meetings, kowtow to benefactress Ada Tibbets, who was still alive.

Shallower professors might have gone to Human Resources, arguing that the hire of the ex-Mrs Hatch would prove awkward. Selfish and smaller people might have characterized candidate French as irresponsible or unfit. But of course my parents didn't. As champions of due process and fair play, they would sooner retire their gavels than put their personal discomfort ahead of an individual's right to life, liberty, and the pursuit of take-home pay. Besides, they assured each other, how often did they socialize with any incumbent house-mothers now?

Maybe Laura Lee had finally grown up, they theorized, and was thinking of Frederica and her undernourished college fund.

'What does that have to do with anything?' I asked.

'I think it's time we told her,' said my father.

My mother said, 'We live in a litigious culture. People need to exact a fee for pain and suffering, no matter how long ago or how fleeting or how big their trust fund.'

'So?' I said.

Here was the fact of life they were saving for the precise moment that my psyche could absorb it: David paid alimony. Now, under their separation agreement, his monthly payments could be reduced one dollar for every two Laura Lee earned – an unfortunate disincentive that had kept her dabbling in dance since 1950.

'How much?' I asked.

My mother hesitated before answering carefully, 'Several hundred dollars a month, plus cost-of-living adjustments, plus health insurance premiums.'

'Dental?' I asked.

My father shook his head.

'Do you understand what we're telling you?' asked my mother. 'That for decades we've practically been supporting her?'

I understood perfectly: books from the library, piano lessons bartered with the music department in exchange for babysitting, bikes from yard sales, haircuts from a school of cosmetology, every meal on the meal plan. What I had or didn't have was due less to political philosophy and anti-consumerism, and more to a skimpy bank account.

'Now can we buy a car?' I asked.

7

P.S. I Love Someone Else

A COLLEGE PORTER PICKED Laura Lee up at the airport, failing to recognize her at the baggage carousel because – my guess – she bore so little resemblance to any previous physical embodiment of a housemother. Her red-gold hair was long and beribboned in Alice-in-Wonderland style. She wore sunglasses despite the dim lighting and was dressed in a leotard and matching wraparound skirt. Rumors of glamourdom were further fueled by her luggage, two steamer trunks, which left the impression that she had been on the stage. Finally, when only the porter and Laura Lee were left at baggage claim, he asked, 'You're not Miss French, are you?'

Laura Lee hugged him, sagging against his dark green janitorial uniform with relief. 'I'd given up hope,' she said. 'I thought there might have been a misunderstanding and I'd have to get back on a plane.'

I had answered the phone when someone called earlier, sounding overwrought. 'Is David there? Tell him it's Laura

Lee.' I stood by his elbow, on the one hand thrilled and on the other mildly disappointed that she hadn't greeted me, her pen pal, in chummier fashion. My father advised her to get a taxi. Someone would reimburse her. Or just sit tight. The porter was probably having trouble parking. Was there a balding man wearing a green uniform in her sights? 'Dewing College' would be embroidered above his left pocket. After hanging up, he told me this call was an example of Laura Lee hysteria. 'Not "I was about to get into a taxi." Not "I was about to call the school,"' he relayed at dinner. 'A grown woman panics when her ride doesn't show up on the dot! I hope we've raised you to handle things better than that.'

I said, 'She did call the school. She thinks *you're* the school.'

'Our daughter is anything but helpless,' offered my mother. 'I think, if you landed in a strange airport, you'd not only get where you were going, but save the taxi fare and get there by public transportation.'

'I don't know how I'd feel if I got to my new job and there was no one there to meet me.'

'You're a teenager. She's a grown woman,' said my mother. 'All Daddy is saying is that this behavior isn't new to us. She can be needlessly helpless.'

'Which has its own appeal,' said my father.

My mother and I looked at him. He said, 'I'm not talking about myself. I'm talking about the world in general. Chivalry is not dead. People always tended to rush to her aid.'

'Daddy's saying that it was hard being married to someone so childlike. That's why, ultimately, he was drawn to someone who was competent and independent.'

'You?'

'Yes, me.'

'Go on,' I said.

My mother took a breath. 'Women who play up their so-called feminine wiles or, worse, feign incompetence—'

'Not that,' I said. 'I meant that I want to hear more about Dad's being drawn to you.'

She looked to my father. They said nothing.

'Did he sweep you off your feet? Was it love at first sight? Or did it begin as a friendship but slowly grow into something deeper that you finally couldn't deny?'

'That's Hollywood love,' said my mother, 'imbued with an added layer of teenage romanticism.'

'Why is talking about love called romanticism? You left your wife for Mom. She wasn't pregnant with me. I know that. Was there some other big reason besides love that I'm not getting?'

'Let's be frank,' said my father. 'You're a young, impressionable girl. We engaged in some behaviors that we wouldn't want you to emulate. We want you to see marriage as inviolable.'

'He means for life,' said my mother. 'Like Canada geese.'

I craved the low-down. David and Aviva were so deliberately plain, so earnest and interchangeable, that I needed to imagine them as two separate people radiating animal magnetism at detectable levels. 'You've always been honest with me,' I tried. 'And I think I need to hear your whole story. As a cautionary tale.'

When they continued to sit there, exchanging silent signals, I added, 'Is it the sex part? Because you don't have to be specific. I'm just trying to get an idea of your history: you met in class. You met at a party. You met at the malt shop. You met on a picket line.'

My mother smiled first. 'It's almost a cliché how we met.'

I said, 'I love clichés.'

'David?' she prompted.

'There was a blackout,' he began.

'And you were stuck in an elevator together?' I asked eagerly.

'Almost,' said my mother.

'We were in a lab when the lights went out. We waited for a while, assuming someone had blown a fuse, or, if it were the real thing, then a generator would kick in. After a while—'

'Maybe a half hour—'

'We groped our way along the corridor to the stairwell—'

'Were you lab partners?'

My mother smiled and said no, not lab partners. This was a neuroscience lab, so not the kind with Bunsen burners. Nonetheless, they were there at night because they both had experiments in progress.

'Did you know each other at all before this?'

'Only by sight,' said my father.

'Which of course is so ironic,' my mother continued.

'Why?'

'Because – and I just recognized this for the first time – we knew each other only by sight. So it took a blackout to bring us together. In other words, sight didn't bring us together. Which we think says so much about our relationship and the depth of it.'

I didn't say aloud what I was thinking: yes, because sight brought people together when they were attractive. 'So you made it to the stairwell . . .' I prompted.

'And I fell down the stairs!' my father exclaimed.

'Slight exaggeration,' said my mother. 'He was going ahead

of me to be gallant. Almost immediately he slipped – they were old, worn stone steps – and I caught him by the back of the shirt.'

'I still fell. Not any distance, but I landed on my coccyx. And I wasn't very stoic about it.'

'Please don't tell me you cried.'

My mother answered like the good note-taker that her field required her to be, 'No crying. Just a little hysterical paralysis for a few minutes.'

'Now *she's* exaggerating. I just sat where I'd landed. But for a very sound reason—'

'He didn't want to move in case it was a spinal injury.'

'Because,' my father rushed to explain, 'we had just finished experiments on animals with spinal cord injuries. So that was me being my sensible self.'

'He did stand up eventually, but he didn't want to risk going down the stairs. We walked back up to where we were so he could explore his various sore spots.'

'I sustained bruises and abrasions through my clothes. It wasn't just a little nothing. It was even bleeding a little bit. I didn't think it was safe to—'

I said, 'Dad! People climb up mountains and rappel down them! Couldn't you hold on to the railing and keep going?'

'Six flights,' he said solemnly. 'I made a rational decision. It wasn't as if the building was on fire. We'd stay put until someone fixed the problem.'

'Was it romantic?' I asked.

'It could have been,' my mother answered.

'Except I was a married man.'

I was deeply disappointed in their romantic genesis. It didn't dramatize anything I didn't already know about my father: that there had never been a younger David reckless enough to walk down six innocent flights of stairs in the dark.

They were smiling at me expectantly. I said, 'I'm missing something.'

They looked surprised.

'The *affair*. What happened between the blackout and Dad's divorce.'

'We fell in love,' said my father.

'Were you a scandal?'

'Very much so,' said my mother. 'Some of my classmates thought I should lose my fellowship for moral turpitude.'

I liked that. I asked if she'd been a virgin before David.

'This is where the privacy line gets crossed,' she said.

I pointed out that they loved the topic of sex. Hadn't they brought it up light-years ahead of when anyone else's parents even thought of passing on pamphlets? Like in fifth grade?'

'We talk about human sexual response when it's educational,' said my father. 'Not to satisfy a prurient interest.'

I said, 'I think I have a fair question that's somewhat educational and not that personal.'

Okay, they said. Go on.

'How did you tell Laura Lee? I mean, was it "I'm in love with someone else, so I'm moving out and divorcing you"? Or was it "I think we should take a marital sabbatical. Nothing personal"?'

'To the best of my recollection, I took the coward's way out. I was never good at confrontation.'

I pointed out that he was president of the Dewing Society of Professors and therefore *extremely* good at confrontation.

'That's different,' said my mother. 'That's professional and political. He means he's not good at confrontation when it's personal. Can you imagine what it takes to sit down opposite your spouse and say, "I don't think this marriage is right for either of us"?'

'And "P.S. I love someone else"?' I asked.

My father turned to my mother. 'Why does she need me to reconstruct, word for word, such a terribly difficult and painful period in my life?'

My mother turned to me. 'Frederica? Can you answer David's question?'

'Not until he answers mine.'

My father took a deep, tragic breath. 'I don't remember word for word, but I put it in a letter.'

'Tell me you didn't,' I said.

'It was beautifully written,' said my mother.

'You helped him with it?'

'I wanted the woman's point of view,' said my father.

'You don't break up with someone in a letter or over the phone. Everyone knows that.'

'Then how did the expression "Dear John letter" enter the lexicon if it weren't a common practice?' asked my father.

'You were married! Didn't you owe her a face-to-face explanation?'

'I gave her the letter in person and I stayed while she read it.'

'But—'

'Your father was afraid that she might storm out as soon as she understood the nature of the discussion, whereas if it were in a letter, she'd read the whole thing. And could reread it as many times as she needed to.'

'Did she go berserk?'

'Why are you asking?' my father said.

'I just want the whole story. She could have stormed out of the house to find Mom and kill her. I never would've been born. Maybe you'd have stayed together and she'd be my mother.'

They both looked alarmed. My father said, 'You take biology! If Laura Lee and I had had a child together, it couldn't have been you. You have half of Aviva's DNA. Were you serious? Or was it a form of poetic license to say that if we'd stayed together Laura Lee would be your mother?'

Et cetera. That's what I was up against, the psych.-soc. team of David Hatch and Aviva Ginsburg Hatch, Ph.D.s. Watergate had provided me with the gerund 'stonewalling', which I employed whenever my questions provoked a string of theirs. They didn't mind: it showed I was paying attention to current events.

8

We Meet

IT WAS I WHO SLID my tray onto her table the Monday following freshman orientation.

'I'm Frederica,' I said. 'Mind if I join you?' – the formulaic question I'd been taught to murmur, earnestly or not, when approaching an established table.

Laura Lee stood up. She was wearing a black dress that rustled and seemed from another century, with an ivory cardigan that was beaded and sequined. I expected the limp hand that adults usually offer children, but instead I got a hug of the overly long variety. I couldn't help but notice a faint body odor behind her cologne, which I would come to recognize as her signature smell: not so much a failure of personal hygiene as a reluctance to visit the dry cleaner. She said, sounding almost tearful, 'Of *course* you would be Frederica.'

We were still standing. I repeated, 'Mind if I join you?'

'I'd adore it,' she said.

As I arranged myself, my silverware, the four skimpy paper napkins it took to cover my lap, Laura Lee asked, 'Is it very hard – this existence?'

I looked up.

'Being not only a faculty child, but a dormitory child? Is it both public and lonely at the same time?'

I said, 'I don't know. I've never lived anywhere else.'

'But when you go to school, and you hear about your friends' living in a normal family, in a house or an apartment, do you wonder if something is missing?'

'Like what?' I asked.

'Privacy? Space? The undivided attention of your parents?'

I split open my baked potato, pushing butter into its crevices with a teaspoon. I could sense that Laura Lee was studying my potato ritual, searching for clues to my upbringing. Her plate, I noticed, matched mine: the roast pork, the beige gravy, the baked potato, the crinkle-cut carrots. After my first bite she asked where my parents were this evening.

I said, 'They eat later. They have what they call their cocktail hour, then usually run over at the last minute.'

'So you usually eat by yourself?'

I gestured around the room. 'I never eat by myself.'

'Do you ever wait for them?'

I said no; I preferred to come early so there were still choices left.

'Choices?'

I pointed back in the direction of the line. 'If you show up too late, you get the baked scrod or the tuna surprise.'

'And you don't like fish?' she asked.

I was beginning to see that any meaningless answer I

supplied – fish too often – would lead to another question that probed underneath what she considered the surface of something telltale. I said, 'I don't like the fish *here*. It's always the same.'

'And you like variety? A little more excitement than a steam table provides?'

I said, 'Are you a psychologist?'

She said, 'No,' then smiled as if I had offered a compliment.

I asked, 'So, how are you finding the new job?'

'I'm passionate about it,' she said.

I had expected something closer to ambivalence, based on every freshman's hesitant answer one week into the first semester. Laura Lee reached down to the floor and took a quart jar from a book bag. Its label said WHITE GRAPE JUICE, and its contents were the color of champagne. She poured an inch into an empty water glass and took one sip.

'You can get juice here in the machines,' I said.

'Not this kind,' she said, smiling.

'Is it wine?'

'Chablis. Are you scandalized?'

I said, 'Not at all.' I returned to my food, buttering my roll, then drinking from one of my two glasses of milk.

'Something's wrong,' she said.

'Like what?'

'Something changed when I brought out the wine.'

'There's a rule about bringing alcohol into the dining hall.'

She actually asked: 'Pro or con?'

'Have you ever heard of a school that served wine at meals?'

'Not "served". This is B.Y.O.B.'

If I were charting the course of my acquaintance with Laura

Lee, here was where the graph took its first dip. I said, 'Not that I agree with the rule, but you might consider having your glass of wine before you come here.'

'And that's okay? Drinking in the dorm? When anyone could be having a crisis any minute? These kids can smell alcohol a mile away, or so I'm told.'

Would I ever have a clean, simple, pleasant conversation with an adult? Question, answer, question, answer, your day, my day, the weather, the Sox, good-bye.

'Does everyone call you Frederica?' she asked.

I said yes, here they did.

'But elsewhere?'

'Some people call me Freddie . . .'

Laura Lee broke a piece from her roll, abandoned it, dusted off her fingertips. 'Why do you say that as if it's a confession? Do your parents object to the nickname? Do you want to be called Frederica or Freddie?'

I said, 'Both. Either.'

'Well, here's a test: when you leave home and go away to school, will you introduce yourself by your proper name or your nickname?'

I said, 'I'll see what comes flying out of my mouth when I get there.'

A student approached our table, but before she could set her tray down, Laura Lee held up her hand. 'I hope you don't mind, Claire, but Frederica wants me to herself. I promise that I'll extend the same courtesy to you anytime you need my full attention. *D'accord*?'

Claire didn't retreat. Laura Lee said, 'I understand, I truly do: you're thinking that the dining room is a place for communal meals, come one, come all, aren't you? I've disappointed you.'

'It's cool,' said Claire.

I waited for Claire to be out of earshot before saying, 'The dining hall rule is that empty chairs are empty chairs. You're not supposed to discourage anyone from sitting down. That leads to tables becoming little cliques. Besides, her parents pay a lot of money for room and board.'

'What about privacy? Where does one carve out a sanctuary if one lives, works, sleeps, and dines at Dewing College?' asked Laura Lee.

One doesn't, I thought. One doesn't live in a dormitory or eat in a cafeteria if one is seeking privacy. And this was the teeming Curran Dining Hall, always a few tables short of ideal social groupings.

She leaned over and said, 'Twice so far in our rather short conversation you've called me on the rules. Do you feel that living in an ivory tower is suffocating?'

I asked, 'Do I look like I'm suffocating? I'm here, all by myself. I can sit anywhere, with anyone, have five desserts, talk about whatever I feel like talking about.'

She poured another inch of wine and took a sip before asking a little too serenely, 'And what did you hope to discuss when you put your tray down at my table?'

I said, 'I didn't have a plan. Honest. I saw it was you, so I stopped.'

She studied me as I drank half a glass of milk, then asked, 'Who do you look like? I don't see your mother at all.'

'No one.'

'Remind me how old you are,' she said.

'Sixteen.'

'What sixteen-year-old,' she asked, 'wouldn't have gotten right to the point?'

I asked what point that was.

She leaned closer to confide, 'Don't you think the reason you put your tray down on my table was so that you could interview, investigate, scrutinize, drink in, the woman who used to be married to your father?'

'You were eating alone,' I said weakly. 'You're new. I'm famous for being sociable.'

'Which I suspect is the result of being raised communally: all for one and one for all, like on a kibbutz.'

I skidded my chair backward and asked if she wanted anything. I was going up for a brownie before they disappeared. It was pretty much their best dessert. She said no thanks, then touched my forearm as I passed her chair. 'When you come back? We'll talk about something comfortable, neutral. What might that be? Your friends? Your love life?'

I took my time, put both ice cream and whipped cream on my brownie, detoured to the salad bar for pineapple chunks and coconut flakes.

Laura Lee smiled warmly when I returned. 'How about this as a safe conversation? Our fellow resident heads. What can you tell me about my predecessor? Priscilla . . . I can't recall her surname, even though it's sewn into every tea towel.'

'Knight,' I supplied.

'Were you and Mrs Knight friends? I mean, to this degree – like you and me. Did you eat meals with her when you needed some adult companionship?'

I said, 'I get plenty of adult companionship.'

'Of course,' she said. 'Sorry.'

'What adolescent would eat three meals a day with her parents if she didn't have to?'

She tapped my hand. 'Shall we get back to Mrs Knight? I'm curious about the woman whose shoes I'm filling.'

I said, 'I used to feed her fish when she went away weekends.'

'To where?'

I said I didn't know.

'She must have left a number where you could reach her in case of emergency.'

I said, 'I wasn't left in charge of the dorm. I was only left in charge of the fish.'

'Don't you find fish as pets to be a very telling facet of a fish owner's personality?' she asked.

'Not really,' I said.

She cut a tiny piece of her neglected meat, chewed it daintily, and washed it down with a sip of wine before continuing. 'No feedback. No warmth. Swimming around in cold water. Do they ever give anything back? Do they even know you're there? What does a person living alone get from a relationship with fish?'

I said, 'I think she loved animals, and fish were the only things allowed in the dorms.'

'If I were an animal lover, you know what I'd do? I'd sneak my dog or cat in and out of the dorm in a big straw pocketbook. I'd buy the smallest breed of dog and keep her a secret. And, if possible, teach her to use a litter box. I would *not* settle for fish.'

'She gave them names, and she didn't feed them fish food.

They ate chicken and lettuce and wholewheat bread because she thought fish food was poisonous.'

'Poisonous,' she repeated. 'She actually *believed* that manufacturers of fish food would want to kill off their clientele?'

'We didn't discuss it. She mentioned it once to explain why she fed the fish people-food.'

'Did the girls like her? Because I get the impression that I am something of a breath of fresh air.'

'Girls *tell* you that?'

'No. What they tell me are things like "Mrs Knight used to go to bed at nine o'clock. Mrs Knight" – they call me Laura Lee by the way – "used to cut out pictures of fashion models and hang them on her door."'

I said, 'Only one model, her nephew.'

'Her nephew? Are you sure? How could you prove that a magazine cutout was an actual relative? Did you ever meet him?'

I said, 'No. He went to Brown. Brown students don't come to Dewing, even if their aunt lives here.'

Her face registered something that I, the daughter of social scientists, knew well: an onlooker prospecting for greater meaning in what I'd said than I'd ever intended. *Frederica is implying that Dewing is inferior. She must be ashamed of her home, her kibbutz.* I could see that a follow-up question was perched on her lips. But she looked up, past me. Someone was approaching our table directly behind me. 'Dr Hatch,' my tablemate said in greeting.

'Mind if I join you?' my mother's voice asked.

'Please,' said Laura Lee. 'Your daughter and I have been having a most interesting conversation.'

My mother put her tray down next to mine. Her plate held only the evening's carrots, baked potato, and raw cauliflower florets from the salad bar. She looked her dowdiest, her gray hair bushing out from two mismatched barrettes of mine, her reading glasses dangling over a faded brown cotton turtleneck, torn along one shoulder seam.

'Are you a vegetarian?' asked Laura Lee.

My mother looked at our plates and said, 'I don't eat pork. They ran out of Salisbury steak.'

'Oh, that's right,' said Laura Lee. 'I forgot.'

My mother said, 'I was raised that way, and old habits are hard to break.'

'She's never, in her entire life, eaten a cheeseburger,' I volunteered.

'The laws of kashrut,' Laura Lee said. 'I know them well. I was seriously involved with an Orthodox Jew, or thought I was. But of course it couldn't last.' She paused before asking, 'Yet you don't mind that your daughter drinks milk with her meat?'

My mother reached over and moved my glass of milk onto her tray. 'Usually we beat her if she drinks milk with her meat, but not in public. Certainly not in the dining hall.'

I laughed.

Laura Lee did not. 'I doubt very much,' she said, 'that you and David, of all people, ever beat your child.'

'It was a joke,' I said. 'Possibly her first.'

Laura Lee cocked her head and gazed at me in analytic fashion. 'She's very bright, isn't she?' she asked my mother.

'*We* think so.'

'She was telling me about her high-profile existence and its attendant responsibilities.'

'Such as?' my mother asked.

'Strict attention to the rules. Never discriminating against less-than-desirable company in the dining hall.'

'How do you mean?' asked my mother.

'Always offering a seat to anyone who approaches your table, no matter how deep in personal conversation you appear to be.'

'You find that odd?' my mother asked.

'I value my privacy,' Laura Lee said.

'As long as no one's feelings are hurt,' my mother said. 'Imagine arriving here, possibly your first time away from home, and you see a girl from your English class or from your dorm, maybe not a friend yet, but at least a familiar face, and an empty chair next to her, so you work up the courage—'

Laura Lee had lost interest in the subject of dining hall protocol. 'Is David here tonight?' she asked.

'If he were here,' my mother said quietly, 'he'd be eating with his family.' She hesitated before adding, 'He has a meeting.'

'He must have a lot of meetings,' murmured Laura Lee.

'Usually they have meetings together,' I offered.

'Oh,' said Laura Lee. 'That's right: your activities on behalf of your faculty alliance.'

Her tone sounded like my grandmother's, condescending and anti-union. My mother said, 'Sometimes.'

I said, 'Too bad housemothers can't join the union.'

My mother, who ordinarily would have said, 'Hear, hear,' to any unit-expanding sentiments, didn't respond.

Laura Lee asked my mother how she and David got so deeply involved in the union, or was it just in her blood?

'My Jewish blood, you mean?'

'Is that a terrible thing to say?' Laura Lee asked.

'Acculturation is one thing,' said my mother. 'Genetics is something else entirely. I don't think you meant that Jews are driven by biology to be, for example, shop stewards or Freedom Riders.'

'I'm not a sociologist,' said Laura Lee.

'When you attribute someone's flair for union activity or sports or math to certain ethnicities and races by saying it's in their blood—'

'No need to lecture me, Aviva,' said Laura Lee.

I said, 'She can't help it. Life is pretty much Sociology 101.'

'We raise her to see the big picture,' my mother explained. 'The sociologist, according to Charles Wright Mills, should hold three sets of values: the first is truth, the second is reason, the third is emancipation and freedom—'

Laura Lee held up one finger, reached down to her book bag, and came back with a slip of paper. 'Criminology and Penology,' she said. 'I signed up for it. To audit. I need your signature.'

My mother took the registrar's slip and studied it as if she had never seen such a thing. Laura Lee produced a pen.

'There's a prerequisite for C and P,' my mother finally said.

'To *audit*?' asked Laura Lee.

My mother handed the slip back to her. 'You might enjoy an introductory course, like Contemporary Society. Or Youth and Youth Cultures. That might be particularly relevant—'

'I want *this* one,' said Laura Lee. 'And if I can't take Criminology and Penology, I'll sign up for Abnormal Psych.' She paused. 'From what I know of David, he's willing to bend the rules.'

I took the permission slip. 'You like older students,' I reminded Aviva. 'You always say they bring life experience into the class.'

'That's certainly true,' said Laura Lee.

'Okay?' I asked my mother. She shrugged.

I took the pen, checked to see if anyone in Curran Hall was watching, then discreetly scribbled my mother's initials on the correct line. I returned the slip to Laura Lee with the advice we gave all auditors: do the reading, don't cut class, and don't hog the office hours of our overburdened faculty.

9

Less Than Full Disclosure

WHAT ELSE COULD I EXPECT from a walking role model like David Hatch other than his enveloping his ex-wife in a selfless hug upon their first private meeting? I saw it from my first-floor window, an early-morning exchange on a deserted sidewalk. It was an awkward moment brought to life: he stopped, she stopped. My father spoke first, presumably no more than *Hello, Laura Lee*. She seemed to say something more acidic, probably *Well, we finally come face to face*. The hug came next, peacekeeping without warmth. Laura Lee said something – *I met your daughter*? *I dined civilly with your wife*? – her head erect, followed by separation and mutual businesslike nods. They were both heading in the same direction, but didn't walk together. I drew back from my blinds.

Of course I had to spook David after school by telling him I'd observed the hug and asking if, in the course of it, he'd apologized to Laura Lee.

'For what exactly?'

I was writing a draft of a paper on 'The Lottery' in my multi-subject binder and didn't look up. 'Falling in love with your next wife while still married to her.'

He led me to our sofa, underneath our college-provided portrait of the founding Dewing. 'Divorce,' he began, 'is very sticky. And very difficult because it is essentially a legal matter. Apologies become something else once they're on the record, before a judge. It gets into the area of fault. Do you understand what I'm saying?'

'It's worse if you fall in love with someone else than if you just don't want to be married anymore?'

'At the time we were going through this, yes. I was the adulterer and your mother was the correspondent, which is the correct legal term for the party who committed adultery with the defendant.'

'Cool,' I said.

'It was very humiliating. Extremely.'

'For who?'

'For whom,' he corrected, but without his usual grammatical gusto. 'For everyone concerned.'

'Why did you let Laura Lee come here?' I asked.

He exhaled a deep, regretful breath and said, 'Pity. I knew how much it meant to her – after a very spotty job history – just to be a finalist. And, truthfully? I never thought she'd get the job once they met her. I thought I'd do the honorable thing, sit back, not interfere. Besides, with a pro-management administration like ours, a bad reference from me would act as a green light to the powers that be.'

I asked him why he thought Laura Lee wouldn't get the job once they met her.

When he didn't answer, I turned around to address founding mother Dewing. It was something David and Aviva were fond of acting out when either wanted to make a moralistic point after some act of selfishness or thoughtlessness on my part. I said, 'Mary-Ruth? Don't you want to hear why Dr Hatch thought Laura Lee was not qualified to be one of your dorm mothers? By "dorm", I mean dormitories. Which were built after you died. With your money.'

'Laura Lee French . . .' my father began, then stopped.

'Is she not responsible enough to be a houseparent?' I prompted. 'Is she . . . not smart enough? Not nice enough?'

'She can be very nice,' he replied.

'So what's the worst thing you can say about her?'

Ordinarily, he'd duck such a question, citing nobler instincts, but this time he answered rather indifferently, 'Self-absorption. Self-regard. Egocentricity. Vanity.'

This was better, a note more vitriolic than I had expected from Mr Fair-minded and Equal. I egged him on. 'I noticed a little of that myself when I ate supper with her.'

'Even that! I don't love the idea that my ex-wife is taking a proprietary interest in my daughter—'

'She wasn't. I was the one who sat down with her.' I added lamely, 'It was pretty crowded.'

'You're a young, impressionable girl – which I'm sure you'll disagree with. But I know from my research that you're at the age when adolescents, especially girls, find ways to break away from their mothers in order to assert their independence. To separate one being from another.' He illustrated this principle by entwining his fingers, then pulling them apart. 'What worries me is that Laura Lee will strike you as a very attractive alternative to the parents you have.'

'Do you think she's attractive?'

'I didn't mean in that sense. I meant as a magnetic figure – with her stories and her costumes.'

I said, 'They're not costumes. They're antiques. I like them.'

'Her appearance is irrelevant. I'm just saying that at your age, you're easily taken in by flashy alternatives to the family you were born into.'

'Do you *not* want me ever to eat a meal at her table? Is that what you're saying?'

'No. I just want you to be aware that Laura Lee – and I believe this wholeheartedly – came here for the sole purpose of insinuating herself into your life.'

I was thrilled, despite my previously stated lack of affection for Laura Lee, because I was sixteen, vain, and experienced in making friends with all varieties of dormitory unlikables. I could change my mind about Laura Lee yet. I certainly could give her a few more audiences at Curran Hall. I said in an effort to be modest, 'Why me, though? A total stranger. I could have been an awful kid. Why change your life for a total stranger who could be a real pill?'

My father smiled. 'I think your grandmother may have communicated over the years that you weren't a real pill.' His smile disappeared. 'And mostly, Laura Lee has no one else.'

'Does Mom know?'

'Know what?'

'That Laura Lee came here because of me?'

'It's more complicated than that. Aviva thinks she came to

make us – Aviva and me – uncomfortable. That she wanted to be a thorn in our sides.'

I said, 'Did you know she registered for one of Mom's courses?'

His eyes narrowed slightly, unaccustomed as he was to less than full disclosure between union co-chairs. 'Which one?' he asked.

'Crime and Penisology.'

He let that pass, as ever. Enlightened fathers didn't wash their children's mouths out with soap. 'That's an upper-level course,' he said. 'You need the instructor's permission.'

'She got it! I was a witness.' I pantomimed a scrawling of initials, adding a little John Hancockish bravado.

'I can see you're enjoying this,' my father said.

'Mom can handle it. That class always attracts the crackpots. It's the field trip to the prison, I think. Maybe she shouldn't put that in the catalogue.'

My father said, as if to himself, 'This is going to be harder than I thought. More intrusive. I'd hoped that between my classes and the union, I wouldn't have more complications to deal with.' He sat up straighter, shook that off. 'Did you hear what I just said? "No more complications to deal with"? I can't believe I said that. That is not who I am. You know that, right? Your old dad is not a shirker.'

I said, 'Don't worry. She's got a whole dormitory full of kids now. I'm sure one of the lost souls will adopt her.'

He seemed to perk up a bit with that. 'And every year there are at least a dozen or so on campus from broken homes with no mothers. Maybe someone could steer those girls in Laura Lee's direction.'

'We could,' I said. 'You and Mom can spot those sad cases a mile away.'

Flattered, he squeezed my hand.

I said, 'That wasn't a compliment. I meant that you spread yourselves a little thin.'

'At your expense?'

'Sometimes.'

'But you've always come first! Even though we have a hundred girls under our roof, whom we may, on occasion, refer to as daughters, that's hyperbole. As long as we wear the dorm-parent hat, then these boarders, by definition, are our surrogate daughters. But that's fleeting, isn't it? They arrive, most a little needy, and then before we know it, they graduate.'

'Or flunk out.'

'My point is, we adopt them temporarily, superficially. No one lives here for more than four years.'

'No one except us! We'll never move, unless it's to another dorm.'

'Or across the river,' he enthused. 'Maybe Harvard will be calling one of these days. Did you know that your mother is a guest at one of their sociology colloquia next fall?'

'Dad,' I said. 'How many of our faculty have gone from Dewing to Harvard?'

He said then what he always said when Dewing crowded in too closely and he remembered that our living arrangement was voluntary, correctable, and not the way of the world. 'Maybe we should think about a real home,' he said.

Marietta Woodbury started off on the wrong foot at Brookline High School. It wasn't entirely her fault: her homeroom teacher introduced her with too much admiration as 'the daughter of the new president of our neighbor, Dewing College.' Immediately the high school arithmetic progression sprang into action: thirty kids told thirty more kids, and so on, until I heard that that new Marietta girl was high, mighty, and stuck-up. The real crime was hubris: being the daughter of Dewing's president was nothing to crow about at a public school whose PTO boasted dozens of Harvard and MIT professors.

I decided to help, not out of altruism or fairness – she *was* high and mighty – but because I valued the rides in Mrs Woodbury's car on rainy days, and perhaps (I now recognize) out of loyalty to Dewing. My first thought was to enlist Patsy Leonard, popular, athletic, younger sister of a much-admired senior. On my left I had Marietta, kohl outlining her prominent gray eyes, brown hair dyed black and styled like a flapper's; while on my right I had Patsy – cheerful, peppy, freckled, with ginger-colored bangs above the Caribbean blue Leonard eyes.

I didn't sugarcoat it. I told Marietta in the presidential pantry, as we snacked on duck liver pâté left over from a trustees' cocktail party, 'It's not your fault, but people think you're stuck-up.'

'Maybe I am,' she said. 'And why would I care what the drips at Bullshit High School think about me?'

I said, 'I've seen this all around me, my whole life: new girls arrive, and some rumor swirls around them – they missed freshman year because they were pregnant; they're here because they flunked out of Radcliffe, Wellesley, Vassar, you name it, or were thrown out because of drugs, sex, grades, alcohol, insanity, whatever, and their father bribed someone to get his kid in here.' I tapped the rim of her gilt-edged hors d'oeuvre plate. 'Besides, it'll make *my* life easier if you're not an outcast.'

'I don't notice you being queen of the hop,' said Marietta.

'I get along,' I said. 'I play soccer in the fall and basketball in the winter. I went to the junior prom when I was a freshman. I'm considered a good kid.'

'Congratulations,' said Marietta.

'You're talking to a trained professional,' I said. 'I know what works and what doesn't. So far you've been a disaster, which isn't necessarily bad.'

'And why is that?'

'Because if you were homely and pathetic, no one would pay any attention.'

Marietta seemed to like that. 'And?' she asked.

'First, I'm going to get help from Patsy Leonard, who's in your Spanish class, and pretty much does whatever I ask her to.'

'Isn't she a cheerleader?'

'Only jayvee.' I hastily explained: it was the culture within her family. It would be unthinkable not to have tried out. She had pinned to her bra the handkerchief that her mother had worn when she was elected co-captain somewhere many decades ago.

'How touching,' said Marietta.

I told her that she shouldn't feel superior to Patsy, whose family was so normal that they could win a contest: two boys, two girls, a mother, a father, two sets of grandparents, and they'd never lived anywhere but in a white house with red shutters as long as I'd known them.

'What does the father do?' Marietta asked.

I walked to the big refrigerator to take inventory and came back with a half-empty platter of smoked salmon and its trimmings.

'I'm waiting,' said Marietta.

'He's the manager of a men's clothing store downtown.'

'Good-looking?'

Was Mr Leonard good-looking? His hair was better cut than any professor's on campus. He was beautifully dressed, certainly, even when he wasn't working, and his shoes were always shined. '*Pretty* good-looking,' I said. 'Why?'

'I always ask,' said Marietta. 'Due to the superficial nature of my existence.'

I changed my mind at that moment: sweet Patsy Leonard, deaf to irony, was the wrong missionary to convert Marietta Woodbury to popularity. I asked, 'How did you do at your previous school, friendwise?'

'I had friends,' said Marietta.

'Girlfriends?'

'All my friends tend to be male.'

I said, 'If you lived in a dorm the way I do, you'd see what happens to girls who say, "All my friends are male."'

Marietta blotted her lips with a cocktail napkin bearing the seal of the college and arched her eyebrows above it. 'They have a lot of sex?'

I was flattered to be asked a question like that. I said, as airily as I could, 'No, just the opposite. They get lonely.'

Marietta asked a very insightful and progressive question then: was she supposed to conform, to lose her individualism, all for the sake of winning friends at Birdbrained High? Didn't she have enough to worry about at home, where she was on display whenever she set foot on campus, where everything she wore or said was fair game? To wit: there had been complaints from some touchy boarders about her not waving, appearing unfriendly, some asinine dorky thing like that. Now her father wanted her to dine at Curran Hall two nights a week, to sit down at a table with total strangers, introduce herself, then actually eat the food. 'Can you imagine?' she asked. 'How is a person like me supposed to survive *that*?'

I decided then to stop applauding her princess-and-the-pea routine. I asked, even though I was wrapping smoked salmon around a nucleus of caper and chopped egg, 'Where do you think I eat every night? The Ritz-Carlton?'

She had manners enough to backpedal slightly. 'I don't mean literally survive. I meant my father's job comes with a cook. Why do I have to eat in a cafeteria? I'll have four years of that in college.'

I knew the cook was part-time and suspected that Mrs Woodbury was farming Marietta out on the nights she had no help. I said, 'It's not hard: you walk out your front door, walk a hundred yards, show your ID, and there's dinner. You have two entrée choices, a salad bar—'

'I'll eat with you,' she said. 'You can initiate the conversations, and I'll throw in the occasional bon mot.'

I said I had two pieces of advice: get there early, and take a brownie the first pass through the line because they go fast.

'What about the company?' she asked. 'Is there anyone worth getting to know?'

The first face that came to me was Laura Lee's. 'Miss French,' I said. 'Laura Lee. She's new, too. Not a fan of the dining hall experience. I think you'd have a lot in common. And she'll shoo away the undesirables.'

She frowned. 'You call the students "Miss"?'

'She's a housemother.'

'How old?'

'Forties,' I said.

'Married?'

'Divorced.'

'Is she attractive?'

'Quite. Long reddish hair.'

'Dyed?'

I said I didn't think so.

'What happened?' asked Marietta.

'What happened when?'

'Who wanted the divorce? The husband or this house-mother?'

I lowered my voice, even though we were alone in her empty house. 'He came home one day and told her he'd fallen madly in love with someone else and wanted a divorce as soon as humanly possible.'

Marietta was helping herself to the pâté with the aid of only her index finger. That declaration stopped her in the middle of a long, disgusting lick. 'Completely out of the blue?'

I nodded.

'Has she ever remarried?'

'Never.'

'Do you think she ever recovered?'

I said I didn't know her well enough, but I doubted it.

'Does she have a boyfriend now?'

I handed Marietta a piece of bread, a knife, and a napkin. 'Why so fascinated?' I asked.

Marietta snapped, 'You're the one who brought it up. I couldn't care less about some stranger's love life or ex-husband or her divorce.'

When I didn't respond immediately – it seemed like a conversational Möbius strip that began with Laura Lee and turned itself into my father – she asked, 'Did the ex marry the other woman?'

I said yes, actually, he did. And that has been a long and fruitful marriage. I stood up and got my books from the kitchen counter, saying I had a test to study for and was heading for the library, which was also a good place to mingle with fellow campus dwellers. At the door I stopped. 'I probably shouldn't have told you. No one on campus is supposed to know the details.'

She asked eagerly, 'Because the ex is someone famous?'

I said no, just a teacher.

'You know a lot,' said Marietta.

If I had liked her more, I would have confided that Aviva Ginsburg had been the other woman and I was the fruit of that second marriage. I might have enjoyed saying, 'Hold on to your hat. Here comes the best gossip in the history of Dewing College.' But I hadn't been a party to my father's first-wife big secret long enough to uncork it with any pleasure. And Marietta was getting on my nerves.

10

We Don't Do That Here

TO EVERYONE'S EXTREME GREAT INTEREST, especially mine, Laura Lee appeared to be entertaining a gentleman caller in the parlor of Ada Tibbets Hall. He was a man of the cloth and rather effeminate, traits that were helpful in staving off gossip within our fishbowl. 'A family friend,' Laura Lee would say in her introductions to Father Ralph Zitka – until the pair moved outdoors and several students witnessed them walking hand in hand across a footbridge that led to a secluded stone bench with a reputation.

Who else but I could take her under my wing and explain the problems inherent in being seen walking with a man in the direction of the kissing bench? This was a women's college, and girls could be mean. I was giving her my advice in the library, sharing a table as I was studying for my US History test, and Laura Lee was reading articles on reserve for Criminology and Penology. If rumors had reached me, a mere adjunct resident, she could be sure that every girl in

Tibbets had her binoculars at the ready.

She looked up and asked mildly, 'Why should I have to refute rumors that aren't true?'

'Because you're new. Because the administration worries about appearances. Because parents might hear that you're dating a priest and make a giant fuss.'

'Who do you mean when you say "administration"? Does that include the president?' she asked.

I said probably. Administrators. Those who weren't in any collective bargaining unit.

'Aren't you friends with the president's daughter?'

I said I was. I had to be. She was my age exactly, lived on campus, and went to Brookline High.

Laura Lee said, 'In other words, in a sea of girls, you're starved for friends your own age. She wouldn't be your first, second, or third choice of a bosom buddy, but she'll do.'

I sighed and didn't answer. I'd discovered over the course of several meals that I didn't need to answer on point. Laura Lee liked to interrogate more than she cared to pay attention to the feedback. Whatever I answered, whatever curve I threw, would become the new conversational starting line. Accordingly, I said, 'She has two sisters, both older. One is studying voice in New York.'

'How much time do you spend over there?'

I said, 'We almost always stop there after school if I don't have sports. They have two refrigerators, and there's always food left over from some reception.'

'So you're saying they're good hosts?'

I shrugged.

'But you *do* know the parents?'

I said yes I did.

'Would it be possible, then, casually, maybe over a drink, to say something that would put these rumors to rest?'

I said, '*Over a drink*? I'm a kid. I don't have drinks with anyone, especially the college president. He'd get arrested.'

She hesitated. 'I didn't mean literally over alcohol. I meant . . . when you were having a social moment.'

I said, 'Why don't you arrange for your own social moment?'

'Because! When do housemothers intersect with the college president? Never.'

I asked what I was supposed to say to Dr Woodbury if the opportunity presented itself.

She closed her eyes and moved her lips silently.

'What?' I prompted.

She opened her eyes and announced, 'You wouldn't need to say anything to Dr Woodbury. You'd be very subtle. One day, maybe walking home from school with the daughter, you could say, "Have you heard about Miss French and her friend?" To which she'd say yes or no. And then you could say, "There are rumors flying around about them being a couple, but they're just acquaintances."'

I said, 'People have seen you holding hands.'

Laura Lee stared forlornly, as if mourning the loss of my good sense. 'Frederica. Do you think holding someone's hand is necessarily a sexual act? Especially if that person is a Roman Catholic priest?'

'Sort of,' I said.

'He's human. And going through a difficult period. Just because he's a priest doesn't mean one can't reach out to him.'

'How often does he come by?' I asked.

'Not that often,' she said. 'Maybe every other day for a few hours.'

'In the parlor, right? Never in your apartment.'

'Absolutely in the parlor. With an occasional visit to my kitchen for a cup of tea.'

'Why does he always have to visit you? Why can't you visit him?'

'Because,' she began, 'his place of residence doesn't have the equivalent of a beau parlor. I'd have to visit him in his room, which Ralph could not explain to his landlady.'

'Landlady?' I repeated. 'Doesn't he live in a special house for priests?'

'Ordinarily, yes.'

'But . . . ?'

'He's currently on sabbatical,' said Laura Lee. She returned to her homework for another few seconds, then made a note in the margin. I refrained from saying, No defacing reserve articles. They belong to my mother.

'I'd rather people not know that he's on hiatus,' she said.

I asked if priests could *be* on hiatus. Wasn't employment a built-in kind of thing, like housemother?

For the first time, her voice dropped to a whisper. 'He's leaving the Church. Need I say more?'

I nodded that she *did* need to say more. Had he been fired because he wanted to date? And what about due process?

'One doesn't just walk out the door,' she said. 'One applies to leave. The Holy Father has to give you the green light. And priests don't have signed contracts like Teamsters. It's much more' – she made circles in the air with one wrist – 'divine or esoteric, or whatever you want to call it.'

I went back to my own reading – manifest destiny and western expansion. Before long, her pencil tapped the top of my page.

'In order to squelch this silly rumor,' she said, 'I'm going to nip it in the bud.'

'How?' I asked.

'In a dignified manner. To be announced. Possibly a letter to the editor of the *Daily*.'

I shook my head in a decisive no.

'Then what are my options? You tell me what works around here.'

'I can't now,' I said, as the empty seats around us began filling up. 'In fact, I'm separating the two of us.' I moved one table over, my back to her for minimal distraction, and began my chapter for the third time.

Within minutes, she was at my side, asking for a piece of paper. I ripped two from my notebook – even that noise attracted dirty looks. She mouthed her thanks and returned to her place. She came back to drop a folded note on my textbook. I opened it and read, 'When do you want to take a break?'

I flashed my fingers in a pantomime that I hoped meant thirty minutes. She checked her watch, made a notation with her pencil, and sent me back a thumbs-up.

Halfway to our appointed rendezvous, a folded note flew from her table to mine. I shook my head – *we don't do that here*. I opened it and read, 'I'm thinking about a tea at Tibbets for all the VIPs.'

I looked up. Laura Lee was nodding, eliciting my approval. I whispered, 'I have to read.'

A girl at the next table shushed us. Laura Lee stood up and motioned that we should move to a friendlier corner. I took my wallet from my book bag, motioned her to do the same, and led her past the long oak reception desk and out the front door. It was October and cooler than it had been on my walk over.

'What did you think of my idea?' she asked.

I said, 'There are teas on campus every week. I don't think another one will attract the VIPs.'

'This would be special. I'd think of something – a theme or a chamber group or jumbo shrimp – but the *raison d'être* would be interpersonal relations, so that President Woodbury and his fellow higher-ups can see me in action, by which I mean as an intelligent, mature, thoughtful, responsible *in loco parentis*.'

I said, 'Would you get up and make a speech?'

'Wouldn't need to.' She smiled. 'I'd mingle. I'd pour. I'd circulate with trays of whatever delicacies my entertainment budget can cover. I'd include my fellow houseparents—'

'Mine, too?'

That stopped her and put her into her favorite mode: parsing sentences. 'How funny. To think of them as your *houseparents* rather than as your mother and father. As if you were a paying student rather than their daughter.'

Ignoring that, I said, 'Run some more names by me. I know who can be fun at parties.'

'Do you think I should invite the old lady?'

'Which old lady?'

'Ada Tibbets!'

I said, 'She won't come. She only goes to things she can take her dogs to.'

Laura Lee said, 'That wouldn't be a problem. Let her bring her dogs. Ralph loves dogs.'

I must have winced because she added, 'Isn't that the whole point? To defuse the situation and show that he is simply a male presence in the dorm? At a school that doesn't have a chaplain, I might point out. Everyone who meets him will come away completely charmed and harboring no more sexual suspicions.'

'Why not?'

'Because.' It was dark on the steps of the library. I could barely see her smile, but I could hear it in her voice. 'Because I'll introduce him as my cousin! Poof, end of rumors.'

I said, 'Some people have sex with their cousins. Some people even marry them.'

'Noted,' she said. 'And may I point out that your father's first marriage to me is always one degree away from any topic I raise with you.'

I said, 'Fine. Do it. Have a party. Invite your make-believe cousin. He can meet all your other cousins at Dewing. And bring on Ada Tibbets. Maybe I'll get to meet the legend.'

'You haven't met her? After all these years? Even across a room at an inauguration?'

'Probably,' I said.

'A really ancient dame with wrinkles on either side of her mouth like a marionette's?'

'Maybe I was looking for the young Ada Tibbets, the one in the oil painting in your foyer.'

'Even in that dewy rendering, she looks like a battle-axe,' Laura Lee said.

'She doesn't approve of the Hatches,' I said.

'Not surprised,' said Laura Lee.

'And we don't like her.'

'Let me guess: because she's not fair and open-minded and doesn't love her fellow man as much as her corgis? And because she smashes to smithereens the labor relations commandments? That kind of thing?'

'Correct,' I said.

It was widely believed that Ada Tibbets liked only people of her own kind. Finalists for the Tibbets Hall job who lunched at her Chestnut Hill mansion returned with reports of long silences and challenging food requiring mysterious Victorian utensils. When the college tried to wrest the hiring decision from Mrs Tibbets, gently citing federal laws and state guidelines, she stared back in a manner that suggested that any changes in protocol would mean changes in her will.

My parents had contemplated a switch to Tibbets Hall one year, to what they viewed as a more like-minded, picket-friendly, avant-garde population. Lunch at Ada Tibbets's long dining room table, during which her dim view, though unexpressed, of a man living among her girls became obvious, had squelched such a move permanently. She didn't like the fact that my father had been divorced; additionally, she served both shrimp and ham in one meal, which my mother pronounced deliberate and malicious. Pointedly, they never reapplied after being turned down in favor of Mrs Knight, an animal lover, a former resident of tony Manchester-by-the-Sea, and a Dewing alumna from the days of certificates rather than diplomas. Aviva and David hoped that future non-pursuit of the job would be perceived as a protest against inherited wealth, against narrow-mindedness, against the silver bell used to summon her doddering housekeeper to the dining room.

Later, as Laura Lee and I chaperoned each other back from the library, I asked her how her own interview with Ada Tibbets had gone. Was it horrible, the way I'd heard?

'I'm here, aren't I?' she said.

'Lots of people don't get hired after that lunch,' I said.

'You know why? Because when she asks, "Do you mind if the dogs eat with us?" and then feeds them from the table – I mean fingers in their mouths, truly disgusting – some people don't handle it well. I not only smiled as if they were adorable, but I fed each one a couple of scraps as well.'

'That's it?' I asked. 'That's the test?'

'At least half of it.'

'I've heard that she doesn't talk. That she sits there and stares so you'll feel uncomfortable.'

'That's part of it – filling in the conversational gaps. Which is utterly reasonable when you consider that you'll be working with brooding adolescents.'

'Especially at Tibbets Hall,' I added.

Laura Lee said, 'You know what's ironic? She has the last word on who's hired, but she has no idea who the population of Tibbets Hall is. She thinks everyone wears crinolines and goes to sleep at lights out. If she ever knew what went on in the beds of Tibbets Hall, she'd call the police.'

'What's the rest of the test?'

'You won't like it,' she said. 'And you'll probably go running to your parents.'

I said, 'I will not.'

Laura Lee looked around to see if anyone was close enough to hear her declaration, then whispered, 'She quizzes you about your means.'

It was so widely acknowledged, so untitillating, that I laughed. 'Everyone knows that,' I said. 'She's famous for being a snob.'

'Of course I lied to her. What possible correlation is there between a person's bank account and her suitability for the job of houseparent – except that a wealthy person wouldn't need it? But I told her my late father owned Dole Pineapple, because I'd had a tour of the plant in Hawaii – did your father ever mention that? It was the first thing that flew into my head, and apparently it hit exactly the right note.'

'Someone should tell her that being judged by how much money you have in the bank is against the law,' I said. 'One of these days, a candidate is going to sue the college.'

'Unlike you,' said Laura Lee, 'I wasn't raised to talk back. Besides, I saw it as an opportunity to be creative.'

That might have been an excellent time to challenge her definition of creativity, to ask, 'Do you ever tell the truth, Laura Lee? Do you think someone young and impressionable should be hearing how much you enjoy telling lies?' But why would I? At sixteen, before her lies ricocheted off my family, I found her flair for fiction altogether charming.

11

My Job

CONSIDERING MYSELF AN AUTHORITY on all things Dewing, I felt entitled to append myself to groups touring the campus. The actual guides, both the hapless and competent ones, offered their audiences a variation of 'This is Frederica Hatch. She lives here. Ask her anything.' If no one responded, I'd volunteer that my mother and father were dorm parents and professors. Griggs Hall, straight ahead, the brick building with the fake white Doric columns, was my first and only home. The food was pretty good over there at Rita Curran Hall, named after a girl who had drowned in a campus pond, now drained and landscaped. We had a salad bar and a soft-serve ice cream machine that could mix the flavors so you could get chocolate and vanilla swirled together – on and on until the guide suggested I finish my homework or get back on my bike.

I offered myself as an unpaid intern the first summer I was over five feet tall. With no students on campus, it was the low season for tours. If a family visiting Boston from far away insisted – leaving tonight, it's now or never – Admissions called on me, their one-man skeleton crew. Feedback was excellent, due to my store of trivia and the charm I summoned from the inner actress I'd been cultivating since birth. When I moved from volunteer to paid guide at age sixteen – thanks to staff shortages during a nasty flu season and over Christmas break – I developed a nose for the smarter-than-average applicants, sensing from their disdainful attitude that their rank in class was too high for Dewing.

'Your safety school?' I'd mouth.

The girl would nod. To which I'd silently convey, *Good. We both know you can do better than this new iteration of the Mary-Ruth Dewing Academy.*

Accordingly, my yield was poor; the lackluster legacies followed through with applications, while the overachievers didn't. Yet appreciative parents unfailingly checked the boxes that deemed me informative, engaging, and loud enough to be heard by those bringing up the rear. I wasn't supposed to take tips, but I couldn't see the harm. No one turned me in for either disloyalty or greed.

Soon after Laura Lee arrived, and with her blessing, I brought the odder applicants, the artistes and potential misfits, to Ada Tibbets Hall. Like all colleges in the 1970s, Dewing had its share of leftover hippies, vegetarians, and flower children. I'd lead the tour through the Tibbets living room, with its floral-labial wall-sized canvases of unframed student art, then knock on the housemother's door. 'Ms French is one of our most active and involved houseparents,' I'd confide.

Laura Lee always managed to look surprised – the dressing gown helped convey that – even though Admissions alerted its hosts to pending visits. 'Come in, come in,' she'd cry. 'I apologize for the mess, but I do feel that my girls come first.' If there were dirty dishes in the sink, Laura Lee would say that she'd just entertained her foreign students for lunch – not easy to give every girl her native cuisine – so please excuse her kitchen. If clothes were draped over her furniture she would say, 'I help out in the theater department, with wardrobe. Nothing official, just as a volunteer. That's my background: the stage.' We had no theater department at Dewing, just an annual variety show to fund a new bike rack or a rape hotline.

She and I were a good team: she told tall tales and I egged her on. I might ask, 'What play are we doing this term?' and she would answer effortlessly, *Moon for the Misbegotten* or *Flying Down to Rio*. Depending on my mood, I might ask, 'How do you handle homesickness, especially with foreign students?' to which she would rattle off a sentence that sounded soothing in a few different languages. If the chaperoning parent was male, not unattractive, and without a wedding ring, she would switch into another mode: 'Please! Ask me anything. Don't be shy. Parents always wonder: *can* a housemother be married? Is there a Mr French? Do I get any privacy?'

If no one bit, I would ask, 'Um. Ms French? What's your schedule like? Do you ever get a night off?'

She'd say, 'Although I feel married to my job, I insist on every other weekend off. We houseparents cover for each other, and of course we have resident advisers on every floor, chosen for their maturity and reliability.'

'Some of you could become RAs,' I would say to the slack-jawed visitors. 'It gets you a reduction in room and board.'

'Didn't you say *you* lived in a dorm?' someone would inevitably ask me, meaning, Why are we seeing *her* apartment and not yours?

'My parents have office hours every afternoon,' I would lie. 'They're both professors.'

'*Brilliant* professors,' Laura Lee would add. 'Very involved in campus . . . doings.'

'It sounds like you really love it here,' a parent usually noted to one or both of us.

Laura Lee would answer sounding solemn and vaguely widowed. 'I haven't had an easy life. I was married young. Here, at last, I've found a home. A family, really. I've been on my own for a long time, and now I've got a mission.' She'd pause until someone prompted, 'Mission?'

The answer changed with each visit. It might be in the realm of the imaginary ('to bring the New England small college theater medal to Dewing'), academic ('to keep the silver bowl for the highest collective grade point average of any dormitory'), medical ('to keep my girls safe, healthy, fit, and substance-free'), or – of most interest to me – highly personal ('to have a home at last, to find the daughters whom God didn't see fit to bless me with, to touch the lives of young women who can learn from my mistakes and benefit from the wisdom I gained in all my yesterdays, on stage or off, for richer or poorer, in war and in peace').

She never seemed embarrassed by her own soliloquies or her loungewear, never exchanged a knowing glance with me acknowledging our act.

'We've taken enough of Ms French's valuable time,' I'd say, leading my group outside.

*

While not stating explicitly their disapproval of my expanding relationship with Laura Lee, my parents asked, 'Is she such an ambassador of goodwill that hers deserves to be the only dorm you lead your tours to?'

I pointed out that they had always hated coming back from class, tired and hungry, to find a coterie of nosy parents in their parlor. Laura Lee didn't have classes to teach or wrongs to right, so she viewed my visits as within her job description.

'Is her place tidy?' my father asked.

I said, 'Not tidy. But not so bad.'

'From what you tell me, she seems to welcome the interruptions,' said my mother, 'whereas I dreaded those knocks on the door. No matter how many times I pleaded with the Admissions Office to stop sending tours through Griggs, I couldn't stop them.'

'I think it was a form of harassment,' said my father.

'It wasn't you they were showing off,' I said. 'It was the piano. They think it makes a nice impression—'

'At a school with no music department, no orchestra, no chamber group? Not even a marching band?' my father asked. 'Seems a little misleading.'

I said, 'I thought I was doing you a favor – knocking on Laura Lee's door instead of ours. She really likes to talk.'

'What do you say when people find out you're only in high school and don't actually go here?' my father asked.

'I get that out of the way. I tell them, "I'm only in high school. I don't actually *matriculate* here. But I was born and raised on campus. They'll probably name a dorm after me when I die, which is quite a tribute because most buildings are named after rich people who donated big fortunes." '

'It was a serious question,' said my father. 'I didn't need a facetious answer.'

'Even more tricky,' said my mother, 'must be the question "Will you be staying on for college?" '

'Not so tricky. I smile and say, "I hope so." Or "If they let me." '

'Did the Admissions people ask you to say that?'

'Not in so many words. But when I rehearsed in front of Mrs Friedlander, she asked me that question – "Do you intend to stay here for college, miss?" It seemed pretty clear that the answer should be yes.'

'What if a parent in your group taught in Brookline? Or was your guidance or college counselor? Do you want to leave the impression that you're aiming only as high as Dewing?' my father asked.

I said, 'In the unlikely event that anyone from Brookline High shows up, I'll take them aside afterwards and tell him or her it was all public relations. I have no intention of staying here for college.'

'We hate your lying,' said my mother.

'Do you want me to quit my job – a job for which I hold the record for the youngest employee ever? Is that what you're trying to say?'

When they hesitated, I knew exactly what to invoke: principle. 'Because you didn't raise me to be a quitter,' I continued. 'You want me to take on challenges and problem-solve. This is my first job, if you don't count babysitting and feeding Mrs Knight's fish. I had to make it work, even if it involved a little creativity. Which I thank you for – my setting goals and not giving up.'

For two such unadorned and allegedly vanity-proof parents, they were quite susceptible to flattery. They both looked a little dreamy, as if recalling heart-to-hearts that imbued me with my unwavering work ethic and cast-iron values.

My father beamed. 'You stick with it,' he said. 'Every job has worth and dignity.'

'No matter how seemingly thankless,' said my mother.

'It's not like I'm cleaning toilets,' I said.

A strategic mistake. I'd forgotten to pay lip service to the belief that all jobs, even if disgusting, were noble. 'Never disparage anyone's occupation,' intoned my father.

'I usually don't.'

'It smacks of snobbery,' said my mother.

'And elitism,' said my father.

I said, 'I'm no elitist. I'm just normal. Normal people know it's better to be a college professor than a chambermaid.'

My mother put her hand over her heart and closed her eyes. The gesture meant either *Where did we go wrong?* or, more likely, *Power to our oppressed sisters toiling in the bowls of the rich.*

12

Legs

LESS THAN A WEEK LATER, Laura Lee French made the acquaintance of Marietta Woodbury. It wasn't at a table for two in Curran Hall, as I had envisioned, but on a tree-lined lane, recently paved with speed bumps, that bisected the campus. Mrs Woodbury was at the wheel of her brand-new silver-mauve Cadillac, with Marietta sulking in the passenger seat. Laura Lee was walking down the middle of the road, not only holding her novel, but also reading it, the spine at eye level in the cartoon manner of a bookworm on parade. Mrs Woodbury felt it was her duty to stop the car, lower her electric window, and say, 'Miss? You're weaving while you're walking. This is a road. Wouldn't it be safer to walk on the grass? Or safest of all: not read while you walked?'

Laura Lee peered into the car and knew immediately who was dispensing advice. She said, in what I can only imagine was her silly-me, absent-minded-professor voice, 'I'm so sorry. Did I scare you? I was a million miles from here. In a gulag, in fact'

– she held up *One Day in the Life of Ivan Denisovich*. 'Such are the perils of being a bookworm.'

'Are you in our English Department?' asked Mrs Woodbury.

If the question had been posed by a visiting parent, Laura Lee would certainly have said, 'Why, yes. I teach Siberian literature. Have you read Solzhenitsyn?' But she knew this was the First Lady of Dewing, and the sullen but rather stunning passenger was the First Daughter. 'I'm Laura Lee French,' she said, slipping her hand for a ladylike squeeze through the half-open window. 'I'm the director of Ada Tibbets Hall.'

'You'd better walk on the left so you can see the oncoming traffic,' Mrs Woodbury advised. 'And save the reading for indoors.'

'I'm hoping to have people over to Tibbets Hall very soon, a welcome party for all of us newcomers.'

Mrs Woodbury must not have grasped that a gracious response was called for. She murmured something like, 'I'm sure the students will enjoy that.'

Marietta said sharply, 'Ma. We're late.'

Her mother's toe pressed the accelerator and the car shot away without, in Laura Lee's view, a proper good-bye and, simultaneously, exceeding the five-mile-per-hour campus speed limit. Mrs Woodbury hadn't even projected a silent apology, a roll of the eyes or a tilt of the head to signal, *Excuse the scowling teenager*. Laura Lee reported that she was left by the side of the road like an undesirable hitchhiker, as the Caddy sped its way to Griggs Hall and waiting passenger Frederica Hatch.

As I slid into the back seat seconds later, Marietta said, 'We just passed your best friend.'

'Who's that?'

'The new housemother. The one you told me about.'

'Is she a little batty?' asked Mrs Woodbury.

I thought so but knew better than to agree with a negative evaluation that might end up in Laura Lee's personnel file. 'What gave you that impression?' I asked.

'She had her nose in a book while walking up the middle of Longfellow Lane. And she appeared to be wearing a raccoon coat.'

I said, 'I haven't seen any raccoon coat yet, but I know she collects old clothes.'

'October is hardly fur coat season,' said Mrs Woodbury. 'I think it's a sign of schizophrenia when a person overdresses to that extent.'

'October in New England can be chilly,' I said. 'In fact, they're predicting an overnight frost.'

'Is she the one I'm supposed to look for at dinner?' Marietta asked.

I said, 'Yes. Did you introduce yourself?'

'Didn't have to,' said Marietta.

'And you're on friendly terms with her because she's a neighboring dorm parent?' asked Mrs Woodbury.

I said yes. We ate together occasionally when my parents were busy.

'I've met your parents, haven't I?' she asked.

I said yes, and for good measure underscored that the doctors Hatch were not only dorm parents but also tenured faculty of long duration. Perhaps she remembered that they had marched in her husband's inaugural procession? In matching purple and white doctoral hoods? Or perhaps she'd noticed a round-shouldered middle-aged man on a bike, briefcase strapped with bungee cords to the rear fender? That was David Hatch.

'Do they have to live in a dorm?' asked Marietta.

I said no, it was their choice. They liked the convenience. And honestly? Who could wean themselves off free room and board? They wouldn't be good at living in a real house, having to shop and cook and call a plumber and buy light bulbs—

'They're hippies,' Marietta informed her mother.

'We have a hippie,' Mrs Woodbury said pleasantly. 'Our older daughter Monica. She wants to be a farmer after she gets her Masters in Social Work.'

'Good for her,' I said.

'She thinks she has a good recipe for making cheese from goats,' Mrs Woodbury said.

I looked out the car window. Three tall Griggs Hall sophomores were walking single file, toes pointed, along Longfellow Lane. Three high-fashion umbrellas, red, pink, red striped, were raised to identical heights. 'I think Laura Lee was a Rockette,' I said.

'You think, or you *know*?' asked Marietta.

'I'm not positive. All I know is that she owns Rockette shoes.'

'See?' said Mrs Woodbury, patting her daughter's thigh. 'Who said there were no interesting people at Dewing? Here we have someone who stepped down from a New York stage to share her experiences with the residents of . . . which hall, Frederica?'

'Tibbets.'

'Tibbets and beyond. The dancing certainly puts a different spin on that ratty coat.'

'Why?' Marietta asked.

We had left campus and were at a traffic light. Mrs Woodbury addressed me in the rearview mirror. 'You know what I mean, don't you, Frederica? Wardrobe department versus Salvation Army?'

I said, 'Absolutely. She arrived here with her clothes in two big steamer trunks.'

'Green light,' Marietta barked.

Mrs Woodbury edged forward in distracted maternal fashion. 'I wonder if Eric knows that we have a retired Rockette in our midst?' she murmured.

I said, 'Historically, the president of the college hasn't had much to do with dorm parents.'

'I know Eric wants very much to change some of the preconceived notions about who fraternizes with whom. In fact, I think your parents may have expressed an opinion about that.'

I said lightly, safely – Mrs Woodbury didn't think me capable of irony – 'Really? They're usually so supportive of the status quo.'

'There's no reason why I couldn't plan something myself, an afternoon tea. Dr Woodbury doesn't have to preside at every college function.'

I said, 'Laura Lee is planning some sort of get-together in Ada Tibbets Hall. We discussed it the other night at the library.' I might have added, She loves the limelight. She wants everyone to know her and to admire her. She can show off her vintage shawl with missing fringe that purportedly belonged to Gypsy Rose Lee's sister, Dainty June.

'Does she still dance?' asked Mrs Woodbury.

I said, 'Not professionally.'

'I wonder if our Dance Department knows.'

I said, 'Dewing doesn't have a dance department. We have two levels of modern dance, offered through Physical Education.'

'How do you know this shit?' Marietta asked.

'Language,' murmured her mother.

I said I was a substitute campus guide. We knew a lot of . . . stuff.

'It won't be long before Marietta is just as well informed about our new home,' Mrs Woodbury said.

'Don't count on it,' said Marietta.

'Imagine if you came here as a potential applicant, and the daughter of the president was your campus guide? Wouldn't that be something?' her mother asked.

'Not if it was me,' said Marietta.

We were two blocks from Brookline High. Marietta, who didn't like being seen in next year's Caddy, or as someone too young to drive, said, 'Pull over!'

'What for?' her mother asked.

'Just pull over. We'll walk from here.'

'It's sprinkling,' said her mother. 'Let me get a little closer.'

'This is fine,' I said. 'Thanks for the ride.'

I had one foot on the curb when I heard Mrs Woodbury say, 'Tell me the name of the new housemother again.'

'Laura Lee French.'

'I took the girls every year to the Christmas show at Rockefeller Center when they were little. Do you remember, Marietta?'

Marietta had already closed the passenger door. I said, 'I'm sure she remembers very fondly.'

Marietta and I had walked up Sumner and turned onto Greenough before I asked, 'Why is your mother so interested in Laura Lee's dancing career?'

'She's not,' said Marietta. 'She's jealous. Have you ever noticed my mother's ankles? She doesn't have any. She's obsessed with other women's legs. And what are Radio City Rockettes world-famous for?'

'Great legs,' I said.

Therein lay the problem: Mrs Woodbury's preoccupation with thick ankles, and Dr Woodbury's unfortunate habit of pointing out better-turned sets to his wife. Marietta said it was incredibly stupid of him. Why couldn't a man with a paranoid wife learn to keep his mouth shut?

I said, 'She doesn't seem paranoid.'

'You didn't notice how the whole conversation turned into Rockette, Rockette, Rockette?'

'I didn't think it was that odd. People get excited about show business.'

Conversation ended as soon as we passed through the double doors of the front entrance. 'See ya,' Marietta said, slowing down to her promenade pace, a signal that I should leave her unchaperoned.

'Game today,' I said. I refrained from adding, 'Home. Against Dedham. Which hasn't lost a game this season,' because Marietta wasn't interested or listening. We were inside the building, and boys were walking past.

*

Since learning about my father's divorce, I'd become particularly interested in adultery among the unlikely. As best as I could observe, Dr Woodbury exhibited no signs of anything improper that would explain his wife's apprehensions. Husband-wife tension hardly existed under my own roof, where much was made of freedom of expression. My harmless, gravy-spotted father could nudge my mother and note companionably, 'Now *there's* a pretty girl,' eliciting only a mild 'yes' or 'no' or 'I can see why you'd say that, but I disagree.'

Who better than David Hatch, in-house psychologist and administrative watchdog, with whom to discuss Mrs Woodbury's low self-esteem? I visited during office hours, feigning a casual drop-in to his famously messy office in the old wing of Hogan Hall. The posters on his wall – yet to be identified by a single Dewing undergraduate – were black-and-white photographs of Erik Erikson, Sojourner Truth, and Eugene V. Debs. The visitor's chair had disappeared under manila files spewing union business, and the room smelled of bicycle chain lubricant and rotting fruit. David was on the phone when I arrived. He puckered his lips in a silent kiss and made a sweeping gesture that I interpreted as *Move the crap and have a seat.* I transferred the files to my lap and opened the top one, which argued the case of a female assistant professor (business math) allegedly denied tenure due to same-sex cohabitation. As soon as he got off the phone, I said, 'Dad! This stuff shouldn't be lying around for the whole world to see. Now I know that Helene Lanoue is a lesbian.'

He blinked hard, one of his astonished, lesson-dispensing tics. 'Are you saying that Professor Lanoue's sexual orientation changes your feelings about her?'

'First of all, I don't know her. Secondly, I'm saying that you should clean up your office and not leave confidential information lying around for spies.' I stood up, opened the top drawer of his unlocked file cabinet, and asked, 'How do you want them? Alphabetical by complainant's last name?'

'I would,' he said, 'if I hadn't run out of room five years ago.'

I didn't bother suggesting he excavate and prune his archives, because I knew the argument: twenty years from now an alumna might need a recommendation for grad school, or an unsuccessful grievant might want to refile.

'Nice to see you, by the way,' he said. 'To what do I owe this honor?'

'Practice canceled.'

'Due to . . . ?'

'Drainage problems. The field is practically underwater.'

'And of all the possible alternatives, you chose a visit to your old dad.' His bright smile faded. 'Your mother has office hours now, too. It might be nice to pay her a visit as well.'

'Why?' I asked.

'You know,' he said. 'One child, two parents. We like everything fifty-fifty.'

'Which can be very annoying to the child.'

'Should I give her a ring and tell her to run down to say hello?'

I said, 'I wasn't playing favorites. Your office is on two, and hers is on five.'

'How about if she runs down here?'

I asked, 'Am I not allowed to have a private audience with my father?'

'Frederica! How could you even ask—'

'Do you have some kind of deal, like, "I want to be there when you and Frederica discuss Laura Lee"?'

'No, we do not. Nor is the topic of Laura Lee the least bit sensitive between your mother and me. Nor, I might add, has that name come up today.'

It was a challenge I answered with, 'Mrs Woodbury met Laura Lee this morning and became totally fascinated.'

'On what basis?'

Before I could answer, he asked, worried, 'Not because you mentioned our . . . family connection?'

'The cousin part? Or the first-wife part?'

He leaned forward to say, 'Please don't think I'm encouraging you to lie. It's just that having an ex-wife living virtually next door to Aviva and me leaves the impression that I'm something of a . . . Romeo.'

I said, 'Honestly, Dad, I wouldn't worry about Mrs Woodbury taking you for a Romeo.'

He thought this over before asking, 'Then what's the reason for this alleged total fascination?'

'Simple,' I said. 'She passed Laura Lee on campus and thought she was weird because she had her nose in a book. I explained who she was, and that she'd been a dancer. Mrs Woodbury has no ankles, so she views women with nice legs as a threat.'

'How do you know that?'

'Marietta told me.'

'How odd,' he murmured.

'Odd because you disagree about Laura Lee's legs?'

Years of standing before roomfuls of girls had trained him not to blush at anything vaguely sexual, but I knew the signs of discomfort. He bought a few seconds' delay by coughing into his fist before saying too merrily, 'I should probably mention that Laura Lee stopped by to tell me about her roadside encounter with Mrs Woodbury, who she felt was patronizing and rude because she drove off without a good-bye or a "Nice to meet you."'

'What did Laura Lee want you to do about it?'

'I think she was looking for a little perspective, along the lines of "Don't take it personally. She's rude to everyone."'

'But she's *not* rude to everyone.'

'Of course not. I said the Woodburys were meeting and processing new names daily, so it was too early to characterize any behavior as typical.'

'Wait'll Laura Lee hears that Mrs Woodbury worries about other women's legs,' I said.

'And how would she hear such a thing? Not from her best bosom buddy at Dewing, I hope.'

I said, 'Certainly not. But I wouldn't be surprised if Marietta squealed over dinner some night.'

'So you're saying she'd betray a private conversation in order to undermine her mother?'

'Maybe she thinks the leg thing is stupid. Maybe she wants her mother to grow up.'

He liked that. It prompted him to state in his most earnest and pedantic style, 'It's hard to believe that a mature woman who seems otherwise so self-possessed, married to a college president, could be jealous of a total stranger's legs, even exemplary ones. If Marietta isn't exaggerating, I'd find her mother's reaction perplexing and deeply disappointing.'

I leaned forward in my chair and said, 'You don't find it a *little* fascinating?'

'For what reason?'

I had nothing to cite except my fondness for potential campus scandal. 'Woodburygate?' I answered.

David was trying to project paternal gravitas, but I knew he was muffling union-related glee, composing a mental note for the folder labeled AMMUNITION.

I added, 'Marietta doesn't think her father fools around. He just appreciates attractive women.'

My father tried to look pained by his fellow man's foibles, but I was not convinced. I knew he'd be watching Dr Woodbury for any extra attention devoted to dues-paying female faculty. And that the minute I left, he'd be calling upstairs.

13

The Dirt

HAVING PENCILED 'ROCKETTE' onto Laura Lee's résumé and single-handedly aroused Mrs Woodbury's curiosity, I felt obliged to mention my career claim to Laura Lee.

'Haven't you learned yet that I think on my feet?' she asked. 'I'm surprised you'd worry about me ever missing an easy lob like that one.' She was sitting in a wicker lounge chair on the veranda of Tibbets Hall, a yellow highlighter poised over her secondhand copy of *Crime and Punishment*.

'The word just flew out of my mouth,' I said.

'Do you know why?' she asked.

'The Rockette shoes. You once told me they were your proudest possession.'

'No. I meant the impulse. You were trying to counteract Mrs Woodbury's failure to recognize my existence, and you – loyal and very democratic person that you are – wanted to present me as an intriguing person.'

I said, 'I think she already found you intriguing.'

'Based on . . . ?'

'The fact that you can read and walk at the same time without looking up from your book.'

Laura Lee said mildly, 'I've known Grace Woodburys all my life, and that is not a set of skills she and her type find intriguing. My guess is that you introduced the notion of me as a dancer because she was saying something dismissive.'

She leaned back against the faded striped canvas cushion – brown and pink, Dewing colors – and marked her place with a Juicy Fruit wrapper. 'The Rockette thing is not so far-fetched, you know. I auditioned, and I got a callback. And the only reason I didn't make it was a technicality. I added a half inch to my height on the application because I knew the requirements, and I'd prepared myself by stretching – I mean seriously, with equipment, hanging from a chin bar with weights around my ankles. But as soon as I was measured, I was out.'

'Where'd you get the shoes?' I asked.

She smiled. 'You know where those shoes came from? The actual green room at Radio City Music Hall! They were lying next to a wastebasket, as if someone was throwing them out but missed the toss. They were only a half size too big, and because I was a little peeved, I helped myself.' She raised one leg; I sensed she was pointing her toes inside her frayed espadrilles, recalling the feel of her secondhand Capezios.

'Do you still have them?' I asked.

'Of course! And, ironically, my feet have expanded, so they're a perfect fit.'

'Can I see them?'

'They're unremarkable,' said Laura Lee. 'They were clearly shoes used in practice rather than performance. Black leather, medium heel, strap across the instep. You've seen a hundred pairs just like them.'

I asked, 'Where would I have seen a hundred pairs of tap shoes?'

She looked past me and stared unhappily at the late-October scene ahead: grass going brown, dwarf trees and shrubs denuding, men raking leaves as fast as they fell. 'You've never taken tap or ballet?' she asked. 'Never been around women who dance for a living?'

I said, 'I took piano lessons instead. My parents didn't believe in ballet lessons.'

'Because . . . ?'

'Because every other girl in kindergarten took ballet, and where did it ever lead? Nowhere. They get to high school and start playing lacrosse and field hockey.'

'And your parents see no relationship between the stage and the playing field?'

I said, 'They considered dance lessons to be a waste of money. They never bought the poise-and-posture argument.'

Unfortunately, those two words inspired Laura Lee to rise from her chair in an exaggeratedly fluid and upright motion. She pulled me to my feet and began ministering to my shoulders and spine, bending my elbows into what she labeled the first position port de bras. 'Not bad,' she said, taking an appraising step back. 'Although it's ridiculously late to start.'

Girls were coming and going through the front door of Tibbets. To each I sent a look that said, Not my idea, not trying to be a ballerina.

'Now feet,' she directed, kicking off her espadrilles, joining her heels impossibly to form a straight line, five coral-tipped toes facing east and five facing west.

'No can do,' I said.

'Fifth position,' she said, maintaining it, her arms rising to form an arc around her head. 'Completing fifth position,' she narrated.

I said, 'Let's go back to the *seated* position. I'll pull up a chair.'

Laura Lee dropped her arms abruptly. 'You know what I've noticed about you? You're confident in a verbal sense, even a smart aleck. But when it comes to anything physical, you hold back. For example, you like to shrink down to nothing in the library, shushing me and worrying what the librarians will say. And that thing you do in the dining hall, making room for the most boring little mouse that wanders toward you looking lost. I used to think it was timidity, but now I think it's just the opposite: you bear the burden of constantly being on display. You think you have to be perfect, like someone who's running for office.'

As ever, no response to this soliloquy was called for. I didn't bring up my physical exploits: soccer, basketball, and two weeks at sailing camp in Maine. I yawned, then patted my mouth to project theatrical boredom before guiding the conversation back to her. 'Were you ever a professional ballerina?' I asked.

She had returned to her seat and was sulking. 'If you mean, did I ever bring home a paycheck as a ballerina, I'd have to say no. But I've been onstage since I was four, and I've danced nearly every romantic ballet ever choreographed. Mostly in the corps, but I was Clara for my entire adolescence.'

'Clara?'

She closed her eyes. 'Please tell me your parents took you to see *The Nutcracker* once in your culturally deprived life.'

I said, 'I've seen it a million times on PBS. I didn't know you meant *that* Clara.'

'I'm taking you this Christmas. I don't care how old you are, or who's in it. I'm getting us tickets as soon as they go on sale.'

'Thank you,' I said.

She opened *Crime and Punishment*. I could tell by the twitching around her mouth that she wasn't done with me.

'How's your book?' I asked.

'It's not required. I'm sure no one else in the class is tackling anything under "Recommended Reading".'

'I'll tell Aviva. Everyone wonders why she wants them to read a novel for a sociology course.'

She didn't answer, except to scowl at what I took to be disappointment with the mean IQ of her Dewing classmates.

'I guess I'll go start my homework, too,' I said.

Laura Lee inserted the gum wrapper and closed her book again. 'Just so you know: I'm not going out of my way to retract your Rockette claim. Besides, it's the way memory works: as you look back, jobs expand and contract. You try out for one show and get hired for another. You dance your heart out, ruin your feet, and pretty soon twenty years pass and auditions blend with rehearsals . . .'

'Fine,' I said. 'As long as you don't lie on your résumé. An instructor was fired for that last year.'

She repeated my sentence in a prissy voice. 'Where do these worries come from? A footnote in the ethics handbook of the Dewing Society of Professors?'

I said, 'People get fired for making up jobs they never held. They think no one will double-check.'

'The word "Rockette" does not appear on my curriculum vitae. Never has, never will. Okay? Does that make you feel better?'

I said yes, it did.

'Don't think I'm not touched by your concern, Frederica. But you can relax. Mrs Woodbury has already forgotten the Rockettes. Next time we meet, she'll look right through me.'

'Betcha not,' I said.

Laura Lee's feet slid off the padded footstool, an invitation to sit.

How could I resist relaying tidbits that would give a fellow dorm dweller a boost? I asked if she'd ever formed an impression of our president, or ever noticed his wife's legs.

'Rosalynn Carter's?' she asked. 'Or Grace Woodbury's?'

'Woodbury's.'

'Go on,' she said.

I hesitated. It was hearsay about the roving eyes of Marietta's father, and I hadn't even gotten a good look at the much-maligned legs.

'We don't leave this porch until I get the dirt,' she said.

As of that afternoon, Mrs Eric Woodbury may just as well have had a bull's-eye silk-screened on the back of her beaver brown cashmere coat. Laura Lee realized – perhaps I'd unwittingly set the example – that Dewing College, like all small schools, was a stage, and that she needed a larger role than the one for which she had originally been cast. The irritant that spawned her grudge was nothing more than Grace Woodbury's rubbing her the wrong way. And the minor coincidence that took the grudge public was the debut appearance of President Woodbury at Curran Hall the very day his wife had left Laura Lee in a wisp of Cadillac exhaust.

She would call it fate: why else, seven weeks into the semester, would Eric Woodbury suddenly undertake an outreach campaign in the form of once-a-week dining with students? And what force besides kismet would have changed Laura Lee from the afternoon's blue trousers and concession-shop Pucci blouse to a dress of zebra-striped jersey that draped and clung in a manner designed to provoke?

From the salad bar, tongs in hand, I saw it all: President Woodbury emerged from the food line, blinking into the fluorescence of Curran Hall, his tray overloaded like a first-timer's. The tall, attractive ex-ballerina sipping Chablis alone glided upward to a standing position and waved. Maybe, from a distance, the president mistook Laura Lee, with her long red-blond hair and her frozen yogurt, for a mature and friendly senior. He smiled, nodded, moved toward her. Face to face, he must have realized that she was not his target tablemate, not a payer of tuition. An exchange followed nonetheless. I guessed he was saying, 'I'd love to join you, but the point of my visit is to meet and mingle with our students. Another time?'

I knew Laura Lee's dining hall smile, and this one was different, even brighter than those bestowed on touring dads without wedding rings. She said something in return. Possibly: *I'm disappointed, but I understand. Such are the demands on those of us who are slaves to social intercourse*. I didn't have to be Margaret Mead to note the time they devoted to each ritual –

the protracted shaking of hands, and the gaze that lingered after their release.

Would a bona fide mating dance be this obvious? Could life be this fast, and this frank? I moved closer, pretending I was searching for an empty seat, noticing nothing, caring less.

'French,' she was saying. 'Laura Lee *French* ... like the nationality, like the fries—'

'Like the *kiss?*' murmured our president, this father of three, this long and publicly married man.

'Hi, Mr Woodbury,' I said.

He didn't mind. 'Hello, Frederica. Do you know Miss French from Tibbets Hall?'

'Sure,' I said.

'Of course you do! She's a resident head, and you're the official resident teenager.'

'And Marietta now, too. Don't forget her.'

'What a coincidence,' said Laura Lee. 'I met your lovely daughter for the first time today.'

I put my tray down without asking permission. 'Two good choices for a change,' I said. 'I picked the veal cutlet.'

'Too much breading,' said Laura Lee.

'You're careful about such things,' he said. 'I couldn't help notice.'

'It's my background as a dancer – a courtesy to the partners who had to lift me over their heads and promenade across the stage.'

'That's right! I've *heard* we had a professional dancer on campus,' he said.

'From Mrs Woodbury?' I asked.

'We should talk,' he said to Laura Lee. 'There's so much that could be done toward enriching our dance program.'

'Even a field trip once a season to the Boston Ballet would be an improvement,' said Laura Lee.

'I'll call you,' he said. 'We'll brainstorm.'

'I'm passionate about dance,' she said, 'and I'm always available: five-five-oh-six. My direct line.'

For my benefit he proclaimed, 'Isn't it wonderful that someone who comes onboard to fill one job can bring a whole other, unanticipated form of enrichment to our campus? That's what I love about Dewing: the talent and enthusiasm I'm finding at every turn.'

'I feel exactly the same way,' said Laura Lee.

Did they think I was deaf or blind or born yesterday? After thousands of uneventful and forgettable meals at Curran Hall, here was one for the Dewing archives: the night President Woodbury and Housemother French virtually announced, publicly and brazenly, the launch of their affair.

14

Everyone

WHAT DID WE OBSERVE, those of us who were watching hungrily, and accepting at face value the public displays of libidinous affection? By Veterans Day, there were reported sightings of President Woodbury entering Laura Lee's apartment in Tibbets Hall unchaperoned; similarly, sightings of Laura Lee leaving his inner office, the one with a leather couch and a private bath, wearing what a promiscuous senior in my dorm described as 'that just-laid look'.

Wouldn't you think they'd go off-campus for their assignations, or at least stagger the dinner shifts to avoid each other in Curran Hall? Their indiscretion became a secondary topic of discussion, not just *Are they or aren't they . . . ?* but also *How much does a man have to hate his wife to publicly humiliate her?* And *How long will he last?*

Condone or condemn? What do parents do when they've been ivory-tower sweethearts themselves? Mine couldn't appear too

exercised about public philandering without appearing hypo-
critical, so until the rumor became fact, they employed it for
pedagogical purposes.

'We think you'll take away from this the following: that
nothing in life is this simple or this transparent,' said my
mother.

'Besides,' added my father. 'It's inconceivable that they'd be
sleeping together. He's too smart for that. And too ambitious.'

'Maybe they're in love,' I said. 'Maybe they can't help
themselves. Maybe it's no rumor.'

My mother bestowed on me a noble and indulgent smile. 'In
the original Latin, "rumor" was a synonym for "noise". I think
you know the culture of the campus as well as anyone, so you
know that rumor and gossip are forms of idle, destructive
chatter.'

'Everyone else thinks they're sleeping together. If they're not,
they'd better stop making a spectacle of themselves.'

'Who's "everyone"?' my father asked. 'Because you know
how we feel about your citing that pronoun as the subject of a
sentence proclaiming some trend, some fashion, some allegedly
majority opinion.'

Were they not the most annoyingly evenhanded parental
team in the history of civilization? 'Students,' I answered. 'His,
hers, yours.'

'We want you to think for yourself,' said my father.

'In our respective fields, observation is everything,' said my
mother. 'Months and years of study in the field. We don't draw
conclusions until we can back them up.'

'Why are you being so nice about this?' I asked.

'How could you even ask?' said my father.

'Because he's management. You hate management. And she's your ex-wife, who's getting more famous by the minute.'

'Do unto others . . .' said my father.

'Innocent until proven guilty,' said my mother.

Even those who weren't majoring in the rumor, as I was, saw tête-à-têtes and penetrating eye contact in the dining hall, spoons stirring coffee dreamily in a manner that would make any reasonable eyewitness conclude that no due process was going to save the jobs of these Ten Commandments scofflaws.

Within a week, one manifestation of the alleged affair worked its way into my immediate family: Dr Woodbury signed up to audit the seemingly irresistible Criminology and Penology.

No one had told me until I heard it at breakfast from a sociology major, obliging me to circle back to our apartment. 'You think it's a coincidence?' I demanded, standing at the foot of my parents' bed. 'Can you still say with a straight face that nothing's going on?' Aviva sat up, her quilt clamped under her armpits – she and David slept in the nude – to announce that it was not a *fait accompli*. Dr Woodbury had visited one class, hardly what one would call auditing. In fact, she'd appeal his regular attendance on the grounds that his managerial presence and note-taking constituted a form of intimidation.

I said, 'This isn't about intimidating you. This is about two students playing footsy.'

'Let's be logical,' my father said. 'If two people were having an affair, especially in this hothouse environment, would they advertise it by auditing the same course?'

My mother turned to him and said quietly, 'Although, you'd have to admit, if these two are having an affair, the audacity is fascinating. He's acting like a male peacock, strutting as if it's a full-time job and his *raison d'être*. I'm just wondering: what does he have to prove?'

'Why else would he want to audit a course that's already half over?' I asked.

'His stated objective is some kind of three-pronged plan to rub elbows with students – in the classroom, in the dining hall, and by coaching a team,' my mother explained.

'And he just happened to pick your class?'

'As I said: to harass me.'

'To harass *us*,' my father corrected.

'What's his Ph.D. in?' I asked.

'Classics,' said my mother.

I had been going to suggest that he sharpen his classroom skills by teaching, but there was a problem with his field: we didn't offer Classics at Dewing. Our Math and English departments had only recently dropped the modifier 'Business'. Psychology and Sociology in those days pretty much represented the school's conversion from clerical to intellectual. I asked my father, 'Do you agree with her? That it's harassment rather than his crush on Laura Lee?'

He said, with a blush that went down his neck and with a truly dorky chuckle, 'I was thinking it was because he has a crush on your *mother*!'

What daughter wants to see her parents in bed, knowing they don't wear pajamas, knowing that as soon as she leaves for school they'll have sex because it was Tuesday and their intertwined schedules gave them the morning off?

'We thought you'd already left for school,' said my mother.

'Aren't you going to miss the bus?' asked my father.

'Yes. And if you had a car, you could drive me.'

'Don't be bratty,' said my mother.

'Did they sit together?' I asked.

My mother said, 'So far, in the one class he attended, no, they did *not*.'

I said, 'It's not a coed school. Maybe you could get rid of him on the grounds that he's disturbing the class's chemistry.'

My father said, 'We're keeping out of it. In our position, you pick your battles.' I saw movement under the covers, the smaller foot nudging the larger one, a prod that induced him to ask, 'Do you think it's more important to continue this conversation, or more important that you get to school on time?'

More tedious psychology at work. I picked up my books and said, 'You're allowed to say, "Go. You're late. You'll miss the bus."'

They smiled uncertainly. I said, 'Never mind. You're doing fine.'

I would have been enjoying our own *As the College Turns* with more relish if it hadn't been for the female Woodburys. Their public faces grew painfully dignified, highly uncharacteristic of the snappish Marietta. I knew she was pushing me away, and I went along with it. It was best, I thought, and kinder if I pretended that the honeymoon was over, that Marietta had found me lacking as a cool girl's friend. Mrs Woodbury phased me out of the carpool when rain turned to snow in November. As a transplant from the south, she explained, winter driving scared her. I said, 'I understand completely. In fact, it's better if I take the bus and get to school a little earlier.'

127

'Marietta likes to walk,' she said. 'Even in bad weather.'

When the silver-mauve Cadillac passed me on its future trips to Brookline High, Marietta slouching in the front seat, I pretended to be engaged in animated popularity with whoever was standing next to me. Left on the curb, I could have waved somberly, but I thought it was the least I could do – to fake bus-stop contentment – for the victims of the humiliating campus romance I might have triggered.

We were losing Mrs Woodbury to a lower and lower profile, sad for a college that had lived under a no-frills bachelor administration for a decade and a half. Mrs Woodbury's First Lady bearing didn't disappear altogether, but it sagged. Where there had once been imported hors d'oeuvres on polished silver trays, now there were cubes of Jarlsburg alongside clumps of grapes. The strain of being cuckolded manifested itself in weight loss. She began to look drawn, then thin, then emaciated by the time the jig was up. We who were watching from the cavalier sidelines didn't take the disturbance as seriously as we should have. What did we sixteen-to-twenty-one-year-olds know of true, debilitating distress? We onlookers had seen heartbreak of the televised and cinematic kind. Bad behavior was for watching and enjoying, for dissecting and disdaining. We were, for a long time, entertained.

What proved to be unique and publishable about the most famous affair in the history of the college – later my parents squeezed two papers out of the mess – was the willful indiscretion of the principals. Where was the classic sneaking around? The shame and the guilt? I still marvel over it today: that Laura Lee seemed proud of her conquest, and her paramour did his share of the preening. At sixteen, I thought someone like me, someone who didn't need months and years of note-taking in order to draw a conclusion, should speak up. After all, who besides Mrs Woodbury was going to confront the truth? And who among the faculty, for reasons of various past indiscretions, would want to throw the first stone?

With only a two-burner stove and limited cookware, we weren't a family who entertained. Dinner parties were out of the question, but I thought, in the face of a campus crisis, we could put candles on the kitchen table and drag an extra chair in from the smoker.

I chose a Saturday on which my parents had an executive committee meeting of the Dewing Society of Professors, took the bus to Star Market, bought a good-sized chicken, some potatoes, some lettuce, and a pint of fancy ice cream.

David and Aviva weren't pleased to hear that company was coming at seven, but I was firm: yes, they were picking their battles and keeping their distance, but did they want to put themselves through another presidential search? Laura Lee needed a talking-to. Grandma would want us to step in. We could end up with someone with an anti-union animus, someone opposed to three people living in a dorm apartment meant for one.

'You should have asked us,' they said. 'Don't we run this family democratically?'

My parents dropped their worn leather satchels and flopped onto kitchen chairs. 'Did you stop to think that we are hardly the two people Laura Lee would want to take advice from on the subject of the sacredness of marriage?' my father asked.

'Yes, I did. But who else is going to sit her down and tell the truth?'

'Which is what?' asked my mother.

'That he'll wake up one morning embarrassed, and not only will he break up with her, but he'll fire her. He won't want her as a reminder, and his wife will insist they get rid of her.'

'Rather sophisticated analysis,' my mother said to my father. 'And compassionate.'

'Astute, even,' he agreed.

'And then who will write her a reference? She'll be back on the dole,' I pointed out. 'Yours. I'll have to go to Dewing because my tuition will go to alimony.'

'Gross exaggeration,' said my father.

'And she accepted this invitation of yours?' my mother asked.

I said, 'Yes, she did. She seemed happy to be invited.'

'What are we serving?' my mother asked.

I told her that the man behind the meat counter at Star Market had told me how to roast a chicken and when to take it out of the oven. Did we own paprika?

'I could have told you how to cook a chicken,' my mother said.

'She's roasted a lot of chickens in her day,' my father said proudly.

'It's not that hard,' I said. 'I think you could have showed me when I was, like, six.'

'I'm guessing your mother felt it would have been a sexist thing to do – to teach a daughter how to roast a chicken as if that were a mother's duty and a daughter's role.'

My mother nodded appreciatively. 'Now I'm thinking that if

we had had a son, we'd want him to know how to cook and iron and sew buttons on his shirts. Whereas with a daughter, we didn't want to send the mixed message, "Strive and learn and achieve, but you won't be a truly fulfilled woman unless you can roast the perfect chicken."'

Blah blah blah. We, we, we. No wonder I was raising myself.

One three-pound chicken and one pint of mint chocolate chip does not stretch five ways. Laura Lee, my parents and I, and her uninvited dinner date, Father Ralph, wearing a navy blue blazer and an ascot at the neck of his perfectly ironed Oxford blue shirt, politely ate the first course of chicken and the emergency backup of pot roast and succotash imported from Curran Hall.

A stranger's presence made the discussion of anything substantive more difficult, so we talked about the downward spiral of his job. My parents adjusted happily. They debriefed Father Ralph with zeal, since his complaints were job-related. What was the Church analogue of tenure? What about seniority? Benefits? Retirement?

The problem, according to plain-clothed Ralph, was that the bishop maintained that his directives about hours, wages, and working conditions came from God.

I laughed, the only one. Father Ralph asked, 'Why is that funny, child?'

'She wasn't raised with any religion,' explained Laura Lee.

'I'm Jewish,' said Aviva. 'And David is a non-practicing Presbyterian.'

'We're agnostic human secularists,' said my father.

I pointed at Laura Lee and my father, back and forth a few

times for emphasis. 'These two used to be married,' I heard myself say.

'I know,' said Father Ralph.

As my parents glared, I protested, 'He's a priest! He's not allowed to repeat anything he hears in confession, right?'

'That's right,' said Father Ralph.

'This is hardly confession,' said my mother.

'*I've* never understood what the big secret is,' said Laura Lee. 'Modern people like us? It seems utterly Victorian.'

'Was it unilateral?' I asked.

'Was what unilateral?'

'The decision to keep it a secret?'

'More or less,' said my father.

'Your parents decided. I was the new girl in town,' said Laura Lee, 'and they were the experts who believed that having an ex-wife on campus was going to be hard for you.'

I prodded the chicken carcass with the serving fork and was rewarded with a strand of dark meat. 'Anyone want this?'

'It's yours,' Laura Lee said. 'I haven't had much of an appetite lately.'

'It was delicious,' said Father Ralph.

'Why was it going to be hard for me?' I asked.

'Gossip,' said my mother. 'You know this place is first and foremost a rumor mill.'

'But it's not a rumor: they were married and now they're not. He married you, and you had me. Isn't that like every family in America?'

'Heaven forbid,' murmured Father Ralph.

We all looked at him. He said, 'I didn't mean that as a personal rebuke. I said it as a pre-Vatican II Catholic.'

'It wouldn't have lasted,' said Laura Lee. 'And this may be as good a time as any for me to say that I've made peace with the past. Frederica should know that her father and I would not be together today, even if Aviva hadn't jump-started the process.'

'How do you know that?' I asked.

'Children,' she said simply. 'He wanted them and I couldn't have them.'

'Laura Lee—' said my father.

'Couldn't, wouldn't . . . not much difference in the end if the woman doesn't feel she's equipped to be a mother,' said Laura Lee.

In normal families, that declaration would have been met with a self-conscious silence, whereas in mine, even in front of a celibate dinner guest and a minor, we had to explore its nuances.

'It wasn't a question of infertility, was it?' my mother asked.

Laura Lee smiled. 'Do you mean *infrequency*? Because I was starting to wonder if David was all that interested in me. Or women in general. Strictly from that point of view, it was almost a relief to know he was having an affair.'

Was this my fault? Had bringing up the divorce led us to this embarrassing topic? Or had I forgotten that all discussions around the Hatch table were embarrassing? I looked at Father Ralph. His expression was so purposefully neutral and pious that I had the urge to puncture it.

'Are you and Laura Lee dating?' I asked him.

No one gasped or scolded me. 'Priests don't date,' he said. 'I think everyone knows that.'

'Ralph and I are just friends,' said Laura Lee.

'What about you and President Woodbury?' I asked her.

I half expected that she would sputter, 'Dr Woodbury and I? I don't know what you're talking about.' But instead she answered, head held high and eyes glistening, 'You four are the only friends I have in this city. It's why I brought Ralph tonight, so we could talk. I mean, really talk. The way Frederica and I do.'

I had been sliding my chair away from the table, about to excuse myself as a mere teenager at the threshold of a seriously adult powwow, until my not-quite-stepmother fingered me as her number one confidante.

'Before you speak, please know that you're putting us in a rather uncomfortable position,' my father began.

'Bullshit,' said Laura Lee. 'You and your wife spend half your waking hours listening to other people's problems. I'd like to know what goes on at Dewing that you *don't* know about.'

'That's true, Dad,' I said.

'Perhaps Dr Hatch meant the uncomfortable position of listening to personal problems rather than *personnel* problems, which generally don't involve the commission of mortal sins,' added Father Ralph.

His was just the right note of religious condescension to drive Aviva and David into the ally camp. Minus a gavel, my mother rapped her knuckles on the bare pine of the table. 'Let's hear from Laura Lee now,' she said.

15

All Ears

GRACE WOODBURY, Laura Lee repeated earnestly and pseudo-scientifically, had been for the full term of the marriage – sorry, no other word – 'frigid'. Hence, Eric's inevitable turning to a woman who could offer him what he'd long been denied.

My mother said, '"Frigid"' isn't a medical diagnosis, Laura Lee. It's a word that men use to describe their wives to their mistresses. I hope you didn't believe him.'

Laura Lee asked, 'Is it all right to speak in this vein in front of Frederica?'

I said, 'They like it when every conversation contains a little sex education.'

Father Ralph said, 'What a different world we live in now. My parents wouldn't even spell the word "sex" in front of us, let alone tolerate it coming from the mouth of one of their children.'

'It's our fault,' said my mother. 'We treat her like an equal, which backfires on a daily basis.'

'You should have had a bunch of kids,' I said. 'Then we'd be an old-fashioned family with no back talk.'

'He grew up in a big Catholic family,' said Laura Lee.

'How big?' I asked.

'Eight children.'

'How many girls and how many boys?' I asked.

'She's fascinated by big families,' my mother said.

Laura Lee smiled. 'Only children. I was exactly the same way.'

'Where were you in the lineup?' I asked Father Ralph.

'Third child, oldest son.'

'And you know what that means,' said Laura Lee.

My mother said, 'You're Ralph Junior?'

'What I meant was he had virtually no choice except to become a priest. Nothing else would do for the oldest son of a devout family. Nothing made them prouder.'

'But what did the oldest *son* want to do?' asked my father.

'Me?' asked Father Ralph.

My father nodded.

'Please his parents. Not to mention his grandparents and two aunts who were nuns.'

'Didn't you have a guidance counselor?' I asked.

'They were priests,' said Father Ralph. 'I went to Catholic schools my whole life.'

Laura Lee, in a voice that managed to convey *enough about him*, asked if we had tea bags.

My father rose to fill the kettle and to clear the dinner plates.

'He never used to be a help around the house,' Laura Lee murmured.

'I was teaching, writing my thesis, and burning the midnight oil in two labs, while your days were a little freer,' my father answered.

'I think you mean "burning the midnight oil at your soon-to-be second wife's studio apartment,"' Laura Lee said pleasantly.

My father sent back a grimace of a smile that I knew was meant to say, Touché.

I said, 'Can we get back to the Woodburys?'

'One minute. I need my tea,' said Laura Lee.

Father Ralph immediately picked up where he'd left off, lamenting the career decision he'd made as an overage altar boy purely to please every adult in his orbit. 'The presumption is that you'll stay in the Church and die in the Church so that you won't need a mortgage or a credit rating, barely even a Social Security number. I'm turning fifty in two weeks,' he said. 'I have no job, no house, no wife, no children, no nest egg.'

My mother said, 'And is that what you're inclined toward: women? A wife and children?'

'Ma!' I said.

'Did I say something wrong? Because you know I ask that question without any prejudice or any subtext. None.'

'As your guest,' said Father Ralph, 'I'll give you the benefit of the doubt, and I won't assume that you meant that question as a slur. But it felt as if you were impugning my . . . my—'

'Masculinity,' Laura Lee supplied, eyes on the tea bag she was dipping.

I knew what was next: my mother's pro-homosexual speech. I coughed to draw her attention, then narrowed my eyes to convey, *He doesn't want you to think he's gay, so drop it.*

'Just say it, Frederica,' my mother chided.

I asked, 'Is it out of the question for you to apologize to our guest?'

My mother said, 'Case in point: my daughter thinks she's the arbiter of family etiquette.'

'High self-esteem,' said my father. 'Nothing we'd really want to do differently, hon.'

Laura Lee turned to her guest. 'Ralph? Is there anything else you want to say to Aviva?'

He was frowning, his gaze lowered to his place mat. 'Only to reiterate that I'm not gay. If I were, I wouldn't be leaving the Church to find warmth and companionship with a woman.'

'I apologize,' my mother said. 'At the same time, I never understand why the question of one's sexual proclivities would ever cause offense, because I see it as as benign a question as asking someone his blood type. But I can see that I offended you, and I *am* sorry.'

My father asked, 'Now what happens? Is there some kind of exit counseling the Church offers?'

'Or termination pay?' asked my mother.

'Unfortunately not,' said Ralph.

'I've been urging him to look into dorm parenting,' said Laura Lee.

'Here?' I asked.

My mother said, 'We're fully staffed, and we've never had a male dorm parent.'

'Isn't that your husband's job?' asked Ralph.

'I meant they don't allow single men. It would be breaking new ground at a women's college.'

Laura Lee said quietly, 'I could speak to Eric about it. He's not averse to breaking new ground.'

Finally, after ninety minutes of conversational hopscotch, we had circled back to the very reason I'd gathered everyone at our under-utilized table. 'Did you mean you can speak to Dr Woodbury because you two are dating?'

Laura Lee leaned sideways to bump shoulders with me. 'Is that not the sweetest question – "Are you two dating?" Three cheers for the Frederica who on some levels is still a sophomore in high school.'

'Which levels?' I asked.

'She's saying that, on occasion, you act your age, and she finds that endearing,' said my father.

'As do I,' said my mother.

'I was trying to be polite. I didn't want to offend anyone by saying "sleeping with" or "having sex with".'

'The word you're looking for is "euphemism",' offered my father. 'You were employing a euphemism.'

Laura Lee drained her cup, blotted her mouth, then asked, 'Where do I begin?'

'With whatever you need us to know,' said my father.

'*Need*?' asked Laura Lee. 'I find that a little patronizing. This isn't me looking for talk therapy. This is me in the middle of a crisis that affects hundreds, maybe thousands of people.'

'Wow,' I said.

'An entire university!'

No one corrected her; no one reviewed Dewing's standing as a barely full-fledged college.

Suddenly, as if emoting into an open mike, Laura Lee cried out, 'I love him!'

'How do you know?' asked Ralph.

She pointed to her head, her heart, and, most embarrassingly, her lap, all the while narrating, 'I love him here, and here, and here! Every way that one human being loves another.'

'This fast?' asked my mother.

'There's only one word that describes something this huge and instantaneous,' said Laura Lee, 'and that word is "electric". Which neither Eric nor I had experienced in our entire lives; not to this degree, anyway. What were we supposed to do? Walk away?'

'Does that mean that every time there are sparks between two people, you act on it?' asked Father Ralph.

'It's complicated,' said my father. 'One reads the signs; one examines one's own loyalties and commitments, one's own various codes of ethics and mores. One asks, Is this merely hormonal, or is it something more profound?'

'Are those inquiries one makes aloud?' Ralph asked.

'No,' said my father.

'Well, wait,' said my mother. 'Mating dances in humans can be very elaborate and varied—'

'It wasn't a mating dance,' said Laura Lee. 'It was combustion.'

'I wish I'd been there,' said Ralph.

'When did he call you?' I asked her.

'That night. October twenty-seventh. He must have gone directly to his office and called my extension. I knew he would. I'd gone straight home myself – took a tea bag and a congo bar with me so I could have dessert by my phone. That's how sure I was.'

'What did he say?' Ralph asked.

Laura Lee closed her eyes. 'He said my name. Actually he said just "Laura", which he's since corrected. He said something neutral, in case he'd overestimated the, the – how would I define it? – opening fireworks. He said, "This is Eric." Just "Eric." Not "President Woodbury." Not "Dr Woodbury." Just "Eric." I said, "I know." And then of course, it was on to the practical stuff.'

'Which is what?' asked Ralph.

'The wheres. The hows. The whens.'

'Can you be specific?' Ralph asked.

'Well, first I'll state the obvious: Eric and I both knew the subtext of any meeting. We weren't talking about a professional chitchat between a housemother and her boss—'

'Technically, he's not your boss,' said my mother. 'You report to the dean of residential life.'

'I know that, Aviva,' said Laura Lee.

I asked, 'How long after that night did you and Dr Woodbury sleep together?'

Laura Lee looked around the table. 'Do I have her parents' permission to answer that? Because I can just as easily say, "Never. He's a married man. We're just colleagues and very good friends."'

'We always prefer the truth,' said my father. 'Even if it's unsavory.'

Laura Lee turned slightly in her seat to face me squarely. 'The night we met, October twenty-seventh.'

'No. When did you *do* it?'

Ralph swallowed audibly. I remember thinking that regular, non-professional parents would adjourn this meeting now, or at least forbid me to say another word.

'I just told you,' said Laura Lee. 'Thursday, October twenty-seventh.'

'That same night?' I asked.

'Why is this so amazing? We met at dinner, no later than six P.M., and we were off the phone before seven-thirty.' She counted on the fingers of her left hand, 'Bathe, dress, find my way over to the Olmstead.'

'The Olmstead?' asked Ralph.

'The Olmstead Hotel? It's outside the city, in a suburb I'd rather not name, which is exactly why we chose it.'

I looked at my parents and saw two faces projecting a single conclusion: *We've brought an amoral and exceedingly indiscreet woman to Dewing.*

'Have I offended someone?' asked Laura Lee.

'They didn't want to believe the rumor,' I said. 'They're a little stunned that you're admitting everything.'

My mother silently nominated my father to speak for the Hatches.

'Aviva and I are looking for some self-doubt,' said my father. 'Some hesitation, some remorse over the fact that innocent people may be hurt.'

'Not if they don't find out!' said Laura Lee.

Ralph weighed in with the inevitable religious view of an all-seeing and all-knowing God, that more was at stake than a wife's sorrow or a wife's catching on, i.e., eternal life in the kingdom of heaven.

'Perhaps the word David is looking for is "culpability",' said my mother. 'We hear you talking about this affair as if you're congratulating yourself.'

Laura Lee said, 'Both of you will excuse me for not feigning remorse when I'm the happiest I've ever been in my entire life.'

'And you don't want her to lie, do you?' I asked the table.

'I want her not to sin,' said Ralph.

'I'm not even Catholic,' said Laura Lee. 'I couldn't even tell you what sins fall under which categories.'

'Thou shalt not commit adultery,' said Father Ralph. 'Is that not a part of your religion?'

Laura Lee said, 'I belong to the Church of You Only Go Around Once in Life.'

She wasn't trying to make a joke, but I giggled, causing Father Ralph to take the whole business out on me. 'Do you know what blasphemy means? You don't make up churches to fit your romantic leanings, and you don't brush aside the Ten Commandments for carnal convenience.'

'Maybe she's kidding,' I said. 'Maybe Laura Lee's exaggerating.'

'Maybe I am,' said Laura Lee. 'Maybe I know a captive audience when I see one. Maybe I like to shock people. Or I'm inventing tales just to tease David and Aviva.'

'Which would make perfect sense,' I pointed out, 'since they slept together while he was still married to Laura Lee.'

'That's quite enough,' said my father.

'Aren't I a good actress?' said Laura Lee. 'Didn't I have everyone on the edge of their seats?'

'*Excellent* actress,' I agreed.

'Trust me. No one's breaking any commandments, Ralph, and no one's disrupting any happy marriages,' said Laura Lee.

For once, my parents let a sentence pass without regurgitating or torturing it.

'I pray you're right,' Ralph said.

'You need a new name,' said Laura Lee. 'A symbol of your new beginning. How does that feel? Strange? Parental? Liberating?'

He smiled shyly. 'My middle name is Joseph. I always liked that. I always wished that had been my first name, and people could call me Joe. Like a regular boy . . . like an outfielder.'

'Mint chocolate chip, Joe?' I asked.

16

December

HISTORICALLY, WHEN THE DORMS closed for Christmas, we went to my grandmother's house in Adams, Massachusetts. She took her acculturation duties seriously, intent on exposing her half-breed granddaughter to as many Christmas table linens, heirloom cookies, and Yuletide songs as one uncommitted Presbyterian could provide. Holidays had meant five of us when my grandfather was alive. Since then, we would recruit the occasional stranded foreign student, who didn't mind hearing which ornament signified what passage in my father's infancy. The year Laura Lee came to Dewing, my grandmother proposed a plan of transportation that was so logical that no son or daughter-in-law could find it objectionable: we would drive Laura Lee as far as Adams, where her mother would pick her up for the last leg of the trip to Schenectady. Surely we were all comfortable around each other by now, correct? Bygones had become bygones?

'That's it?' my mother asked my father. 'We drive her across the state?'

'Not entirely,' he answered. 'We may have to factor in Christmas dinner with the extended family.'

'Call her back right now,' said my mother.

My father looked at his watch. 'She was heading for bed,' he said.

Aviva dialed just the same, advising me between numbers, 'You might want to observe how I handle this.'

Her bare feet slapped the kitchen linoleum as she paced, winding her finger in the longest curly cord on the market. After a businesslike 'Jane? Aviva,' my mother listened, winced, opened her mouth, closed it, and finally said, 'If you're saying that it's her rightful place at the table, then why don't I stay behind? It can be like old times – you, David, and Laura Lee. Frederica and I can go to my brother's in Montclair.'

I stopped pretending that I wasn't listening. '*Can* we?' I asked. My Montclair uncle had two teenage sons with drivers' licenses, a Cairn terrier who acted in a soap opera, and a collection of arcade-worthy pinball machines.

'That's true,' my mother was saying. 'He *doesn't* celebrate Christmas – being both my brother and a Jew.' She held the phone out to me. I declined with a shake of my head. 'Your grandmother wants to talk to you,' she pressed.

My grandmother went right to the cross-examination: would I want to break tradition and spend Christmas celebrating Hanukkah at my uncle's house rather than come to Adams?

I said carefully, eyes on my mother, 'I don't think Aviva was serious about changing our plans. She's used to taking votes and doing everything by committee.'

'Tell me the truth,' said my grandmother. 'Is it going to be very awkward for all of you to travel together?'

'Not *very* awkward,' I said.

'Bibi and I just assumed that your parents are educated in the social sciences and deal with awkward situations and disgruntled professors every day, so this wouldn't upset any apple cart. Twenty-four hours shouldn't be a strain.'

'The ride only takes three hours,' I said.

'I know that.'

'But you said, "twenty-four".'

In a voice that conveyed *let me put this into plain English*, she continued. 'You'll arrive on Christmas Eve. Bibi is coming for Christmas dinner on Sunday. I hardly thought it was fair to ask her to make an extra trip to pick up Laura Lee on *Saturday*, especially if the roads are bad. We'll eat in the dining room. I ordered a fourteen-pound turkey.'

I said, 'That sounds like a lot of work – feeding us on Saturday night, then another big meal on Sunday.'

My unsuspecting mother gestured, *No, don't ask her to change plans. Christmas Day, Christmas Eve – what's the difference?*

'I can't imagine Christmas Day without Christmas dinner,' my grandmother was saying. 'And I can't imagine Christmas dinner without extended family. Bibi is my only living first cousin in New England. Oh, and bring a dress.'

Strictly speaking, Bibi and Jane were second cousins, and Schenectady was not in New England. I asked why I'd never met this Bibi at previous holiday meals.

'Timing,' said my grandmother. 'I think you know to what I refer.'

147

'Has she ever met Mom?'

'Who?' asked my mother. 'Has who ever met me?'

'Bibi. Laura Lee's mother.'

'Never,' said Aviva from across the room, as my grandmother was saying, 'Bibi came to your parents' wedding.'

'Did she crash it?'

'Of course not.'

'Did she make a scene?'

'Bibi? Of course not. I invited her on the condition that she behave. She didn't stay for the reception.'

'How come you never told them?'

'Where's your father?' my grandmother asked.

'At a meeting.'

'At this hour?'

'There was a crisis somewhere,' I said.

'Don't let your parents forget about Laura Lee,' said my grandmother.

'Unlikely,' I said.

'If you don't go, I won't either,' I heard my father pledge the following afternoon. School had recessed at noon for Christmas vacation and I was wrapping presents in my room. 'We'll put Frederica on a bus, and you and I will spend the holiday at a hotel.'

It was my own fault. Second honeymoons were easy when you had a daughter who could fend for herself, who could now roast a bird, and whose ID card gave her entrée to an unchaperoned life.

I left my room and sat down on the piano bench. 'You'd refuse to go to Adams all because of Laura Lee?' I asked my father.

'No. Out of respect for your mother,' said David.

'I'm the wife of record,' said Aviva. 'I know your grand-mother will never make peace with the divorce, but I've been happily married to her son for eighteen years, and I've produced a daughter that any open-minded grandmother would say was worth the rupture.'

'Really?'

'Have we not conveyed that?' asked my mother. 'Because if we haven't, I'm very concerned.'

'Not so much lately,' I answered. 'Especially that part about putting me on a bus.'

'That was conjecture,' said my mother. 'That was Daddy being gallant in the face of his mother playing favorites.'

'Has anyone even passed along this Christmas invitation to Laura Lee?' my father asked. 'Wouldn't it be ironic if all of this was the plotting of the two mothers, and no one had brought the proposal to the table?'

'Interesting question,' said my mother.

'Call Laura Lee and ask her directly,' I volunteered. 'Or I will.'

'For once,' said my father, 'would you consider keeping out of this matter?'

'Fine,' I said. 'I'll leave you two to your executive session. I hope I haven't used up too much space or oxygen in the past sixteen years.'

One or both asked where I was going.

'Out.'

'Don't leave campus,' said my father.

'Do you have your ID?' asked my mother.

I patted it, through my clothes, against my sternum.

'Let's have dinner together,' said my father. 'Six at Curran?'

'No, thank you,' I said.

'Then you name the time,' said my mother. 'Because we're definitely eating together tonight so this doesn't escalate.'

'We could go out to a restaurant,' my father offered.

I was slightly torn, remembering there were éclairs on the campus menu. 'What restaurant?' I asked.

'Coach House?' he wheedled.

'Maybe,' I said. 'If you insist.'

As I headed for our front door, my parka bunched under one arm, I heard, 'Another father might tell you to put that coat on and zip it up.'

I turned around. 'Just tell me, then! Pretend you're the kind of father who tells his kid to put on her coat so she won't catch a cold.'

'We don't tell you what to do,' said my father. 'If you want to get chilled, it's really none of our business.'

I said, 'Since when does reverse psychology work on me?'

'Do you want to talk about it?' he asked.

I said no, I did not.

'Are you going over to Marietta's?' my mother asked.

I wasn't, but visiting Marietta struck me as an excellent suggestion, armed as I was with parental grievances, and in the relatively bad mood that would make us more compatible.

Mrs Woodbury's Cadillac was parked askew in the circular driveway. Ordinarily, by dusk, someone would have lit the omni-denominational holiday bulbs, but the house was dark. Even the front-porch light, meant to symbolize an open door and round-the-clock hospitality, was extinguished. I rang the bell once, a long peal. When no one appeared, I tried the three-beep signal we guides used to announce *tour in progress*. The door was open. I let myself in.

'Anybody home?' I called. 'Hello?'

What was I looking for, possibly even hoping for? Brothel noises, evidence, sights and smells? Or dramatic nothingness, an abandoned house, which I would thrill to report: *The Woodburys left town! Mrs Woodbury must have issued an ultimatum: that housemother or me. Leave everything, leave the Caddy. I won't spend one more minute in this soulless and frozen place.*

What I found was worse: the distinct sound of sobbing from upstairs.

I tiptoed to the stairway, then up to the first landing, past the Currier and Ives skaters on the Boston Common that I bragged about in the art-appreciation portion of my tours. 'Is everything all right?' I called.

I climbed higher, another landing, a grandfather clock, the gift of the loyal class of 1950. 'It's me. Frederica,' I tried, louder. The crying stopped abruptly.

What was my duty? Since childhood, I'd been taught the protocol: keep an eye out for the depressed and the disheveled. Tell David or Aviva or alert an RA. If no adult was present, call the dean of students, the infirmary, or, if the girl's safety was in question, 9-1-1.

From the top step I said, 'Mrs Woodbury?'

'Not here,' said the voice.

'Grace?'

'I told you: my mother's not here!' said the voice.

'Marietta?' I tried.

Mrs Woodbury's unmistakable voice came back in a brighter tone. 'Yes, that's right. It's Marietta.'

'Is everything okay?'

'I have a bad cold. I can't say another word, so you have to leave.'

'Sure. Sorry. Okay.' At the halfway landing I yelled back upstairs, 'I'm leaving. I won't tell anyone I was here.' And then, so she'd think her impersonation had succeeded, 'Call me later if you can sneak to the phone, okay?'

'I shall,' the faux Marietta warbled.

Where would I take this information? Home to my parents for a political discussion on the rights of privacy? And what would I say? That I had let myself into Marietta's house, assuming she was closeted in her room and, as usual, deaf to the doorbell? Oh, and incidentally? I found Mrs Woodbury sobbing.

'You don't know the context,' they would say. 'She was probably watching a sad movie or reading a sad book. We have to respect an adult's right to cry in the privacy of her home.' I would have had to frame it as a union matter or a dormitory dilemma: someone under your wing, Mom and Dad, someone on the verge of buying a term paper or filing a grievance sounds seriously depressed.

I went looking for Marietta, first in the library, then at the student center, the commuter lounge, and the bookstore, where she was known to buy gum and candy bars, and finally at her father's office. His secretary, still named Bunny in her late sixties, was a holdover from the previous administration, and had been in the same creaky desk chair since I was born. 'Is Dr Woodbury in?' I asked Bunny.

'Do you have an appointment?'

I said, 'It'll take one minute.'

'Someone's in with him,' she said.

'Can I wait?'

She looked at her watch. 'It's late. I don't know how long this appointment will take.'

I said, 'You don't have to wait. I can watch the office for you.'

Bunny, who'd never lived on campus, who reportedly threw away union notices contractually required to be posted on the bulletin board in her custody, and had never doted on me, huffed a *no thanks*.

I crossed the royal blue carpet and its Dewing seal to a leather chair. 'How's our new president doing?' I asked.

Bunny didn't look up. 'Why?' she asked.

'Do you think he's happy here?'

'Extremely.'

'He's auditing one of my mother's seminars.'

'I know that. Tuesdays and Thursdays, three to four-thirty.'

'Does he like it?' I asked.

'We've never discussed it,' said Bunny.

'What about Mrs Woodbury? Do you think she's just as happy here?'

She looked up. 'I wouldn't know, Frederica. And it's not our business.'

'But you talk to her all the time, right? And don't you sometimes work over at the house?'

Bunny didn't answer. She swiveled away from me to face her typewriter and fed two sheets of paper, a carbon between them, into it.

After a few moments I said softly, 'I think she must be miserable, don't you?'

I studied her shoulders and the back of her head for any sign, any twitch of agreement, but she, a pro, wouldn't give me that.

'Should I knock?' I asked after a few more silent minutes.

'No.'

What did I think I was going to say to the president of the college? *I hope you know that your wife is upset. Possibly having what laymen call a nervous breakdown. I was going to tell Marietta, but I can't find her. I think you should go home and see if she's all right.* 'Maybe I'll come back,' I said.

'Do you want to make an appointment?' Bunny asked.

I crossed to her desk and planted myself in front of her typewriter. 'I don't think that's necessary, do you? We both live on campus, and I'm friends with his youngest daughter. I see him all the time.'

'Suit yourself,' said Bunny.

I walked back to my own dorm by way of Curran Hall. The evening meal wasn't out yet, but one of my hairnetted buddies wrapped three éclairs to go.

Before we'd opened our menus, my father announced that we were all going to Grandma's house, respecting her wishes, like the mature and flexible people that we all knew ourselves to be.

'What happened?' I asked.

'We talked about it and we decided we have enough confrontation in our lives,' said my mother. 'And here was an issue we could shelve without compromising any principles—'

'Knowing that Laura Lee is not our enemy,' my father added. 'She is, in the eyes of the college, simply the newest housemother and she needs a ride home at Christmas.'

'Who are "the eyes of the college"? Someone she told about her plans, so now you can't leave her high and dry?'

My mother's glance swept the room – we always bumped into colleagues at the Coach House – before she said, 'Apparently she told Eric Woodbury that we were taking her home for Christmas, and he was pleased.'

'Did he say why?'

'I would imagine,' said my father, 'that the president of a college does not want any employee to be spending her holiday on a locked-up campus—'

'In a nearly unheated dormitory,' my mother added.

I asked how they knew Woodbury was pleased.

My mother said, 'He came to class today.'

'And mentioned to your mother something along the lines of what a nice gesture it was to extend a hand to the new girl on the block, given that she's all alone.'

'Did you say, "What's it to you, buddy?"'

'No, I did not,' said my mother.

'And that was it? You didn't say anything?'

'Such as?'

'That anyone with two eyes in their head can see he's cheating on his wife, who's just as much the new girl on the block, and probably all alone, too.'

They both sighed, reached for rolls, buttered them. My father said, 'Here is a cold dose of reality, Frederica: how often have we spoken to the man when it hasn't been adversarial? Once? Twice? Never? Yet here he was saying, in effect, that

155

despite pigeonholing the Hatches as pains in the ass, he was now seeing us in a different light.'

'Which one?' I asked.

'A friendly and collegial one. Even an altruistic one.'

I asked if Laura Lee was by his side as he was making his speech.

'They've stopped doing that,' said my mother. 'They sit separately and they hardly exchange glances.'

'Why not? If everybody knows.'

'What everyone knows is gossip. Your mother and I ignore the rumors, especially after Laura Lee admitted at our own table that no one was disrupting any happy marriage.'

'They were making euphemisms,' I said. 'Isn't that when you say something to protect the innocent?'

My mother pointed to a box on my father's menu: 'Bouillabaisse for two persons.' He nodded enthusiastically.

My mother asked what I was in the mood for. Before I could answer she said, 'Let's leave it this way: sometimes adults know what's best. And reaching out to Laura Lee is the right thing to do at this point in time.'

I asked if she meant now, December, the holidays, when lonely people get lonelier and jump off bridges.

'That. And with a cost-of-living adjustment on the table,' she said quietly.

I studied my menu, which I knew by heart. 'Fine. No one's committing adultery in front of your impressionable daughter. No one's noticing, and no one's suffering. As long as the faculty union profits, I'm happy.'

To hinder the cross-examination, I timed my announcement to coincide with the arrival of our smiling waiter. 'I'll have the porterhouse steak, medium, with fries,' I told him. 'For one.'

'Were you being ironic?' my mother asked.

'Did you mean that any benefits that accrue to the union do *not* make you happy?' asked my father.

'I'll come back,' said the waiter.

17

I Hate Them All

ANY ONE OF US WOULD have been grateful for nothing worse than an awkward round trip across the state. Instead, we Hatches were whisking Laura Lee, now the official other woman, out of town after Grace Woodbury attached a vacuum cleaner hose to the exhaust pipe of her Caddy and nearly succeeded in killing herself.

I received the news on December twenty-fourth, waking to find my mother seated at the foot of my bed wearing such a tragic expression that I cried out, 'What happened? Where's Daddy?'

'Daddy's fine. He went to his office.' She dug beneath my covers, found my right hand, and rubbed it. 'But, honey – Marietta's mother attempted suicide.'

'*Attempted*?'

'She's alive. At Mass. General. In intensive care.'

'Is she going to be okay?'

'We don't know much more, except that she's in a coma.'

I asked how, when, where? What else did she know?

'Yesterday. In her car, in their garage, with the motor running.'

'But then changed her mind?'

My mother said no. She was rescued. Thank goodness for an astute and observant UPS man who was delivering a fruitcake from the board of trustees.

'Who told you?' I asked.

'Marietta's father told Laura Lee. Who called Daddy.'

I lay back down, put my pillow over my face, and asked from underneath it, 'Why aren't you saying that she's going to be all right?'

'It's too early to tell,' said my mother. 'And we're getting our information from a fairly hysterical source.'

'Don't people come out of comas? They always do on TV.'

'It depends on the neurological damage. Daddy's at his office right now reading up on carbon monoxide poisoning.'

'Where's Marietta?' I asked.

'Presumably at the hospital with her father.'

'Is Marietta okay?'

'Laura Lee didn't mention her, but that doesn't mean—'

'Did Dr Woodbury mention Marietta? Or is he too busy praying his wife won't make it?'

'Frederica!'

I sat up. 'Wouldn't it be convenient? He'd be a widower. Everyone would feel sorry for him and he could screw every housemother who brought him a casserole!'

She found one of my ankles through the cover and held it. 'You're angry at him. Of course you would be. You enjoyed those rides to school with Marietta until Mrs Woodbury became too humiliated to carpool.'

I said, 'We let this happen. We should have seen it coming. I could have stopped her.'

The resulting expression was a combination of maternal concern and academic curiosity. Finally she said, 'Honey? Why do you think you let this happen? Can you tell me? This is important.'

I lay back down and folded my arms across my face.

'In this family we talk,' she tried.

I whispered, 'She was crying when I went over there.'

'When was this?'

'Night before last.'

'Did you talk to her?'

I said no. Well, sort of. I'd only exchanged a few sentences with her from the stairwell.

'What did she say?'

I didn't want to confess that Mrs Woodbury was impersonating Marietta and I'd played along. 'Not too much.'

My mother sounded relieved. 'How could you possibly have predicted she might do harm to herself? Even a psychiatrist wouldn't have deduced that from the stairwell.'

I sat up again and yelled, my voice choked, 'Maybe I could have put two and two together. Maybe somebody should have noticed that she was depressed. Maybe some professor of criminology could have kicked them out of class for inflicting cruel and unusual punishment on somebody's wife.'

My mother met this with silence. Finally she asked, 'Do you really think that someone in my relatively controversial position could tell the president of this college to behave himself?'

'Somebody should have,' I said.

'And said what? "Cut it out"? "Your wife seems depressed"? Who *isn't* around here?'

I confessed then that I had gone to Woodbury's office to tell him that his wife was all alone in a dark house and sobbing as if her heart was broken.

My mother moved from the foot of the bed to my side. 'What did he say?'

'I didn't see him. He had someone in his office and I decided not to wait.'

'Did you tell Bunny it was important?' asked my mother.

'Important?' I repeated. 'How about urgent? How about life or death?' I flounced onto my side, then into the fetal position, which always got attention in my family.

'Let me point out,' said my mother, 'that Grace Woodbury must have been an extremely unstable and depressed woman if she tried to take her own life. Now I'm going to say something you won't like: you are a child. No one expects a child to fix a marriage or prevent a suicide.' She patted my hipbone through the quilt, then rose from the bed. 'Your father and I will do whatever we can,' she said.

'For who?'

She stopped in the doorway and turned around. 'For everyone, Frederica,' she said.

My father was working hard at rolling down the driver's window of our rental car in anticipation of the tollbooth. Because there was a light snow falling, I suggested he turn on the windshield wipers. There – the black knob. No, the other one. Clockwise. Now give the ticket to me for safekeeping.

Laura Lee had requested the passenger seat because she was prone to carsickness. She was sniffling, and pretending to do it privately. Every ten minutes or so my father would ask, 'Do you want to talk about it, Laura Lee?' She'd shake her head, look out the side window, pass a tissue delicately under her nostrils.

Just beyond the Framingham exit, Laura Lee said, 'I think this is a mistake. I don't think I should have run off like the guilty party.'

'You're going to your mother's for Christmas,' my father said quietly. 'No one would consider that running off.'

'The college virtually shuts down,' said my mother. 'No one stays behind to consider anything.'

I said, 'Maybe Laura Lee meant she should be by her boyfriend's side.'

Laura Lee swiveled around to bark at my mother, 'Your daughter has no right to be talking to me like that. Do you ever tell her that she's too fresh and too big for her britches?'

'All the time,' said my mother.

'It's how they raised me,' I said.

'You're annoying all of us,' said my father. 'So pretend you're traveling with Patsy's family, where children don't weigh in on adult conversations.'

'Our nerves are frayed,' added my mother.

'Who's Patsy?' asked Laura Lee.

'A school chum of Frederica's who has a big nuclear family and strict, God-fearing parents,' my father supplied.

'They're not professors, so they live in a house,' I said. 'With a finished basement and a color TV.'

'Is that what you want?' Laura Lee asked.

I pursed my lips, silence made observable, to remind her that she had requested no communication from me, the brat.

'Answer her question,' my mother murmured.

'Yes,' I said. 'Okay? I would like to live in a house like most normal people do.'

'Patsy Leonard has to share her bedroom with her little sister,' my mother said.

'I might have liked a sister,' I said.

'You have hundreds of sisters!' my father said. 'Thousands, if you add up sixteen graduating classes at Dewing.'

'I hate them all,' I said.

We continued in silence along the Pike. Traffic was always heavy on the two days a year we traveled west, no matter what time we set out. The three-hour trip might be taking four.

'Do we have everything?' my mother asked. 'David? Did you take the shopping bag on the kitchen counter?'

'In the trunk,' he said.

'Did you bring the presents?' I asked.

'Ditto,' said my father.

'We bought Jane an illustrated book on bonsai and a starter kit,' said my mother.

I turned to her and asked quietly, 'Does Grandma know what happened?'

My mother shook her head.

Laura Lee said, still facing front, 'David and I think that Jane doesn't need to know any more than the fact that the president's wife is in the hospital—'

'She'll want to know why,' I said.

'We're saying, "She's in the hospital. Her car broke down and she was stuck by the side of the road, and her tailpipe was blocked by a snowbank and she suffered carbon monoxide poisoning."'

'Who came up with that?' asked my mother.

'We both did,' said Laura Lee. 'David and I.'

'Isn't it a little elaborate?' asked my mother.

I said, 'If the car was running, she wasn't broken down.'

'She was stuck in a snowbank,' said my father.

'Wouldn't she have gone for help?'

My father said, 'Your grandmother is not going to interrogate me. If she has any questions, they'll be about Grace's medical condition.'

'Which is where we can pick up the truthful part of the story,' said Laura Lee.

'Why not tell the whole truth from the beginning?' asked my mother.

Laura Lee answered for them both. 'It isn't necessary. It's Christmas. Why bring up a difficult subject—'

'Like sin,' I said.

My mother looked perplexed: What alien values had her daughter been assimilating outside the home?

'Now that Aviva brings it up, I'm not terribly comfortable with our fabrication,' my father said to Laura Lee.

Laura Lee asked smartly, 'At what point did you tell your mother that you'd left me and were having an affair with Aviva?'

'Promptly.'

'No, you didn't! She called the apartment and asked for you, and I had to tell her you were no longer in residence, but could be reached at the apartment of a Miss Aviva Ginsburg.'

'Is this necessary?' my mother murmured.

'What's our exit number?' asked my father.

I said, 'The last exit on the Pike. You don't even have to think about it.'

Laura Lee said, 'You don't know the exit number for your childhood home?'

'He's got a lot on his mind,' I said.

Aviva asked, 'What about *your* mother, Laura Lee? Don't you think she'll pick up on the fact that you're upset and want to draw you out about what's bothering you?'

She said tersely, 'Not all families work the way yours does, Aviva.'

'She's going to know something's wrong,' said my father. 'I think you should tell her, especially if you're going to extend your stay.'

'She is?' I asked.

'We weren't speaking to you, Frederica,' said Laura Lee.

'Is this something new? You won't be returning with us?' asked my mother.

'That depends,' said Laura Lee.

'Are you talking about Mrs Woodbury?' I asked. 'If she dies or not?'

'No one thinks she's going to die, honey,' said my father.

'You don't know! You haven't talked to her doctors!'

'Poor Marietta,' said my mother. 'We should have taken her with us.'

'You must be joking,' I said.

'Christmas for her will forever be associated with this

tragedy,' said my father. 'Whether her mother fully recovers or not.'

'You don't think Marietta knows her father was fooling around and that's what drove her mother to suicide? Do you think she'd want to spend Christmas with her father's girlfriend?'

My mother said quietly, 'We would have altered our plans. Your grandmother would have understood.'

'I'm telling Grandma the whole story,' I said.

'No, you're not,' said Laura Lee. Then: 'Does anyone have any control over this child?'

'Maybe Frederica is right,' my father said. 'Maybe the lesson of Watergate was "Keep secrets at your own peril."'

'Or you'll have to resign,' I added.

Laura Lee turned around, this time facing me squarely, hands gripping the back of her seat. 'What happened?' she asked. 'We were such good friends. I explained to you, to all of you, about this gigantic, unforeseeable, profound, and, most amazing of all, mutual bond between Eric and me. Don't make me say anything more. Don't make me verbalize what he didn't have with his wife.'

The traitor at the wheel chimed in, 'I guess I don't appreciate, either, Frederica, why you're so hostile to Laura Lee.'

'Maybe she misses her,' said my mother. 'Maybe it's precisely because they were such good friends that Frederica feels the loss so intensely and is masking it with anger.'

I wasn't ready to admit to any such thing. I said instead, 'I don't think the president of a college and a housemother should be having an affair like they're proud of it. And I don't want Marietta's mother to die. Is that so hard to understand?'

Laura Lee clucked and flounced back around to face the road. My mother patted my hand. 'We'll call the hospital from the next phone booth,' she said.

'Try the morgue,' I said.

'Frederica's never been a Pollyanna,' my father announced proudly.

18

Alienation of Affection

OUR HOSTESS SHOWED US to my father's childhood room, still decorated in brown corduroy, still displaying artifacts from his science-club and Eagle Scout days.

'Wouldn't it make more sense for David and Aviva to have his old room, and for me and Frederica to sleep in the guest room?' Laura Lee asked.

'Married people get the guest room,' said my grandmother.

Laura Lee assumed a pained expression. 'I didn't prepare myself for this,' she said.

'For what?' my grandmother asked.

'Sleeping in my ex-husband's bed.' She sighed, crossed the threshold without her suitcase, and turned back to face us.

My grandmother said, 'I bought these sheets well after David ever spent the night in this room. And the pillow, too. There really isn't anything of his left. The towels are new.'

'Which bed did he sleep in?' I asked.

My grandmother pointed to the one beneath the solar system mobile.

'I'll take that one,' I said. Laura Lee didn't answer. She lay down on the spare bed and stared up at the ceiling.

'She didn't get much sleep last night,' I told my grandmother.

'I can speak for myself, Frederica,' said Laura Lee.

I put my overnight bag in the closet, which was now my grandmother's arts and crafts headquarters, stuffed with bags of yarn and bolt ends of fabric.

'Towels in the linen closet. You don't have to use the brown ones. And cocktail hour at five, or whenever anybody comes downstairs.'

Laura Lee lifted her head from the flat pillow. 'Not a party, I hope?'

'*We're* a party,' said my grandmother happily.

I unpacked quickly and quietly. The one skirt I'd brought was brown corduroy, not intentional, but depressing just the same. The sight of it caused Laura Lee to lift her head from the pillow. 'Hand-me-down from your father?' she asked before subjecting me to one of her increasingly cruel laughs.

While no one was explicitly forbidding me a refill of eggnog, the subject was under discussion. My grandmother had set out the seasonal punch bowl with its ten etched cups and a plate of cookies meant, via their blue sprinkles, to be ecumenical.

'You decide,' said my father. 'Think about what you could miss later if you get sick.'

'What would I miss?'

'My yule log,' said my grandmother. 'And carolers from Bible Baptist.'

'I don't understand what you object to,' said Laura Lee.

'I've seen people get sick on eggnog,' said my mother. 'Even experienced drinkers.'

'This is spiked?' asked Laura Lee, taking an insincere sniff from her fourth cup. She'd been drunk since guzzling her third.

'Can't you taste it?' asked my grandmother.

'Here, Freddie,' said Laura Lee. 'You can finish mine.'

'I'd prefer that she didn't,' said my mother.

'It's probably good for her,' said Laura Lee. 'Protein and vitamin D.'

'I should have put some aside for Frederica before I added the bourbon,' said my grandmother.

'Surely not necessary in that family,' said Laura Lee. 'They wouldn't want their teenager to know she was under twenty-one.'

My grandmother looked toward my parents, who were tucked under the same poinsettia afghan on a loveseat. 'Is something going on that I don't know about?'

I stopped what I was doing – my annual painstaking job of draping tinsel strand by strand on the Christmas tree – and checked with my parents. My father fixed me with his sternest stare, a clear request for non-participation.

'Something very upsetting happened on campus,' my mother answered. 'Something that has us all a little shaken.'

Laura Lee grunted in what might have been agreement, except that she raised her glass, not in a toast, but to examine the reindeer etched in the glass. 'I have Prancer,' she said. 'Who has Rudolph?'

'We lost Rudolph,' said my grandmother. 'In fact, I don't think he survived David's childhood. Santa's disappeared, too.'

'It's a shame eggnog's only served once a year,' said Laura Lee.

'She makes it at Thanksgiving, too,' I said.

'This is homemade?' Laura Lee asked.

'Of course,' said my grandmother. 'From fresh eggs, newly laid. And the nutmeg is freshly ground.'

'Do you own chickens?' asked Laura Lee.

'I've thought about it,' said my grandmother. 'But for one person, I'd have too many eggs. And I certainly don't want to get into the retail egg business.'

'You'd need a rooster, too,' I said.

'Even sillier when you consider that Panek's Poultry Farm is a ten-minute ride from here,' said my grandmother.

'I prefer the city,' said Laura Lee, and burst into tears.

My grandmother said, 'Frederica, get Laura Lee a handkerchief from my top drawer. Upstairs. Go.'

They held back until I was out of eavesdropping range. I ran the rest of the way, grabbed the top handkerchief, and galloped back downstairs. My father was delivering the hospital update we'd obtained at the phone booth. 'Critical but stable,' he was saying. 'That's all they tell you at the switchboard.'

'I don't understand,' said my grandmother, turning back to Laura Lee. 'Were you very close to this president's wife?'

Laura Lee ignored the handkerchief from my outstretched hand, letting the tears run down her cheeks for more dramatic effect. I tossed it onto her lap and took a seat on the piano bench. 'What did I miss?' I asked.

Aviva answered, 'Your grandmother knows that the reason the president's wife is in the hospital is because of carbon monoxide poisoning, self-induced.'

'Didn't you just attend his inauguration?' asked my grandmother.

'Induction,' said my father. 'September.'

'So you haven't known her very long,' my grandmother said to Laura Lee.

'I met her once.'

'What are you crying about, then?'

'It's a big mess,' I supplied when no one else answered.

'For the college, you mean?' said my grandmother. 'In terms of parent relations?'

'Parents don't know what goes on,' said Laura Lee. 'At least that's been my experience so far.'

'Did anyone notice that the president's wife was a danger to herself?' asked my grandmother.

'I noticed she was depressed,' I said.

'Their marriage was on the rocks,' added Laura Lee.

'Does anyone know why?'

'For the usual reason,' Laura Lee said. 'Because her husband was in love with someone else!'

'Not with a coed, I hope,' said my grandmother.

'Certainly not,' said my mother.

'Do they have children?' my grandmother asked.

'Only one's still on campus,' I said. 'And she's my friend. We used to ride to school together.'

Laura Lee began sniffling again.

'You know the daughter, too?' asked my grandmother.

Laura Lee nodded bravely.

'I think I understand why Laura Lee is so upset,' my grandmother confided. We waited. Nothing followed except a long sympathetic gaze at the ex-daughter-in-law who'd known a husband's infidelities.

I said, 'Wait a minute? Do you think Laura Lee's upset because she feels *sorry* for Mrs Woodbury?'

Laura Lee was on her feet for what looked like an abrupt exit. Instead, she crossed to the piano bench and swatted at me. I ducked easily. David and Aviva were instantly on the job, restraining my assailant.

'She's a little shit,' said Laura Lee. 'Someone should knock some manners into her.'

'You're drunk,' I yelled.

'Go to your room,' my grandmother said.

Laura Lee didn't obey. She wiggled her elbows free of my parents and plunked herself down next to me on the piano bench.

'Watch it,' I said.

'Frederica?' my grandmother said.

'Me?'

'For once,' said my grandmother, 'I'd like to have a strictly adult conversation.'

I waited for my parents to defend my right to free assembly and to denounce corporal punishment, but they didn't. My mother, still at my side, said, 'I'll go with you.' She said to Laura Lee, 'If you ever hit my daughter again, I'll see that she never comes within a hundred yards of you. Or your dormitory.'

'She means it,' I said, and put my arm around Aviva's waist.

Laura Lee stuck out her tongue after my mother turned away.

'Don't be childish,' my father said.

'I'm dropping your class!' Laura Lee yelled after us.

'I wondered how long it would take,' murmured my grandmother.

'I hope you're not beating up any of your students,' I yelled back.

'Go to your room,' my father barked after me.

I told my mother she could stay downstairs. I'd be fine. I'd read or play solitaire with the door closed so they could have their privacy. 'Call me if you need help in the kitchen, Grandma,' I remembered to add sweetly.

When the living room below me grew quiet, and I could hear meal-preparation noises from the kitchen, I came downstairs and asked my father if he wanted to go for a walk.

'Sure,' he said. 'Does Aviva want to join us?'

'She has to wrap some presents and some must be for me because she doesn't want me around,' I lied. 'She's really trying to get into the spirit of Christmas.'

He liked that. I followed him to the coat tree by the door, where he wound a striped scarf around his neck and chose a tweedy crocheted hat of my grandmother's that I would have forbidden at home.

Once outside, I tried the opener I'd devised during my exile. 'Is Laura Lee okay?'

'In what respect?'

'I'm no expert,' I said, 'but I think she was drunk.'

My father walked half a block before saying, 'It may have been the emotional strain.'

'Is that what you'd say if someone in the dorm drank four cups of eggnog and hit her roommate? That she was under a strain?'

He shook his head sadly. 'No. You're right. She had too much to drink.'

'She brings a flask into Curran, you know. Filled with wine.'

'Not now, Frederica.'

I pointed down the block. 'Same place?'

'Sure.'

We were headed to the small cemetery at the end of the street. When I thought enough time had passed and we'd covered which of his neighbors' driveways he had shoveled in his teenage entrepreneurial days, at what wages, I asked, 'Did you tell Grandma the whole story?'

'After a fashion.'

I asked what that meant: *after a fashion*. Was everything out in the open now or not? Would we be pussyfooting through dinner or speaking honestly?

He took my mittened hand and squeezed it. 'You don't need to keep up a brave front. We know you are extremely fond of Mrs Woodbury. On top of that, Marietta is your chum. And most touching of all, you love Dewing. You're worried that something happened that could touch off a scandal. You don't need dinner etiquette as an excuse to know what Laura Lee said.'

Even with his unblemished record of sensitivity, I wasn't expecting this much help. 'Okay,' I said. 'If that's how you feel, just tell me everything.'

We had reached the entrance to the cemetery and were on the path that led to our favorite spot, a granite bench, the memorial for an Ernest Lawrence Lamport. Confident that the full transcript of the adult powwow was forthcoming, I made some graveyard small talk. Wasn't it nice that Ernest's loved ones would choose something practical like a bench?

'Of course you remember that he was our head librarian,' my father explained. 'I think his wish was that people would come here with a book.'

'Did you know him?'

'Of course! Everyone did. He came from one of the first families of Adams. Everyone knew that his annual salary was one dollar. When he retired, the town had to do some fancy footwork, budgetarily speaking, to finance an actual salary.'

I waited a polite few seconds, then asked, 'Can we call the hospital when we get back?'

'We called. No change.'

'Did you talk to Woodbury?'

'I don't particularly want to.'

'Can't Laura Lee call him?'

'At this point, no news is good news, hon.'

I moved closer to the end of the bench so that I wasn't sitting on Mr Lamport's name. My father put his arm around my shoulder, nudging me toward him.

I asked, 'Does Grandma know that Laura Lee is the president's girlfriend?'

'We told her, but I'm not sure it registered.'

I waited a few moments before asking, 'Can I try?'

'For whose sake exactly would you be doing this?'

'For Grandma's! And for Aviva's. Unless you haven't noticed, your mother thinks Laura Lee is a saint. Better than Mom in every way: not a professor, not a rabble-rouser, not a Jew! It makes me sick.'

He dropped his arm and said sharply that there was no need to raise my voice; it was disrespectful in this setting. And further, how could I accuse his own mother of anti-Semitism when she was sensitive enough to wrap presents in Hanukkah paper and to bake cookies in the shape of six-pointed stars? Never had an unkind word about Aviva's religion been uttered under his family's roof – not now, not ever. See that yellow house with the orange shutters? Mrs Marmelstein was Mother's best friend on the street throughout his entire childhood.

'Sorry,' I whispered.

Immediately, the arm went around me again. 'One more thing,' he confided. 'Your hostility toward Laura Lee. Do you understand it yourself? Do you want to talk about it?'

No I did not. I said, 'How about that fact that she'll get fired, and we'll have to support her all over again because she'll never get another job? Have you thought of that?'

'Woodbury wouldn't dare fire Laura Lee. She'd have a rock-solid case before the Commission Against Discrimination if that came to pass.'

'Is any of this against the law?' I asked.

'Terminating a worker after initiating a sexual relationship with her—'

'Not that. I meant the affair. If someone makes you want to kill yourself, wouldn't that be something you could sue over?'

'Alienation of affection,' he said quietly. 'Also known as grounds for divorce.'

'What if she's stuck in a coma and can't divorce him?' I asked.

He landed a kiss on the top of my head. 'Not your concern,' he said.

Too late for that. I already held the firm conviction that everything was my concern.

19

Dinner Is Delayed

MY FATHER, NOTICING ONE CAR missing from the driveway, said, 'Mother's been known to slip out to Vespers on Christmas Eve.'

She hadn't. Instead, she'd lent the station wagon to Laura Lee, who'd pleaded for a change of venue and time to think.

'You let her drive drunk?' I asked.

'Drunk?' my grandmother repeated. 'I don't think a person can get drunk on eggnog – something to do with the proteins canceling out the alcohol.'

'I wasn't aware she had a license,' said my father.

'She said she needed a change of scenery. I gave her directions to Panek's because she wanted to get some fresh eggs for Bibi.'

'Why would a chicken farm be open on Christmas Eve?' I asked.

We were in the unheated mudroom off the kitchen. My

grandmother pointed to the back door. 'Shake the snow off so it doesn't melt in the house, please.'

'Where's my mother?' I asked.

'In the guest room, grading papers,' said my grandmother. 'Apparently a quiet upper floor is a luxury she has yet to experience.'

My father rubbed his hands together and asked if anyone wanted to join him for a cup of tea.

'All my burners are in use,' said my grandmother. 'But I suppose I could take the potatoes off for a few minutes.'

I asked how long Laura Lee had been gone.

'Ten minutes? Twenty? Not very long.'

'How would you describe her emotional state when she left?' my father asked.

My grandmother was filling her copper teakettle at the sink. 'I don't notice those things the way you do,' she said.

Two hours later, Laura Lee hadn't returned. My grandmother was stationed at a window that overlooked the driveway, while David had gone down the street to stand at our corner. My mother and I were side by side at the stove, keeping four pots of overcooked side dishes from burning. 'We're eating at seven-fifteen, regardless,' said my grandmother. 'Seven-thirty at the absolute latest.'

'Whatever you want to do, Jane,' my mother answered.

'Should I go get Dad?' I asked.

'Please,' said my grandmother.

She followed me into the mudroom, where she sorted through a bushel basket full of boots and rubbers. I agreed to a pair of semitransparent plastic boots that fit over my shoes and ended an inch above my ankle. I stuck one foot, toes pointed, into the kitchen, prompting a laugh from my mother.

My grandmother didn't notice. 'Do you think she could have gone straight to Schenectady with the eggs?' she asked.

'We can call Bibi,' my mother said.

'No reason to get her upset,' said my grandmother.

'Are *you* upset?' I asked.

She sighed. 'I didn't have much gas in the tank. And she was never the kind of person who looked at the fuel gauge.'

'Do you think she ran away?'

'In *my* car? I can't imagine she'd do that without asking my permission.'

'Did she take her stuff?' I asked.

'Go check,' my mother said quietly.

'Her suitcase is upstairs, exactly where she left it,' said my grandmother. 'I already checked.'

My mother said, 'Go get your father.'

He was standing under a streetlight, hatless and gloveless in the snow, hands tucked into his armpits. Several neighbors and one squad car, he told me, had stopped to ask if everything was all right.

'They think you're a vagrant,' I said.

'They were being Good Samaritans,' said my father. 'I told the neighbors I was waiting for our houseguest, who might need help recognizing Renfrew Street.'

'Did the cop believe you?'

'I knew him. Rather, I knew his father from high school, from band. I told him the truth, though – just in case he sees Grandma's Hudson on his rounds.'

'Do you think Laura Lee had an accident?'

'Not at all,' he said unconvincingly. 'We'd have heard. Someone would have called.'

I asked if ex-husbands qualified as next of kin.

'Everyone in this town knows your grandmother's Hornet. Even if Laura Lee didn't remember the address, she'd certainly be able to supply Grandma's name.'

I didn't say the obvious: *Unless she was dead or comatose or at the bottom of the river.* 'How worried are you?' I asked.

Of course he couldn't say a simple 'not very' or 'quite'; he had to put himself on the proverbial couch and puzzle aloud over what he was failing to feel. 'What does it say that I'm more angry than worried?' he asked. 'Because if it were you or Aviva or Mother who'd disappeared for hours, I'd be frantic. I think the best description of my feelings is annoyed.' He nodded. 'Yes, no question: I am feeling acute annoyance.'

I said, 'Let's go back. Grandma made some kind of steak that's rolled up with stuffing so when you slice it you get a pinwheel.'

'Pie?' he asked hopefully.

'That's tomorrow: pecan and pumpkin chiffon. But maybe she'll let you have a slice tonight.'

He continued to peer into the distance, left, right, then back again. A car approached, then another, neither familiar or slowing down.

I said, 'C'mon. You're not going to accomplish anything out here.'

He said, 'I've had it, Frederica. I can't take much more of her drama and irresponsibility. Isn't it enough that I have to wait up nights when students don't come home? And those phone calls I have to make in the middle of the night to parents? Why did I ever let her come to Dewing?'

I asked if he thought something was wrong with Laura Lee – not this, not her disappearance, but what was happening back at school, the affair. All the flaunting and the showing off. Wasn't it creepy? Wasn't there a name for the condition when you don't know right from wrong?

'I think you mean sociopathy,' said my father. 'And you're not far off when you consider that certain characteristics, including personal charm, selfishness, impulsiveness—'

'What about her charming boyfriend? He's flaunting it, too. Where's his conscience?'

'His conscience,' my father answered, 'is undoubtedly suffering a dark night of the soul outside the intensive care unit at Mass. General.'

'Think so?' I asked.

'If I were he? I'd be bargaining with God right now: *Let Grace live, and I'll never see that woman again. Save the mother of my children, and I'll give up my mistress.* Why do you think Laura Lee is so distraught? Because she knows this marks the end of the affair.'

'God?' I said. 'You bargain with God?'

'Figure of speech,' he said.

We ate in the kitchen to be close to the phone, transferring the Christmas place mats, napkins, napkin rings, and crèche centerpiece to the round Formica table. My grandmother took her seat after serving us, then suggested we clasp hands around the table. 'Frederica?' she prompted.

I was good at this. Whenever I joined a religious girl's table at Curran Hall, I participated in and could even ad-lib a few convincing lines. This night I said, 'Thank you, God, for bringing our family together during this holiday. Thank you for giving us a place to go when the dorm is closed, and for food that is not only homemade and delicious but also cross-cultural.' I looked around the table. My grandmother's eyes were closed. My mother winked at me. I continued, 'We're a little concerned right now because one of our party borrowed the car and hasn't come back. It's been several hours. We're hoping for her safe return because she may be driving inebriated. Thank you. And Merry Christmas, which I think translates in your house to Happy Birthday.'

My grandmother added, 'Lord, bless this food to our use and us to thy service and keep us ever mindful of others so they, too, may receive from the bounty of Christ our Lord, amen.'

I looked at my mother, who telegraphed to me, *It's fine. Let it be. She made latkes.*

We had barely cut into our first slice of steak when the phone rang. My father, napkin in hand, tipped his chair backwards and stretched behind him for the wall phone. 'Hatch residence,' he said. After a few moments he calmly asked, 'Where?' Then, 'Does she know you called us?'

Clearly she was alive. But something else besides truancy – a totaled Hornet? a skid across a yard into someone's living room? – was causing a look I knew, rage restrained through houseparent equanimity.

'Can you keep her there? . . . No, I'll come get her.' Then: 'What time does it get over?'

He thanked the caller, hung up the phone, picked up his knife and fork.

'David?' said my mother and grandmother.

'She's fine.' He cut all the steak on his plate into bite-sized pieces, then asked me to pass the rolls.

'Where is she?' my grandmother asked. 'Who was that on the phone?'

'Chuck LeDout, the officer I flagged down on the corner. He spotted the Hudson in the parking lot of Hoosac Valley Regional.'

'Was she with the car?' I asked.

'No, she was not.'

'Is she missing?' asked my mother.

He said grimly, 'He's quite sure she's inside.'

'The school?' said my grandmother. 'What for?'

He smacked a spoonful of apple sauce onto a latke. 'Apparently,' he said, 'there's a special Christmas Eve twilight matinee of *The Nutcracker*.'

'The Hoosac Valley Ballet!' my grandmother exclaimed. 'I think tonight's the final performance.'

My mother said carefully, 'And you're taking your time and finishing dinner because you're confident that she'll find her own way back?'

'Who says she's coming back at all?' I asked.

'I want my car,' said my grandmother.

'Beyond typical,' my father muttered. 'Unbelievably thoughtless, not to mention self-absorbed and immature—'

I stood up. 'C'mon. Let's go get her. She's not going to show up.'

'Sit down,' said my mother.

I said, 'I've never seen *The Nutcracker*! I'm the only child in America whose parents haven't taken her at Christmas.'

'You've seen it six times on PBS.'

'It's probably over soon,' said my grandmother. 'People have lots to do on Christmas Eve.'

My father said, 'LeDout's niece is in it. He said it ends at eight.'

'I'll go with you,' I repeated.

'And you'd serve what role?' asked my mother.

'If Laura Lee ran into the ladies' room when she saw Dad, I could go get her. Besides, someone should drive back with her to make sure she doesn't take off with Grandma's car.'

'Absolutely not,' said my mother.

The driveway to Hoosac Valley Regional was fluorescently lit and plastered with posters announcing FINAL PERFORMANCE! edited with a handwritten TONIGHT! My father and I crossed a courtyard, entered the building, and walked up a few stairs to the auditorium. We opened one door and slipped into the empty back row. She was sitting alone in the second row, dead center, and producing the involuntary twitches of a choreographer-director.

'Can you tell how far along they are? What scene?'

'Near the end. It's the Sugarplum Fairy and her cavalier. Should we go down there?'

'Not till it's over,' he said.

I'd been relishing the thought of something FBI-ish: David would approach down the left aisle. I'd skulk down the right. When we got to the second row, we'd each slide across,

185

beautifully synchronized, and drop into the empty seats on either side of Laura Lee. I said, 'I wouldn't mind seeing the finale up close.'

'You stay here. I know you: you'd sashay down the aisle and demand the car keys.'

There couldn't have been more than a dozen parents in attendance, plus an orchestra that was a mixture of children and adults. We had a clear view of Laura Lee, who was swaying and gesticulating like a true showoff who had danced the role of Clara and wanted everyone to know.

'Why can't she be normal?' I whispered.

'Melodrama,' he whispered back.

'Was she always like this?'

'Always.'

I recognized the 'Waltz of the Flowers' and nudged my father. 'After this comes the finale, and Clara gets taken offstage in a sleigh. If they do the Russian version.'

We were the first to reach the back doors, which we held open for the retreating audience. Laura Lee, last one up the aisle, was half walking, half reliving her starring role. Finally she looked up. She stopped and cried, 'What's wrong?'

'Nothing—'

'Did Eric call?'

'No one called,' my father said. 'We came to collect you. Dinner's on the table.'

'I'm not sure of my evening plans,' she said.

He let the door close so it was only we three left in the auditorium. 'Then let me enlighten you,' said my father. 'You are driving back to my mother's house, where all of us have been fairly certain that a three-hour unexplained absence meant you were dead in a ditch.'

Laura Lee, brow furrowed, looked toward me for affirmation.

'We called the police,' I told her. 'They must have issued an all points bulletin, because an officer spotted Grandma's car and called us.'

She raised her chin slightly and said, 'You of all people know, Frederica, how I feel about ballet.'

'And you know how the police feel about grand theft auto,' I replied.

My father snapped, 'That's enough.' And to Laura Lee, 'Did you give any thought at all to your hostess?'

'And to returning her coat,' I added. Laura Lee was fishing for gloves in the pocket of my grandmother's Persian lamb coat, famous for its magenta lining and for being the sole surviving garment from her trousseau.

'*All* I've given thought to is Eric and what he's going through, spending Christmas Eve in a hospital waiting room, dealing with three hysterical daughters, running a college—'

'What about Mrs Woodbury?' I yelled. 'She could be dead. She could have died while you were watching the lamest *Nutcracker* ever performed.'

'That's very mean, Frederica,' said Laura Lee. 'I didn't think you were capable of such cruelty.' With that, she marched past us through two sets of doors, across the parking lot, and to the Hudson, which she kicked hard with the toe of her patent leather boot.

My father grabbed my hand, and we ran to catch up. Laura

Lee was now at the wheel, ineffectually stomping on the clutch and grinding gears so that each start ended in a stall.

'She can't drive it,' I said.

'She must have driven it here.' He rapped on the window and said, 'Stop it. You're going to damage something.'

'The starter,' I said.

'Go away,' said Laura Lee. 'I can't concentrate when you're hovering.'

I said, 'Don't let her drive it. Tell her she's riding with us. You and Grandma can return for the car in the morning.'

'Good idea,' he said. He gestured to her: *Forget it. You're coming with us.* She opened the door faster than anyone expected and wider than necessary. Some part of it hit my father hard, with a disturbing thwack. He yelped, then crumpled.

'You hit him in the balls!' I yelled.

'Not on purpose,' said Laura Lee.

He was white, every feature contorted in pain. 'I'm okay,' he whimpered. 'Give me a minute.'

'I'll drive,' said Laura Lee.

20

After All That

IT WAS DECIDED out of my earshot: Laura Lee deeply needed to be in Boston. The wages of her early departure would be a bus ticket; no one was going to drive her across the state, loan or rent her a car, especially since her license, we now knew, had expired some fifteen years earlier. Her mother would understand once we explained that there had been an emergency on campus. After her initial shock and disappointment, Bibi would realize that it was better to be spending Christmas with family than alone in Schenectady.

Laura Lee retired early and sulkily after picking at her cold beef pinwheel. I excused myself from the annual checker tournament, simulating yawns, to join my roommate upstairs. She was already in bed, lights out, but tossing noisily. 'If you're going to have a long, drawn-out toilette, please go elsewhere,' she growled.

I pulled off my shoes and my bulky sweater, and slipped into my bed otherwise fully clothed.

'I suppose they're discussing me,' she said.

I said no. The carolers came, we fed them, and then we set up the checkerboard—

'They think it's so black and white! His wife tried to kill herself, so I have to walk away. As if he doesn't need me more than ever. As if she didn't pull this stunt precisely to vilify me.'

'How can you call it a stunt? A stunt is when you take a few sleeping pills knowing someone's going to find you and pump your stomach.'

'Then she needs serious help. She needs to be in a psych ward when this is over – *if* she hasn't turned herself into a vegetable.'

When I could manage a reply I asked, 'Are you the least bit sorry for her?'

She sat up. I could tell, even in the dark, that a lecture was gathering force. 'I'm going to point something out to you, Frederica, a parallel that no one in this family appreciates: I had a husband who left me for another woman. And how did I handle it? With dignity! Did I try to kill myself? Did I fall into a pit of depression and lose ten pounds a month until I looked like death warmed over? No. I picked myself up, called a lawyer, and agreed to a divorce.'

'You were young. You told me that it wouldn't have lasted—'

'And then this miracle happens! In the unlikeliest place, I find the love of my life. And let me point out that there is another side of this, which isn't *my* happiness, but Eric's. Do you know that he's tried several times to leave her? And that she threatened to kill herself if he ever did?'

I said evenly, 'Do you believe everything he tells you?'

The lamp between us went on. Laura Lee was wearing a black lace nightgown, surely from a lingerie department's honeymoon rack. 'Unlike you, I wasn't raised to be a cynic and to mistrust someone just because he has power and authority and a comfortable car.' She shut off the light. A minute later I heard, 'If you're worried about Marietta and her sisters, you don't have to be.'

'Because their mother's going to pull through? Or because their father's found happiness with a woman who isn't frigid?'

'First,' she said, 'their father's found them a suite virtually across the street from the hospital and made them a reservation at the Parker House for Christmas dinner. And secondly, throwing around sexual terms doesn't qualify you as an adult, so stop trying.' I heard the sounds of aged pillows being thumped and fluffed. 'You know what I see happening between us, Frederica? I see you looking back on this week – I mean, at some distant point when you've had some life experience and a few love affairs of your own – and feeling ashamed that you were so quick to judge me and cut me dead. *Especially* when you were the one who did the honors.'

'What honors?'

'The night Eric and I met? I happen to know that he ventured into Curran Hall because he'd heard there was an ex-Rockette on campus.'

I thought of running back downstairs, joining my parents under the poinsettia afghan, and thanking David for conceiving me with Aviva rather than Laura Lee.

'That definitely intrigued him,' she continued. 'That one word: "Rockette."'

I pulled the covers over my head to muffle my hyper-
ventilating.

'Good night, little girl,' she said.

Bibi French was Laura Lee at seventy. She had her daughter's
height and build; her hair was the kind of white that recalled its
strawberry blond past. Her vintage fur coat and wine-colored
dress could have been on loan from Laura Lee's steamer trunks.

We greeted; we shook hands or kissed as was appropriate.
Bibi said without much enthusiasm, 'Well, you don't look like
your mother. I suppose I see David in you.'

'She looks a lot like my mother did as a young woman,'
offered Aviva, who was dressed in her all-occasion black pleated
skirt and white turtleneck sweater.

'A throwback,' said Bibi. 'Those are often interesting.' She
looked past me into the rooms beyond the foyer. 'Don't tell me
my daughter is still asleep?'

'Come sit down,' said my grandmother. 'Aviva made her
special hot spiced cider.'

We were seated around the tree, cider poured, the
soundtrack from *White Christmas* on the hi-fi, musical credit to
Irving Berlin noted. My father pronounced the drink delicious:
warmed one's innards, didn't it? As I circulated with partridge-
in-a-pear-tree napkins and walnut-dipped cheese balls, Bibi
asked, 'Lee-Lee's not helping in the kitchen, is she?'

My father sat up straighter and said, 'Lee-Lee's not here,
Bibi. There was an emergency back at school. She had to leave
this morning.'

Bibi barely looked dismayed. 'Would it concern a man?' she
asked.

'Partly,' said my father.

'Did she make it here at *all*?'

'Of course,' he said. 'We would have given you more notice if she'd stayed behind.'

'Let me guess: a summons – some man saying "drop everything and spend Christmas with me" – so she packed her bags and ran for the bus?'

'She did, in fact, board a bus.'

'When?'

'This morning.'

Bibi said irritably, 'She couldn't postpone her romantic emergency a few hours to have dinner with her mother?'

My grandmother said, 'Maybe when you hear the particulars—'

'What could the particulars change? Is the man on his way to war? Is someone on his deathbed?'

'Sort of,' I said.

My father set his cup down on an end table. 'Here is the situation, Bibi: the wife of our college president, Dr Woodbury, is in a coma due to carbon monoxide poisoning—'

Bibi shrieked, 'She's dead, isn't she! She's not on a bus! There was a carbon monoxide disaster all over that school, and that's what you're trying to say! That's why you had to tell me in person!'

My grandmother rushed to her side to remove the brimming cup near her from harm's way. All of us shouted our various reassurances – no disaster, not dead, alive and well.

My father said firmly, 'Listen to me, Bibi: Laura Lee is fine. Her bus is no doubt pulling into Park Square right now. I would never lie to you.'

193

Bibi's glance shot involuntarily to my mother and back again. 'Then why didn't she call me herself to tell me about her change of plans?'

'That was our selfish decision,' said my father. 'We wanted you with us for Christmas dinner. We thought if you heard she'd gone back to Boston, you wouldn't come.'

'I'm not easily fooled,' said Bibi. 'I didn't drive sixty-seven miles to find out that my daughter had better things to do on the one day all year she doesn't have dorm duty.'

We didn't correct her. My father granted, 'No question: it *is* a round-the-clock responsibility.'

'Do you want to know more about the circumstances back home?' asked my grandmother.

Bibi looked blank enough for me to clarify, 'The president's wife? In a coma?'

'Which you swear is not from anything contagious?'

My father repeated, 'Laura Lee left here in perfect health in order to be with President Woodbury.'

'She's in love with him,' I said.

Bibi seemed to take this assertion in her stride. 'Are there children?' she asked.

'Three.'

'I see,' said Bibi. 'And is he inclined to accept her suit?'

'They're all over each other,' I said.

'If you're asking me if there's an amicable, garden-variety divorce ahead, I'd have to say no,' said my father. 'Apparently, Mrs Woodbury has threatened in the past to take her life if he ever left her.'

'But now she's done it,' said Bibi.

'Unsuccessfully,' said my father. 'She was rescued by a United Parcel delivery man on his rounds.'

'She's in critical but stable condition as of this morning,' said my mother.

'But comatose,' I added.

'Nothing you've told me so far,' said Bibi, 'explains why Laura Lee had to board a bus this morning and rush to Boston.'

'She's been very upset,' said my father. 'Very worried about her relationship with the man.'

'Is she going there to help with his children?' asked Bibi.

'They're grown-ups,' I said. 'One's studying to be an opera singer and the other one wants to make cheese after she gets out of grad school. The youngest is my age.'

'She's mad about him,' said my grandmother. 'She wants to be by his side.'

'She's never been one to play hard to get,' said Bibi.

My grandmother confided, 'From what David and Aviva tell me, they're making a spectacle of themselves.'

Bibi asked what that meant. Obviously the wife knew, and we knew, but who else?

'Everybody,' I said. 'Students, faculty, you name it.'

Bibi shrugged. 'Maybe they had an open marriage.'

My father said, 'Certainly nothing ratified by both parties.'

'Is this a pattern of his?'

My mother said, 'Nothing that the presidential search committee detected.'

'But of course they won't touch him, will they? Lee-Lee will lose *her* job. The man always comes away unscathed while the woman suffers for both their sins.'

My mother said quietly, 'Right now, the crisis at hand is the survival of Mrs Woodbury.'

Bibi picked up her cider, pronounced it still too hot to drink, put it down again, and asked pleasantly, 'Is the wife an attractive woman?'

I could feel the collective unexpressed gasp in the room.

'I guess I don't understand how that's relevant,' said my mother.

'Just trying to picture the triangle,' said Bibi. 'For example, how old is this Woodbury?'

'Old,' I said.

'Fifty. Early fifties,' said my father.

'He limps,' I said.

'War injury?' asked Bibi.

'No one knows,' said my father.

'He was born with it,' I said. 'Marietta told me. Something a little off with his hip.'

'But otherwise attractive?'

My mother stood up suddenly. Surely the time had come for a speech denouncing the cold hearts and shallow values on parade. 'If everyone will excuse me,' said my militant mother, 'it's time to baste the turkey.'

'Thank you, Aviva,' said my grandmother.

'Did I say something wrong?' asked Bibi.

My father, I knew, was doing his diplomatic best for the sake of his mother and a Christmas already undermined by disorderly conduct and rash leave-takings. But enough was enough for a natural-born spokesperson. 'Aviva and I,' he said, 'try never to judge people by outward appearances. And we've pledged to raise our daughter so that she, too, will see beyond the exterior—'

'That's hogwash,' said Bibi. 'Ask her. Go on. I raised a daughter. I gave lip service to inner beauty and not judging a book by its cover, but that's not what makes the world go round.'

I didn't allow anyone but me to ridicule my parents. I, who at sixteen could disqualify a suitor based on the color of his socks, said, 'I always try to look beyond the outside of the package, and I give my parents the credit for that.'

'I couldn't agree more,' said my grandmother. 'But at the same time it would help to know what Mrs Woodbury looks like.'

'Don't ask Dad,' I said. 'He'll say two eyes, a nose, and a mouth.'

'We're asking *you*,' said Bibi.

I said, 'I've seen pictures of her as a young woman and she was really beautiful.'

Bibi snorted. My grandmother asked Mrs Woodbury's present age.

'She turned fifty last month.'

'Did she have a party?' asked Bibi.

I said no, she didn't want one. Her daughters tried. They love their mother, even if they don't always show it.

'Imagine your husband having an affair as you were approaching something as momentous as your fiftieth,' said Bibi. 'No wonder she tried to kill herself. And believe me – this will affect the way the daughters approach fifty, too.'

'What's *he* like?' asked my grandmother.

'Smart. Ambitious. Charming,' groused my father. 'Very smooth. Too smooth.'

'If I know my daughter, he's tall,' said Bibi.

My father, looking increasingly strangled and red-faced, sputtered, 'The mother of his children may be dying over this affair. This is not a question of who invited whom to the prom! This is something that affects an entire campus! I don't have just one daughter to worry about; I have a hundred girls in my dorm alone who have the right to ask me, to ask the college, to go to their parents and say, "Is this the way adults are supposed to behave? Is this a healthy environment for me? Is this how people solve their problems – attach a hose to their exhaust pipe and close the garage door?"'

'David,' said my grandmother. 'Of course we feel for that woman. And we feel for you because of the difficult public relations job ahead.'

Bibi looked puzzled. 'Didn't someone say that this woman has threatened suicide before? She doesn't sound like someone who should be the First Lady of a college.'

'Because you have a candidate in mind?' my father asked angrily enough to draw my mother from the kitchen.

My grandmother murmured, 'This whole conversation got off on the wrong foot.'

'What could be the right foot in a situation like this?' asked Bibi. 'These are the questions I'd be asking my daughter if she were here. Wouldn't any mother want to know, "Who is this man and what is his situation?" And "What besides the wife being on her deathbed was the big hurry?"'

'The holiday bus schedule,' said my father. 'It was either eight A.M. or five P.M.'

'I suppose that the silver lining in all of this is that Laura Lee will get first- or secondhand reports on the wife's medical status,' said my grandmother. She turned to Bibi. 'David's been calling the hospital two or three times a day for updates.'

'Because you're close to the wife?' Bibi asked my father.

'Frederica is,' said my mother, who was standing in the doorway, one hand in a quilted mitt and the other dabbing a paper napkin at grease stains on her white sweater.

'I used to carpool with her,' I said. 'Well, not an actual carpool, because we have no car, but she drove me every morning until she got too depressed to drive.'

'She was always very fond of Frederica,' added my father. 'A very gracious and hospitable woman.'

'Stop talking about her in the past tense,' I cried.

'Critical but stable,' said my grandmother. 'You keep thinking *stable*, sweetheart, and I bet the next thing we hear is "Sitting up and eating solid food."'

Why now? Why after three stoical days did my eyes have to fill and my chin quiver in front of the pitiless Bibi French?

'Frederica,' my mother said. 'Could you come into the kitchen? I need a hand with the turkey, hon.'

'Poultry is Frederica's specialty,' my father explained.

Dinner was strained after my grandmother set a conversational ground rule: no more mention of comas or extramarital affairs. Whenever our hostess went into the kitchen for a new course, Bibi would hiss, 'What else are you not telling me?' Or 'Where do they have their trysts?' Or 'What's his house like?' When my grandmother reappeared, our guest pretended to be midway into a benign conversation: snow tires versus chains; white meat versus dark.

Instead of arguing, debating, whistle-blowing, or psycho-analyzing, we made small talk. My grandmother found multiple topics in the heirlooms on display: this Georgian gravy boat, this handmade Belgian lace tablecloth, these monogrammed fine linen hemstitched napkins, would all be mine one day. Bibi in turn summarized the plot of the previous Sunday's *Hallmark Hall of Fame*, which was based on a book she'd once read at Lake George. My mother addressed us on the subject of whether Parents' Weekend, traditionally convened in the fall, should be moved to the spring. My father found his subject on the plate: what elusive herb or inspired spice was sneaking up on him in these succulent creamed onions? In this incomparable cranberry mold?

I felt sorry for me and sorry for my grandmother, who was pretending that Cousin Bibi's presence wasn't a terrible mistake. Everything felt wrong. At Curran Hall, I could pick up my tray, plead homework or piano practice, and escape. Dinner for a mere five, in private, felt claustrophobic. Without a crowd – those thousand sisters I liked to disparage – I found myself miserable. It was the first time that I felt the separation from Dewing so acutely, and I longed to get home.

21

Sleeping Arrangements

MRS WOODBURY DID NOT DIE. She came home on New Year's Eve, a ghost of herself, confined to a wheelchair and to the second-story bedroom previously shared with her husband. The dean of students announced at a welcome-back assembly that Mrs Grace Woodbury had suffered a stroke, which sounded right to anyone who had seen her wan half smile or the rolled towels that propped her slumping body into an upright position. Next, Dean O'Rourke asked my parents, planted in the front row of the auditorium, to stand. Professor Aviva Hatch would be acting housemother at Ada Tibbets Hall while Professor David Hatch would honorably and capably carry on as houseparent in Griggs. Then, to the astonishment of the one thousand girls in attendance, Dean O'Rourke announced that Miss Laura Lee French, not present that morning, would be acting in the newly created role of emergency hostess to the president, due to the incapacities of Mrs Woodbury and the urgent social requirements of a college president.

We convened a family meeting the minute I arrived home from school, both parents waiting and pacing in the dorm lobby. They said there were so many issues here, so many unilateral actions to be grappled with, that their heads were swimming. 'Is it time we resign?' I asked.

They motioned that our discussion called for privacy. My mother, with a firm flip of the welcome sign to its DO NOT DISTURB UNLESS FOR EMERGENCY side, led us into our apartment and to the sofa beneath our dour portrait of Mary-Ruth Dewing.

Aviva announced, 'We can't resign. They have the right to reassign us in an emergency, and apparently this has been declared exactly that.'

'Rest assured that we know every codicil by heart,' said my father.

'Why you?' I asked. 'Why not another couple with less seniority?'

My mother couldn't help looking proud. 'It's *because* of our longevity. Dean O'Rourke told us off the record that your father's unblemished seventeen-plus years as a houseparent – he actually used the word "housepère" – gave the college utmost confidence in him as the first male to carry out the duties solo.'

'When did you find this out?' I asked.

'This morning. Twenty minutes before the assembly,' my mother said.

'Why didn't you call me?' I whined.

'How? Page you in school? Wouldn't you have thought the worst?'

'This is pretty bad,' I said.

'Tell us what the bad part is,' said my father.

I was too old to admit that I would like my mother to stay put. 'Won't people think you got divorced?'

They looked relieved. I'd come up with a conventional concern, easily refuted by the family who didn't care what the neighbors thought.

'This was conscription,' said my mother. 'Hatches don't volunteer to live apart.'

'And let me point something out,' said my father. 'This is not permanent. We are talking about eight to ten weeks. The plan is, allegedly, to hire a replacement for Laura Lee's dorm as soon as Personnel posts the job. And you know what eight weeks represent?'

I said no, I didn't.

He smiled. 'It's the duration of a summer at sleepover camp! But instead of your being up on some cold lake in New Hampshire, your whole family unit is within a stone's throw of one another.'

I grumbled, 'I'm not a baby. I hardly ever see you anyway. I'm objecting on principle.'

'Such as?' my mother asked.

'They're taking advantage of us. They know you won't quit in the middle of a school year, and you'd have to buy a house, and we can't afford Brookline so you'd have to commute, and we don't have a car, and I'd have to change schools.' I sat back and folded my arms, pleased with my on-the-spot summary to the jury. For further effect I added, 'You should be getting two stipends if you're running two different dorms.'

They said *of course* they'd thought of that. And amazingly enough, so had the administration.

'How much?' I asked.

'Month to month, on a prorated basis: effectively double,' my mother answered.

We three sat in silence, most likely imagining, respectively, a car, fieldwork on a warm island, and a certificate of deposit. My father asked my mother if she'd like a Dubonnet on the rocks.

I said, 'You're not toasting this thing, are you?'

My mother lowered her voice. 'We think we can confide in you. First of all, the temporary assignment is a tribute to your father's character and his perfect track record as a houseparent. Secondly, we are looking ahead, past this bump in the road, to something we all want. We think this will bring the matter to a head. We think it will call attention to the affair, and that President Woodbury cannot survive as president if he ensconces his mistress under his roof. We think that this will be his Waterloo.'

'What about Laura Lee's?' I asked.

'We can think of several scenarios,' my mother said. 'He goes, she follows. Or he blames her for everything and gets her fired—'

'Like Bibi said.'

'Correct,' said my father. 'He'll prostrate himself in front of the trustees: "There's a cancer growing on the presidency that I was too innocent to diagnose. This woman set her cap for me, and I didn't recognize what was going on until tragedy struck." He'll come away with a slap on the wrist and a renewed contract.'

'Unless they run off together,' I said.

'He wouldn't leave an invalid wife,' protested my father, so reflexively that my mother smiled.

'Can she still die?' I asked.

My father said, 'I believe she's out of the woods.'

'Albeit cortically impaired,' said my mother.

I said, 'How's this for a scenario: Laura Lee puts arsenic in Mrs Woodbury's tea.'

My father reached around me to touch Aviva's knee. 'Frederica and I have discussed Laura Lee's sociopathic inclinations,' he explained. 'I should have labeled it narcissism.' He turned back to me. 'No one thinks Laura Lee is capable of cold-blooded murder, honey.'

'Doesn't the whole thing look unbelievably fishy to every single person on campus?' I asked.

'Which facet of it?' asked my father.

'O'Rourke announcing that Laura Lee would now be the official emergency girlfriend of the president.'

My mother said, 'There was definitely a reaction.'

'Positive or negative?'

'Booing,' said my father, 'which Russell handled by pretending it was the splitting up of the Hatch team rather than the reassignment of Laura Lee. He said, "I know. I understand. You Griggs girls can't imagine Mrs Professor Hatch not under your own roof, but don't forget she'll be right next door. And no doubt she'll be spending her free weekends at Griggs," which *of course* turned into a lot of hooting and whistling,' said my father. 'Because the students were reacting as if it implied conjugal visits.'

'Dad,' I said. 'Please.'

'Russell doesn't get thrown by that,' said my mother. 'He just droned in that dry, sardonic voice of his, "Peo-ple. Okay. Enough." And moved on to the particulars.'

'Which were what?' I asked.

My father said, 'Russell explained how they reached the decision, how they asked for volunteers among the dorm parents, and when no one had volunteered, they more or less appointed Laura Lee to the newly created job because she had the least seniority.'

'What a coincidence,' I said.

Another signature look passed between them, one I knew to mean, *Should we tell her?*

'Just say it,' I snapped.

My father said, 'This was told to us in confidence by Woodbury himself, and later confirmed by the dean of residential life—'

'So it can't leave this room,' said my mother.

I stood up, walked to the kitchen sink for no purpose, came back.

My mother continued. 'There's a footnote: they're claiming that the girls of Tibbets Hall hate Laura Lee.'

'Since when?'

'That's the party line,' said my father. 'If challenged, Woodbury can say, "One of my deans had a staffing problem. I had a whole dorm ready to revolt. This was ostensibly about my own family emergency, but in fact it's a solution to a looming residential crisis."'

I said, 'There's no crisis. That dorm is too weird to agree on anything.'

'Welcome to the private sector,' said my mother.

I asked if Mrs Woodbury knew that Laura Lee was taking her place, or was she too out of it to notice?

'We don't know,' said my father. 'I'm hoping Laura Lee will

give me access to Mrs Woodbury.'

'Laura Lee will?' I asked sharply.

'Laura Lee is keeping house,' said my mother. 'Didn't we make that clear? Isn't that what "acting hostess" implies? That when you ring the doorbell, Laura Lee answers?'

I said, 'Please don't tell me that she's actually shacking up in Marietta's house.'

'Of course,' said my father. 'Why did you think Tibbets Hall needed a replacement houseparent?'

My mother volunteered, 'Russell swore that Laura Lee is sleeping in a Spartan maid's room behind the kitchen as if she were hired help. He assured us that Eric is very sensitive to the public face of this whole ordeal. And, according to Russell, Eric sincerely believes that bringing in a housemother for a teenage daughter believed to be wild and in need of supervision won't raise any more eyebrows than the gossip has already raised.'

'Did anyone consult Marietta?' I asked.

'That's the missing part of the equation,' said my father.

'Wasn't she at school today?' asked my mother.

I reminded them that it was a big school, that I had no classes with her, that she'd been avoiding me since her father began sleeping with our family friend. And what do you say to someone whose mother wanted to kill herself? *Sorry? Does she have her marbles back?*

'We could have helped with that,' said my mother.

'We're a little disappointed that you haven't made yourself available,' said my father.

'After all, who else does she have on campus?' asked my mother.

'When was I supposed to barge over there?' I asked. 'Besides, Marietta and I were never bosom buddies.'

'Would you care about that if one of us were gravely ill? If Marietta tried to rekindle the friendship at that point in time, wouldn't you welcome the overture?' asked my mother.

I said yes. Okay. I'd call her.

'You'll be seeing her on the bus now,' said my father. 'You could simply say, "I was away over Christmas, but if there's anything I can do, please don't hesitate to call me."'

I said okay. Hard to see how that could turn nasty.

'I think you know from all of your years living among adolescent girls that unprovoked nastiness is a defense mechanism. You have the tools to rise above that. And don't forget your new common ground,' said my father.

I asked what that was.

'The disruption of your households!' said my mother.

'Temporarily,' my father said firmly. 'Or we file.'

I asked casually, 'Wouldn't it make more sense for Dad to sleep over at Tibbets, and Mom to stay here with me? Not that it applies here, but wouldn't the college think that adolescent girls need their female parent?'

'We tried that,' said my mother.

'But?'

Another delicate subject at hand, her frown conveyed. 'The college felt that a father and his daughter would present a safer, more paternal image to the parents, as opposed to an unchaperoned male.'

'Even *Dad*? You've got to be kidding. The same people who let Laura Lee shack up with the president think Dad is going to seduce the boarders?'

'First of all, thank you,' said my father. 'Secondly, it's all about public relations. Woodbury is effectively saying, "I'm rising above the rumors. I could have sent my wife to a rehab facility, but I want her with me, compromised though she is. The college thoughtfully arranged for a housemother to act as hostess and to keep an eye on my unpredictable teenage daughter."'

I said, 'I live in a certifiably crazy place.'

'It's going to catch up with him,' said my mother.

'Unless he's telling the truth,' I said.

They both looked uncomprehending and mildly offended: had they raised me to think that management could be trusted?

'Maybe he's letting Laura Lee live there as a way to break up with her,' I explained. 'Like, "Okay, we thought we were in love, but you and I have to cool it. Otherwise, we'd be the biggest scandal in the history of Dewing College *or* Dewing Academy, and both of us will be out on our asses."'

'We aren't counting on them cooling it,' said my mother. 'We're hoping that they'll be discreet for the sake of his wife, and for Marietta, and for a very vulnerable student body.'

I said, 'I think I have an ethical quandary.'

'Which is what?' they asked eagerly.

'Marietta.'

'Go on,' said my father.

'Won't it be kind of phony if I go over there and offer my sympathies or whatever you call it when someone's mother doesn't die but comes close, while my parents are secretly hoping that her father gets sacked?'

'No,' said my mother. 'Not when your motive is a sincere offer of renewed friendship.'

'And don't you think it's the right thing to do, regardless? She must be in a great deal of pain,' said my father.

'Putting it off won't make it any easier,' said my mother.

'Am I doing your dirty work?' I asked.

They didn't answer immediately. Eventually my father asked, 'How would you define "dirty work"?'

'Spying on Laura Lee and her boyfriend while pretending to give Marietta a shoulder to cry on.'

'We think you'd be the most welcome visitor to the house as a possible source of comfort to Marietta,' said my mother. 'If that's spying, then we're guilty as charged.'

'Children hate change,' said my father. 'Even those who seem so mature and capable of handling disruption without ill effects.'

'Are you talking about me?'

He said, 'You've always hated change. Remember when they expanded the utility closet into an actual bedroom? For weeks you wanted your bed and toys in the same square footage that you'd always lived in.'

'We'll have dinner together every night,' said my mother. 'And Monday, Wednesday, and Sunday nights you'll do homework with me at Tibbets.'

'And Tuesdays and Thursdays here with me,' said my father.

'And we're really going to make an effort to go to your home games,' added my mother.

'Is it still basketball season?' asked my father.

22

Custody

BEFORE I COULD DROP OVER, before I could approach Marietta at the bus stop or in the halls of Brookline High School, she moved out of the presidential manse into Ada Tibbets Hall, room 209, which had been vacated by a sophomore who transferred mid-year to a school with boys.

Of course it was what any self-respecting melodramatic daughter would do in the face of adulterous activity under her own roof: run away. Conveniently, on a college campus, we boarding offspring could accomplish the sought-after effect – punish the offenders, make a statement, leave home – while remaining within our own gates. I hadn't taken the drastic step myself but had often contemplated the single life, of putting myself on a waiting list in case a spare bed opened up in a dorm not overseen by my parents.

'You don't understand,' Dr Woodbury told his daughter. 'I am at the center of a hideous rumor. Laura Lee's transfer is purely professional. I cannot do my job without a hostess. The dean of residential life chose Miss French for this role, and I had to abide by that reassignment.'

Did he think she was an idiot? Marietta railed. She would never live under the same roof as his slut-girlfriend, and if he didn't get out of her way and help with her suitcases, she'd report him to . . . someone.

'Who would that be?' he asked.

'Your boss,' she tried, not sure if presidents of colleges answered to anyone other than an indistinguishable group of dowagers called trustees.

He asked for a compromise and for mercy: Dewing parents would be horrified to learn that the president's daughter was a runaway. Grudgingly she allowed him to call the dean of residential life, who looked at her color-coded chart and found an empty bed a few hundred yards from the presidential homestead under the experienced maternal eye of Dr Aviva Hatch.

I could see that my mother liked this stewardship. She took in Marietta as if she were a refugee seeking asylum: found her linens, lent her shampoo and soap, invited her to unburden herself whenever the welcome sign was facing out. *The president's daughter doesn't think she'll be compatible with the girl from Emmetsburg, Iowa, who shares the double? No problem! Several corridor mates on Two East belong to the glee club and burst into song too early on Saturday? I'll speak to them about rehearsing elsewhere. That's what sociologist-housemothers excel at – the grouping of individuals who constitute the social world.*

The girls were mean, complained the suddenly thin-skinned Marietta. They were laughing behind her back while her mother could be dying. Housemother Hatch, who had always risen above squabbles, who had always insisted that boarders settle their differences among themselves and without adult intervention, asked for names. Marietta tattled. One by one, Aviva spoke to the offenders. Be nice to the new girl. She's younger than any of you and very vulnerable right now. Try to imagine how she feels: mother diminished, father the center of a rumor that won't go away.

After witnessing one of these scoldings in the naked light of Curran Hall, I accused Aviva of selling out. How could Mrs Fair Play choose sides – she who was famous for treating the daughters of ditch diggers just like the daughters of Hollywood moguls? What had happened to her lifelong commitment to equal justice and no pandering?

'Are you feeling a little neglected?' she asked.

I said, 'I can't talk. I have a ton of trig to do.'

She motioned that I should follow her into the dining room's coatroom, to the farthest wall of pegs. 'C'mere,' she said, my signal to walk into the open-armed hug she bestowed. 'We haven't been exactly faithful to our homework schedule or to our dining contract, have we?' she asked.

I said that I had viewed our custody arrangement as loose and informal. I did my best homework at the library, anyway, sans either parent. And meals couldn't be pinned down, could they, given our extremely independent and overscheduled lives.

'Laura Lee's apartment has a new popcorn popper,' she said, 'which has inspired informal open houses Monday through Thursday nights.'

'Is that an invitation?' I asked.

'Of course! The girls always ask for you.'

'What time?'

'Nine to ten P.M. I also serve soft drinks.'

I asked if Marietta was a regular. My mother said, 'No. She doesn't mingle. At least not voluntarily.'

I asked what that meant.

'I know you won't repeat this . . .' – a lead-in that always got my full and prurient attention. 'Marietta walks around the floor naked. Which our lesbian population finds confrontational, and the others find inconsiderate.'

'So tell her to stop it. What's the big deal?'

'I *have* told her. She says, "It's a women's college. I'm not ashamed of my body. Why is it a big deal if I sleep in the nude? Show me where it says I have to put on a bathrobe to urinate in the middle of the night."'

I said, 'Ignore it. Let the inmates handle it. Why are they bothering you?'

'I represent authority. I'm new here. They're testing me.'

I said, 'It's not you. They certainly don't want Laura Lee back. Maybe they just hate Marietta.'

She rubbed my cheek with her knuckles and said that she appreciated my support.

David and Aviva tried to make us a nuclear family on a regimen – eating together nightly for some or all of the hour between 5:30 and 6:30. Although we didn't explicitly invite Marietta, she had a talent for arriving at Curran Hall ninety seconds after we assembled. To my further annoyance, my mother developed the habit of slipping sample portions onto Marietta's finicky tray, cooing over how she really should experience our twice-baked potatoes or our cheddar cheese soup.

After four straight nights in our midst, I asked her if she ever took meals with her mother.

'Your evil president fired our cook,' said Marietta.

'Wasn't she part-time anyway?' I asked.

'Three days a week. But she cooked stuff in advance and left it for us.'

'Who feeds your mother?' I asked.

'The nurse,' said Marietta.

My father asked, 'Marietta? Is that the entire answer?'

Marietta, her lip curled, said, 'My father feeds her supper.'

'Doesn't that invalidate some of your criticism?' he asked.

'Like what? That he's not a total asshole twenty-four hours a day?'

'Too bad about the cook,' I said, remembering happier days and our after-school raids of the presidential refrigerator.

'I'm sure he's trying to save the college money,' said my mother.

'That's not what I think,' said Marietta. 'I think he wants the house empty so he and his mistress can have sex as soon as the nurse leaves at three.'

'With your mother right there?' I asked.

'She's a zombie. How would she know if they were having sex in the guest room?'

'Is she getting occupational therapy?' my father asked.

'How would I know?'

'Do you want one of us to ask?' he offered.

'Doesn't Bunny work over there now?' my mother asked. 'She would know.'

'Bunny! She's in love with him, too. When my mother used to call, she'd put her on hold for ten minutes. She tried that with me once, and you know what I did? I ran over to the administration building, showed up at her desk, and said, "Is he free yet?" She told me to take a seat. What an asshole.'

I said, 'Isn't Bunny, like, sixty years old?'

'Sixty-six,' said my mother. 'We're the ones who knocked out the compulsory retirement language from the contract.'

'So it isn't just Laura Lee under your roof, but Bunny working there that makes your home uncomfortable?' my father prompted.

'Uncomfortable? Try "beyond belief". Try "fucking impossible".'

'Of course it is,' said my mother. 'No child should be made to feel as if she isn't the most important thing in a parent's life.'

They beamed at me. Marietta said suddenly, eyes lowered to her untouched plate, 'Oh, shit. I can't believe who just walked in here.'

It may not have been Laura Lee's first appearance at Curran Hall since moving into the president's house, but it was the first time we'd seen her with Marietta present. She was dressed in a straight black skirt, several inches above the knee, and a ruffled pink blouse of a semitransparent nylon that I recognized from her Mamie Eisenhower collection. Her black high-heeled shoes had straps across the instep. If they weren't the legendary Radio City Capezios, they were meant to flatter the ankles that had started it all.

After surveying the room, she spotted the object of her search.

'Here she comes,' I murmured.

My father stood, less good manners than sentry duty. 'Can I help you?' he asked.

'I need Marietta,' she said.

'Fuck you,' said Marietta.

Mary-Ruths at the surrounding tables shushed their tablemates and stared.

'What is it, Laura Lee?' my mother asked.

'We need her at the house.'

'*We*? You and my asshole father? Is that what "we" means?'

To my astonishment, Laura Lee borrowed a chair from the closest table and dragged it to Marietta's side. 'I don't think you mean that,' she said.

With an angry bounce, Marietta turned her chair ninety degrees away from Laura Lee.

'I can't get through to her,' said Laura Lee. 'She thinks I'm forcing myself where I'm not wanted, especially with respect to her father.'

'Liar,' said Marietta.

'I am an employee of the college, following orders,' Laura Lee said.

'What order is that?' Marietta spat out. '"*Come fuck me. My wife's a vegetable. She won't notice.*"'

'She is *not* a vegetable,' Laura Lee said calmly. 'She has some neurological deficiencies, and her brain may have reverted to a state when she was a child, but she's still . . . a person.'

'A person who wishes she could kill herself all over again, thanks to you.'

'This is not the place to be having this conversation,' said my mother.

'Then tell her to leave,' said Marietta.

Laura Lee said, 'I came to get you.'

'Why you?' asked my father. 'Didn't you know you'd upset her?'

Laura Lee said regally, 'Her mother is asking for her, and her father didn't want to leave his wife's side.'

'Is it an emergency?' my mother asked.

'He believes it is,' said Laura Lee.

Marietta finally swiveled back to face Laura Lee. 'And you can't even tell me what's wrong? You can't even be helpful for two seconds and tell me what the fuck is the matter?'

Laura Lee said, 'Your mother refused to eat her dinner. Again.'

'So?'

'Your father thinks it may be the beginning of a hunger strike. She clamps her lips together and bats the spoon away with her good hand.'

'Maybe it's the food,' said my father.

'Maybe she thinks someone's trying to poison her,' said Marietta.

'Don't be ridiculous,' said Laura Lee. 'It's political. She's taking a stand.'

'Political?' my mother repeated, blinking furiously.

'Isn't she aphasic?' asked my father.

'She can communicate,' said Laura Lee. 'When she wants to.'

'Can she chew?' he asked.

'We don't take that chance,' said Laura Lee. 'Her swallow reflex isn't a hundred per cent.'

Marietta said, 'Maybe she'll choke to death. Wouldn't that be convenient?'

Laura Lee fished a carrot stick out of my salad bowl, chewed, and swallowed a bite before saying, 'Grace said something that we translated to mean that she wants to reach your sisters.'

'So?'

'Like you, they refuse to talk to your father. He needs you to call them for her before she gets any more agitated.'

'You're the assistant,' said Marietta. 'Why don't *you* call them?'

My mother said quietly, 'Why don't you go home and see if she'll take some food from you. Didn't you tell me she loves coffee ice cream?'

'She can't eat ice cream three times a day,' said Laura Lee primly.

'Fuck you,' said Marietta.

'That doesn't help, Marietta,' my mother said quietly.

'I can't believe he'd send her to get me!'

'Then tell him that,' said my father. 'You two need to talk. And if you need a referral, I know some very good people off-campus.'

'Don't think Eric hasn't begged her for that,' said Laura Lee.

I kicked Marietta under the table. 'Your mother's upset and she's asking for you. So what if you hate everybody else? Go! Get the hell out of here.'

Laura Lee had to ask smugly, 'Frederica? Is the swearing new? Something you've picked up from your mother's new charge?'

Marietta rose to her feet slowly, disdainfully. She said to Laura Lee, 'I'm leaving, but don't you dare follow me.'

'Fine,' said Laura Lee. 'I was going to stay and have a bite. I need to eat.'

Marietta shoved her tray into mine to convey, *You're dumping this for me.*

'Knock on my door when you get back, Mare,' said my mother.

Laura Lee went through the food line and returned to our table. She set her tray down in Marietta's spot and smiled as if no one had cursed her or made a scene. 'How's everyone feeling?' Laura Lee asked serenely.

'Fine, okay,' we mumbled one by one, eyes on the Formica.

'Isn't anyone going to ask how *I* am?'

We didn't have to. I'd eaten at Curran Hall my whole life and knew the signs, seen young housemothers arrive and seen their families expand. I understood immediately what it meant when lined up on a tray, in neon lights, were three full glasses of frothy, prenatal milk.

23

Adolescence, Puberty, and Emotion Regulation

I GOT MY PARENTS' ATTENTION the old-fashioned way: by falling off the honor roll. Of course we had to dissect every psychosocial factor, and the coincidence of me taking up with a boy just as double dorm duty was watering down their parental intensity. Thus the weekly family meeting in our Griggs Hall kitchen, instituted since the bifurcation, had only one unwritten item on the agenda: the correlation between Ritchie Almeida and my C in Honors Chemistry. They spared me the relations-are-a-beautiful-thing speech, which I'd been hearing since I attended my first coed party at eleven, and went directly to their true quandary: what did I possibly see in a boy like Ritchie, who played hockey, who wasn't going to college, and didn't ever – as each of my parents had independently observed – make eye contact with adults? Was it a daughter's cry for help?

They were blind, obviously, to Ritchie's varsity appeal, the light eyes in the olive-complected face, which compensated for his underachievement as far as I was concerned. I said, 'He's shy around adults. And as for going to college, he doesn't have the money.'

'My concern is that he's a senior,' said my father. 'And I am all too familiar with the urges of young men that age.'

'Firsthand?' I asked.

'I was eighteen once, if that's what you're asking. But you know my areas of interest.'

I did: 'Adolescence, Puberty, and Emotion Regulation,' the subject of his doctoral thesis, never published.

'You're barely sixteen,' said my father.

I recognized this as the perfect opportunity to accuse them of being old-school, definitely conservative, possibly even conventional.

The charges induced a few stumped seconds of silence until my mother said, 'Perhaps, earlier, when we said everything is beautiful and awe-inspiring, we were being theoretical, because sex was very far down the road and we didn't want it to loom ahead of you as scary or unpleasant. At the same time, we may have given you the false impression that intimacy could be entered into casually—'

'Whereas what we want to convey is that there's nothing to fear about sexual relations with the right person—' added David.

'At the right *time*,' added my mother.

'Which is why we've made an appointment with your mother's doctor,' said my father.

I said I wasn't sick. And wasn't Dr Frankel still my doctor

until I was eighteen, or whenever it was a person stops going to the pediatrician?

'We meant my gynecologist,' said my mother.

'Would you like me to leave so you two can talk, woman to woman?' asked my father.

I said, 'I don't need a gynecologist.'

'Are you sure?' my mother asked.

My father said, 'We'd like some kind of reassurance that you've internalized what we've discussed through the years—'

'About taking precautions,' my mother added.

I said, 'I don't need birth control. When I do, I'll let you know.'

'*Will* you?' they asked in unison.

I said yes, they could count on me confessing in advance when I expected to have sexual relations. They'd be the first to know.

They smiled proudly. It didn't occur to them that drugstores were invented for such purposes, that parents didn't have to be enlisted except in families like ours.

'Another thing . . .' said my father.

'It's about school,' said my mother. 'About the next two years.' And from nowhere she brought forth a catalogue – shiny, green, cheerful, and preppy, even at first glance.

'No,' I said. 'Not a chance.'

It wasn't the only one. A half dozen more boarding school catalogues and brochures bounced out of a padded envelope onto the table.

'I thought you hated private schools,' I said. 'I thought they were elitist institutions.'

'We work at a private school,' said my father. 'We feel very lucky that we both have jobs in this market, and as much as we support wholeheartedly the notion of public education—'

'We don't think we have to sacrifice our only child to that principle,' said my mother.

I said, 'I am not switching schools in my junior year. If you send me away, I'll come back. I'll live at Patsy's.'

My father laughed. 'Did you read that in a book somewhere? Runaway moves down the lane? Was that *Peter Rabbit* or *Benjamin Bunny*?'

My mother splayed the brochures in front of me. 'Will you at least look at them?'

I said, 'You never even had two minutes' conversation with Ritchie. You're prejudiced because he plays hockey. Too bad he doesn't work at Dewing and have a couple of grievances to file. Then you'd invite him home for dinner.'

'Ritchie is irrelevant,' said my mother. 'This is about your future and your need to recapture your love of learning.'

Ritchie *was* irrelevant; I would never see him after his June graduation, and he'd already been spotted with Debbie DuBois, a senior and a majorette, at *Slap Shot*. I curled my lip and took a brochure. The first one showed a semicircle of girls smiling around a big bowl of chocolate batter. Next to that was a photo of girls in pleated plaids wielding sticks, and below that, girls in fuzzy cardigans listening intently to their language-lab headphones. 'No good,' I said, and pushed the bunch back across the table.

My father picked up the closest catalogue and feigned deep interest in its table of contents. 'What didn't you like about this one? It looks so pretty. You can see mountains behind the playing fields. I think they're the foothills of the Berkshires.'

I said, 'I don't see any boys.'

I knew those faces too well to miss the disappointment. They had tried so hard to do everything right, but they'd been rewarded with a newly defiant and possibly boy-crazy girl.

My mother spoke first. 'Some have brother schools relatively close by.'

'So?'

'I would imagine that means mixers. And perhaps some coed activities . . .'

'Like field trips,' said my father. 'Or volunteerism. Cleaning up public spaces or . . . library privileges.'

I sighed deeply, sadly. 'Is that how well you know me – that you think cleaning up litter would be a selling point?'

'No,' said my mother. 'Not at all. We were thinking aloud . . . about activities . . . where the opposite sex might come in.'

I stared across the room, hoping to convey, *Deep in second thought*. My father asked what I was thinking. 'Maybe I *should* go away,' I answered. 'Lots of kids from broken homes go to boarding school.'

'Broken homes!' my mother repeated. 'What would make you choose those words in relationship to yourself?'

I shrugged. 'Dad and I live here. You live over in Tibbets. Sometimes a person's grades slip when her parents live in separate dormitories.'

'You know this wasn't voluntary,' she said, her voice catching. 'We hate it, too. The thought that you see us as a broken home and yourself as a casualty . . .'

'Do you think any brick wall or any fire door can separate your mother and me?' asked my father.

'Or that boarding school would exile you from this family?' added my mother.

'Look,' I said. 'Not that I wasn't trying in Chemistry, but maybe I could do a little better.'

'We know you can,' said my father. 'That's what breaks our hearts – we know your potential. Since you came home with a C, we've been grappling with the question, "How can we get Frederica back on the right path?" Everything you do now, in a sense, will determine how far you can go later.'

Again I said okay, maybe I could do better. Today's quiz was tomorrow's good job with an excellent benefit package. I'd not only study harder in the future, but I'd go right to my room and read a book.

My mother pointed out that I'd voiced similar promises in the past, which turned out to be lip service.

'Such as?'

'Guitar lessons. And before that, the recorder.'

I said, 'This time I'll put it in writing: "Give Frederica R. Hatch the chance to improve her grades at Brookline High School, one of the top public schools in the country, before we rashly send her away." '

My mother said, 'Or words to that effect, which you'll sign.'

I thought this over, then asked, 'How many honor rolls will I have to make?'

'All,' said my mother.

They adjourned to their bedroom for further deliberations. While they were whispering behind the closed door, I flipped through the catalogues. The school I knew I would hate the most was Harding Academy. Every photograph of its overly attractive students seemed to say, *Give us your rich, your reckless, your promiscuous adolescents yearning to act out.* Marietta could be happy here, I thought.

My parents rejoined me, body language mute.

'How did it go?' I asked.

My mother announced, 'We've decided to let you stay at Brookline High School for the remainder of the school year, but we're keeping the private school option on the table—'

'With a codicil about Ritchie,' said my father.

'In fact, about all boys,' said my mother.

I waited.

'There won't be any going out during the week.'

I asked if this was negotiable.

'We'll revisit that clause after the next marking period,' said my father.

I knew them well; I knew that imbuing their only child with confidence was first or second on their parenting wish list. 'What if I can't do it?' I whispered hoarsely. 'What if I'm not smart enough to get back on the honor roll? What if I do everything right and stay home on weeknights and give up sports and my grades *still* get worse?'

It worked. In the face of the excellent low self-esteem I was projecting, they rushed to reassure me that I was loved, and above all else valued for my intelligence and my . . . my . . . those many attributes too numerous to name.

Sniffling, I raised my miserable face from the nest of my own crossed arms. I may have been substandard in Honors Chemistry, but I could act.

I kept the catalogues. The following week, the principal of Brookline High School called Dr Woodbury to announce that

227

he was suspending Marietta for smoking marijuana in the girls' room. Yes, he did understand that there was a family crisis, to which he was completely sympathetic, but rules were rules, especially when it came to drugs on school property. No, of course he hadn't witnessed it firsthand. But others – reliable and unimpeachable students who'd been putting up with the acrid fumes for months – had reluctantly come forward.

24

Need to Know

WITH MARIETTA SHIPPED OFF and out of the picture, I had more time to indulge my curiosity about Laura Lee's condition. I wanted to know everything: how could anyone who'd lived with my gynecologically astute father let herself get pregnant? Did her serene smile mean that this was no accident? And how far was she broadcasting the news?

I rang the president's doorbell late on a Friday afternoon. Laura Lee answered, looking a little peaked, but dressed as if it were her turn to host the bridge club in a navy blue shirtwaist dress of a lacy knit.

'May I help you?' she asked, her gaze eluding me and resting on some piece of snowy Dewing landscape.

I said, 'You don't sound very friendly.'

'We're working,' she said. 'Bunny's here.'

'I'd like to talk to you,' I said.

Shivering, she wrapped her arms around herself and said,

'It's too cold to be conducting a conversation with the door open.'

'Then invite me in,' I said.

She instructed me to take off my wet boots, after which we could talk for a few minutes in Eric's study, since he was in the administration building interviewing some candidates.

'For what?'

'That's not our business,' she said.

She led me down the hall, took the president's chair, folded her hands on the immaculate blotter, and stared.

'Where's Bunny?' I asked.

'We've got her set up in the breakfast room.'

I sat down opposite her and shimmied out of my parka. 'How's Mrs Woodbury?' I asked.

'No change.'

'Is she with it at all?'

Laura Lee said, 'I'm sure you realize that I can't give you a firsthand report. My work is on the first floor, and she's upstairs twenty-four hours a day.'

'You'd better watch that,' I said. 'She could get bedsores.'

'I'm not her nurse, Frederica. And she's not confined to her bed.'

'Can she walk?'

'With help. But she can't navigate the stairs.'

I looked back in the direction of the kitchen. 'Any chance I could get a cup of cocoa?'

She said, 'You can get cocoa at Curran' – she checked her watch – 'in forty-five minutes. Let's just skip to the reason for your visit.'

I asked, 'How old are you?'

'What does this pertain to?'

'It pertains to my not knowing your age.'

'How old do you think I am?'

I said, 'Somewhere between forty and forty-five.'

'I'm forty,' she said.

'What year were you born?'

'I was barely out of my teens when I married your father, if you're trying to do the math.'

I said, 'I have a reason for asking.'

Laura Lee waited.

'I counted the glasses on your tray, which said one thing to me: only a football player or a pregnant woman drinks that much milk.'

'I'm not having this conversation with a child,' she said, and stood up.

When I didn't move, she sat down again and picked up a pencil from the cluster Bunny sharpened daily.

'What about Bunny?' I asked. 'Has she figured it out?'

'I haven't confirmed your theory, Frederica, so don't try to trick me.' She scribbled a charade of a note on a presidential memo pad.

I said, 'We're a very liberal family. You don't have to worry about us making judgments. And you probably need someone to confide in.'

'Did your parents send you over to make this speech?'

I said, 'Absolutely not. It's all self-motivated. I have a lot of questions. I'm at that age when I need to know if it was an accident or a birth control failure.'

She made another note and said without looking up, 'You

know when you're the most annoying? When you sound like your father.'

I said, 'I agree. But I'm being sincere. If you *are* pregnant, and you're raising the baby alone, you're going to need a lot of help.'

She allowed a small, guarded smile. 'And how would that be?'

'Well, you'd keep it, right?'

'Of course!'

'I've done the math. You're not showing at all, so you're probably in your second month. I figure your due date is late summer.'

'Which would mean what in this hypothetical situation?'

'That I'd be on vacation.' I smiled. 'I'd help. I have a lot of experience with younger children.'

'And?'

'I could give you references.'

'You're telling me that you'd *babysit*? Is that what you meant by help? That's it?'

She was hoping for something bigger, some cunning campaign that would turn her scarlet letter into a blue ribbon and change her last name to Woodbury. I pointed to the bronze nameplate. 'Does he know?'

She asked, 'You're not going to trick me into confirming anything, especially a wild guess based on what you view as excessive consumption of milk.'

I said, 'Time will tell.'

She asked if my parents shared this pregnancy theory. I said we hadn't discussed it out loud, but I knew we had all drawn the same conclusion.

'Because of your tight family bond and their unwavering commitment to treating you as an adult?'

'Guess so,' I said cheerfully.

'How's it working out – the parents living apart?'

I said, 'That wasn't voluntarily.'

'Still joined at the hip?'

I said, 'The biggest problem just got shipped off to boarding school in Connecticut.'

Laura Lee leaned toward me to confide, 'She phones her father now. Of course it's to beg to come back. But he thinks they're making progress.'

I disclosed my own chief Marietta complaint: her kissing up to my mother while boycotting her own. What a brat.

Laura Lee appeared to like that. Sensing that we were slipping back to the old honeymoon phase of goodwill and co-conspiracy, I asked if she had had a blood test or had merely missed a period.

She looked toward the hallway. I crossed the room and closed the study door, carefully and soundlessly. When I returned to my chair Laura Lee said, 'It isn't customary to make an announcement until one has made it through the first trimester. Especially at my age. It's considered a high-risk pregnancy.'

'How old are you, really?'

She whispered, 'Forty-four in May.'

I asked again, 'Does Dr Woodbury know?'

'I'm waiting,' she said.

'Until?'

'He's got too much on his mind. His whole life is one public relations crisis after another.'

I said, 'I read a book once where this unmarried woman, older, went away to have her baby – just from Manhattan to Brooklyn, where no one knew her. After he was born she told everyone that she'd adopted him in Europe, even though she'd never left Flatbush. It had a happy ending because her obstetrician thought she was incredibly noble, and they fell in love.'

'I'm not running away and I'm not hiding. Eric loves me. We didn't think we had to worry about getting pregnant—'

'Because?'

'Because I'd never come close before.'

'But you could have? In between my dad and Dr Woodbury?'

'Are you asking about my sexual history?'

I said, 'I think I'm asking about your medical history.'

'Which you think is your business?'

I said, 'Sorry. No. It's not my business. I'm just nosy. I didn't mean to be fresh.'

Laura Lee said, 'You don't usually apologize.'

'We have a serious situation on our hands. I mean, we're still related. Your baby would be my cousin. Except for your mother, we're your closest family.'

With the first dreamy smile I'd seen in months, she confided, 'I've thought of that. I've pictured the wedding on campus. I've even pictured your father walking me down the aisle. Isn't that silly? But who else would do that? I have no brother, no living uncles, no father figure.'

I said carefully, 'Laura Lee? Wouldn't Mrs Woodbury have to pass away before Dr Woodbury could remarry? And wouldn't he wait a year? For public relations' sake?'

'A baby changes that,' she said. 'Especially when the wife

can't be a wife. Especially if the baby is a boy after three difficult daughters.'

'You can't know that yet,' I said.

'I sense it. I feel it in my bones. It's as if his Y chromosome is sending a message to my brain.'

I said I didn't think it worked that way, physiologically speaking. Besides: wasn't she setting herself up for great disappointment if the baby turned out to be a girl? I said, 'I don't want to burst any bubbles, but maybe you could think of an alternate plan, other than a wedding.'

'Do you mean going back to Tibbets Hall?'

'Or Schenectady. I'm sure your mother would help out.'

'And separate my baby from his father?'

I'd heard about hormones. Laura Lee thought she and her baby would always be welcome on the first floor of the president's house, in a room off the kitchen, or across the green in Tibbets Hall. Was it my fault? Had my family been too good a model? Have a kid, raise her in a dorm, treat her like an undergraduate, create a campus darling. I asked, 'You definitely, positively, want to go through with this?'

'Frederica! I've wanted a baby my whole life. The only regret I have about my divorce is that the marriage didn't produce a child.'

'You told me you weren't equipped to be a mother.'

'Did I? That was my youth talking, and my dreams of being a dancer.'

'What if Dr Woodbury hits the ceiling like he did over Marietta's suspension? What if he ships you off to a home for unwed mothers and tricks you into signing papers to put the baby up for adoption?'

'Out of the question,' said Laura Lee.

'It happens,' I said. 'At least one girl from Dewing gets sent away every year by her parents.'

'I'm not a Dewing girl,' said Laura Lee. 'Eric loves me, and I love him. And in any case, I have a fallback.'

Before I could ask, *Fallback job? Fallback housing? Fallback paternity suit?* Laura Lee asked nonchalantly, 'You remember Father Ralph, don't you?'

25

Walking Papers

VOICES WOKE ME: my father's, and one that wasn't my mother's. I checked the time on my alarm clock – 1:55 A.M. – threw my afghan around my shoulders, and set off to investigate.

Laura Lee was sitting on the couch under the founder's portrait, my father next to her, a bathrobe over the pajamas he'd taken to wearing since my mother was transferred.

'Go back to bed,' Laura Lee snapped.

My father said, 'Laura Lee felt she had nowhere else to turn.'

I didn't have to ask why: her red eyes and clenched hanky told me that President Woodbury had learned of his love child.

'Eric guessed!' she cried.

'He noticed the iron pills and the prenatal vitamins,' said my father.

'Is he furious?'

'He wants her to terminate the pregnancy,' said my father gravely.

Laura Lee nearly shrieked, 'What *don't* you tell her? Is there nothing, ever, that you'd consider to be over her head?'

I let my father answer, as I knew he would, about *Roe v. Wade*, about the term paper I'd written on the subject for extra credit, about how he and Aviva felt perfectly comfortable—

'Oh, shut *up*,' she cried. 'You're a worse bag of wind than you ever were.'

I said, 'That's rude, especially when you came to us for help.'

'You're distraught, Lee-Lee,' my father said. 'Let's all take a deep breath and stop calling each other names. Do you want a cup of herbal tea?'

Laura Lee said she did. 'Do you have anything to put on a sandwich?' she asked.

'Peanut butter and jelly.'

'What flavor?'

I crossed the five strides to our diminutive refrigerator, moved a few things around, unscrewed a few lids to see what didn't have mold growing on it, and called, 'Orange marmalade or elderberry preserves.'

'The latter, please. I'm ravenous.'

'It's white dining hall bread,' I warned.

'Fine,' she said.

As I made the sandwich, my father asked her, 'Can you tell me, word for word, what Eric said when he found your prescriptions?'

Laura Lee wailed, 'He charged into my pathetic little excuse for a bedroom, holding the bottles – like this, like grenades – rattling them, and railing, "Tell me these aren't yours. Tell me they're not for the purpose I think they're for." I collapsed in tears. I knew immediately that the timing was disastrous.'

'Go on,' said my father.

'There was no effort to mask his shock and his anger. No consideration of my condition or my feelings.'

'Had he been under the impression that you were using birth control?' asked my father.

She said sarcastically, 'He was under the *impression* that I was barren.'

'Because you'd never conceived?'

'Correct.'

'Had you ever seen a specialist?' my father asked.

'That is irrelevant! My point is that Eric has changed. Ever since I moved into the house he's been distant and distracted – beyond what you'd expect for a man in his situation.'

My father asked me how the tea was coming, then turned back to Laura Lee. 'Well, let's examine that: "his situation". His wife tried to kill herself over his philandering. She's reverted to a childlike state. He moved his – forgive me – mistress into his house. His daughter was thrown out of high school for smoking marijuana, effectively ruining her college admissions profile, all of which the entire Dewing student body has intimate knowledge of, or thinks it does.'

'Which is why I wasn't going to tell him yet! I was waiting for things to settle down.'

I brought the sandwich on a plate and the tea in a mug. Instead of a thank-you, Laura Lee said, 'Nothing that I discuss with your father, now or ever, is to be repeated. Do I have your word on that?'

'What if I were testifying?' I asked.

'Where do you get these ideas?' asked Laura Lee. 'Is that your view of the world – that everyone ends up on trial?'

'I was thinking of a hearing,' I murmured. 'Some commission somewhere.'

'Can't she go back to bed?' asked Laura Lee.

I would have complied if the next moment hadn't presented me with an interruption I considered too good to be true: through the blinds, behind the security bars, rap-ping on the outside window, President H. Eric Woodbury had materialized in a suit and tie and camelhair overcoat. I was the only one facing him, so I was the only one who didn't startle. 'It's Dr Woodbury,' I said. 'I think he wants to come in.'

My father didn't gesture – *go around, I'll open the door*. He approached the window, raised the blind, and yelled through the glass, 'What do you want?'

Dr Woodbury might have said, I'm the president of this college, sir, and you're being impertinent, but instead he asked politely, 'Is Laura Lee there?'

'She is, but she's not seeing visitors.'

Dr Woodbury said, 'I'm going around to the front door.'

'It's two A.M.!'

'You might as well let him in,' said Laura Lee. She stood up. 'We'll talk in the first-floor smoker.'

'Jesus!' my father exclaimed. 'Aren't you two enough of a sideshow without duking it out in a public space?'

'Then you won't mind if I invite him inside,' said Laura Lee. She handed my father her mug and plate and hurried out of the apartment.

I took her place and rewrapped myself in my afghan. 'She thinks he's here to kiss and make up,' I told my father.

'Don't think you're staying up for this,' he answered.

I knew Dr Woodbury wouldn't talk in front of me, but I also knew that my bedroom was ten uninsulated yards away from what would turn out to be the summit. I could already hear their voices outside our door, sending my father outside to shush them. I scrambled into my room. Seconds later, the trio returned. Laura Lee asked if I'd gone to bed. My father said, 'Of course.'

Laura Lee said, 'With her ear pressed up against the door, no doubt.'

Dr Woodbury said, 'I need to talk to Laura Lee alone.'

My father asked Laura Lee if that was all right with her.

She said, 'I'd prefer if you stayed, as my representative, to take notes.'

'That's entirely inappropriate,' said Dr Woodbury. 'This is not about employee relations, and you know it.'

'If you're going to fire me, I want someone here from the union,' said Laura Lee.

My father managed to refrain from discoursing on the composition of the bargaining unit. He said quietly to the president, 'I know about your predicament.'

Dr Woodbury asked, 'Which one would that be?'

'If you're talking about our child, I resent that!' said Laura Lee.

My father said, 'He hasn't had time to digest your news, Laura Lee. An unplanned pregnancy is rarely embraced as cause for celebration, and when you consider the other pressures Eric's facing—'

'I don't need a third party to speak for me,' said Dr Woodbury.

'I'm family,' said my father.

'I thought a divorce dissolved those bonds,' Dr Woodbury replied.

'We're cousins!' said Laura Lee. 'He has a stake in this baby, too.'

'Who else have you told?' Dr Woodbury asked.

'No one. Not a soul. I didn't even tell them. They guessed.'

'At this stage? I find that hard to believe—'

'Because they sensed something! They know me. They know my habits and my, my ... *modus operandi*. Even Frederica figured it out – from across the dining hall. What does that say about insight and emotional commitment or lack thereof?'

Even with a closed door between us, I could picture Dr Woodbury shaking his head, well on his way to hating me for my high obstetrical IQ and – much worse – as the potential megaphone between him and a thousand Mary-Ruths.

'One question,' said Dr Woodbury. 'Does Marietta know? Did anyone tell Marietta?'

'Do you want me to ask my daughter?' my dad asked.

'No!' I yelled from my bed. 'I haven't told a soul.'

'Don't!' the president yelled back fiercely.

'Where are you going?' I heard Laura Lee ask, causing me to snap off my bedside lamp and pull my covers up to my chin.

In his most presidential manner, Dr Woodbury said, 'If you and your family will excuse me, I have to get back to Grace. I can't leave her alone because she doesn't know day from night.'

'And you're Florence Nightingale!' yelled Laura Lee.

I thought he'd left, but after a few seconds I heard a barely audible, 'Good night, then.'

The door slammed. I waited for my father's counsel.

'Now what?' he asked our guest.

*

I woke up to find Laura Lee asleep on her stomach in the adjacent twin bed. More disturbingly, she was wearing a nightgown from my sleep-in-the-nude mother's rarely used collection. The alarm provoked barely a stir; when I asked how she felt, she groaned.

My father was already up and looking depressed, drinking instant coffee at the kitchen table. He didn't even greet me except to say, 'What choice did I have at two A.M.?'

'You'd better hope that no one saw her coming in or sees her going.'

'She'll leave with you. Besides, is there anyone left on this entire campus with the energy to absorb one more turn of the screw as far as Laura Lee's reputation is concerned?'

'Your current wife,' I said.

'I called her. She's not worried.'

I asked, 'Do you want my opinion?'

He didn't answer.

'She's got to go,' I said.

He sighed, closed his eyes, shook his head.

'No?'

'She says she's not running away. She's going to have this baby. She's not ashamed. She's convinced she'll get her Tibbets Hall job back because it's the least he can do. *And* she thinks she'd have a dorm full of babysitters at her disposal.'

I said, 'Did she mention Father Ralph?'

'Father Ralph?' he repeated.

I said, 'I think she might pin this on him.'

From the doorway of my room, in my mother's cream satin nightgown, not altogether opaque, her painted toenails peeking out, Laura Lee said, '*Pin it on Joe*? I never said that.' She crossed the living room and took a seat at the kitchen table. 'I know what she's referring to, but there would be no deception, no pinning anything on anybody. It would be me saying, "Joe – I'm pregnant. It has a silver lining. You need a roof over your head, and you need a job. In the bargain, you'd get a child, which I know you've always wanted."'

My father asked, 'Someone else's child?'

I couldn't see Laura Lee's face from where I was standing, but I could see my father's reaction to whatever lift of her brow was requesting discretion.

'Want me to leave?' I called from the door.

My father answered, 'Not without Laura Lee.'

'What do you want me to do with Aviva's nightgown?' she asked.

'Put it in the hamper,' I said.

She stood. Smoothed the fabric over one thigh. 'I think it's silk. I think you'd want this dry-cleaned.'

'Just put it in the hamper,' my father said, eyes lowered to the *Boston Globe*.

I said, 'I have twelve minutes to grab a bagel at Curran, so hurry up.'

She said, 'Two shakes of a lamb's tail.'

When David and I were alone, I crossed back to the kitchen table. 'Are we thinking that she had sex with Father Ralph?'

'We're not thinking anything of the kind.'

'But—'

He put a finger to his lips.

I said, 'I can find out.'

'No, you won't. It'll only give her more ammunition for her rantings against you.'

'Not against *me*,' I said. 'It's against you and Aviva. Boohoo. What a horrible crime – treating your child like an equal.'

He tapped his finger against his lips again. Laura Lee came out of my room, tying the bow at the neck of her blouse, and said, 'I didn't strip the bed, just in case I'm back tonight.'

'Take Frederica's coat. It's freezing out,' instructed my father.

She looked over at me as if waiting for the surrender of my parka. 'In the closet,' I said. 'My good coat. It's navy blue.'

As she buttoned my coat and examined the contents of its pockets, I asked my father, taking a stab at sounding age-appropriate, 'Wanna see us play Newton North this afternoon? It's a home game.'

'What time?' he asked.

I squelched my usual impatient answer – *same time that we play every home game on a weekday* – and said, 'Um, three-thirty.'

'I'll see what I can juggle,' he answered weakly.

Laura Lee said she would have joined me for a bagel but didn't feel well, and sure as hell didn't feel welcome at Curran Hall. Did I think a baby would change that? Even the radicals and the artistes had soft spots for babies, didn't they? Hadn't student doting contributed to my high self-esteem?

I said, 'You really should eat.'

'Can't. The very thought of food . . .'

'Sorry,' I said.

'I'm wondering if it's psychological. I was fine yesterday, yet sick the morning after Eric tells me he has no use for another child.'

I said, 'When do you tell Father Ralph that you want to marry him?'

'Soon. The minute he gets his walking papers from Rome.'

I said, 'Any chance this baby is his?'

'No,' she said. 'The timing is way off.'

It was too good a subject to abandon for a cakey bagel. I turned with her onto the lane leading to the president's house. 'Father Ralph must have been really hurt when you broke up with him,' I prompted.

'Not at all. He and I are just friends, which is why I could bring him to your dinner party and freely discuss Eric in front of him.'

I asked if she'd be willing to marry someone she didn't love.

'I love him as a friend.'

'What about the sex part?'

'It was fine,' she said.

I looked behind us on the path before I asked, '*What* was fine?'

'The sex. I don't want to sound condescending, but that was an act of friendship, too – a welcome back from celibacy.'

'But too long ago for this to be his baby?'

'Definitely.'

I said, 'I have to run, but maybe later you can explain where you met him and how the sexual act of friendship happened.'

'We have a board meeting later,' said Laura Lee. 'The thought of all those canapés makes me feel sicker.'

I said, 'Enlist some students. Trustees love that. You put nametags on the girls – class and hometowns – and let them circulate with trays. That's what President Mayhew used to do. Call the student employment office. They'll know who will charm the geezers and who will wear a dress.'

I shouldn't have added that Marietta and I used to gorge ourselves on the leftover pâté and various other delicacies. Her face went a shade paler and registered distress. She put her hand over her mouth and turned away. There was a mild gag, followed by a stronger one, then a heave onto an unlucky yew.

'Watch the coat,' I said as compassionately as I could, and headed for the nearest gate.

26

February

I WOKE TO FIND David and Aviva standing at the foot of my bed, serenading me. They harmonized proudly, wearing smiles that said, *We will try for the next twelve hours to make Frederica think that there is nothing more important on our calendar today than the anniversary of her birth*. I knew the routine: we'd have breakfast at home with doughnuts and crullers, purchased off-campus. They'd give me the option of skipping school to attend their classes, which I'd decline, after which they'd walk me to the bus stop. Hand in hand, they'd wave from the curb until the bus pulled away, despite my annual request that they refrain from doing so, as well as kissing me in front of my fellow commuters. Dinner, they promised, would be at the restaurant of my choice. How about Bo Shing? I loved that place, didn't I? I'd say great, as if it were a novel idea and not the setting of my birthday dinner for five straight years past.

The unwrapping of presents wasn't on the schedule because we didn't believe in birthday presents. When I turned thirteen an unfortunate tradition had been born: before dinner we'd gather around the baby grand, where David would write a check to the charity of my choice. Indeed, they'd remind me, all your dormwide parties, all that doting from the girls of Griggs Hall, and the ice cream and the giant sheet cake and all that attention – yes, you did have a magical childhood. But didn't I agree that I was now too old for a public celebration of what was essentially a private milestone? Gifts were unnecessary for a girl as lucky, as well fed, and as warmly dressed as I.

What were the plans for Frederica's special night? Laura Lee inquired of Aviva. Could she insert herself into the celebration?

'How did you know?' my mother asked.

'A year ago this week,' Laura Lee said proudly, 'I was at the post office, mailing off my wedding pearls to a special stranger who was turning sixteen.'

Aviva reportedly said, 'You're welcome to join us as long as you remember that February the first belongs to Frederica. Let's leave the adult problems back at the college.'

'My treat, of course,' said Laura Lee.

'I'll need her permission,' said my mother. 'That's how we do things in our family.'

'I know,' said Laura Lee.

I thought I had said no. Whose birthday was it anyway? I argued. Did we need David's ex-wife and my harshest critic at our table?

'I may already have assented,' said my mother.

'I'll take care of it,' said my father. 'I'll tell her about the family tradition—'

'And how about "We're living in two separate dorms thanks to you, Laura Lee, so we're keeping it private"?' I grumbled.

'Your father will handle it,' my mother said.

None of us, therefore, expected to see Laura Lee in a mink-trimmed cardigan and Father Ralph in a clerical collar and black suit, engaged in somber conversation at a table for two at Bo Shing.

'What a coincidence,' I murmured.

My father was happily following the owner's wife to our customary table, failing to inform her that we'd like to be seated as far away as possible from those party-crashers directly across the aisle.

'Happy birthday!' Laura Lee called to me as soon as I had taken my seat.

'Thank you.'

'Many happy returns of the day,' added Father Ralph.

'Thank you, Father,' I said.

'The usual?' David asked us, rattling his laminated menu. 'Or something special in honor of the occasion?'

'Peking duck?' offered my mother.

'What's on the chalkboard?' asked my father.

'Eggplant sounds good,' said my mother.

'Not to me,' I said.

'You choose,' said my father. 'In fact, this should be a new tradition: the birthday celebrant makes the selections – thoughtfully, of course, remembering what her tablemates like and don't like.'

'And with some thought to balance,' my mother added. 'Nutritionally speaking.'

I reeled off the standard chicken and shrimp dishes we had

democratically elected in the past and added a pu pu platter, which on any other occasion the senior Hatches would have disdained.

Father Ralph called over, 'I always wanted to try one of those.'

'It's a free country,' I said.

I busied myself by studying the place mat I knew by heart, of the Chinese astrological chart, and reciting compatible animal signs to my parents.

'Don't you think that was rude?' asked my mother.

I glanced over at their table. Laura Lee and Ralph were whispering, eyes darting in my direction. 'How's the food?' I asked pleasantly.

'It's excellent,' said Laura Lee. 'Thank you for the recommendation.'

'What do you hear from Rome?' I asked Father Ralph.

Father Ralph cleared his throat. 'I beg your pardon?'

'The Holy Father?' – the question causing a few of our fellow patrons to glance our way.

'Perhaps it would be better if they joined us,' my mother murmured.

'No way,' I said.

Across the aisle, they had resumed their private conversation. We heard Father Ralph say, 'It would kill my parents.' We heard him say, 'too soon' and 'not equipped.' We heard 'sin' and 'God' from him. We heard 'job' and 'parking space' from her.

My mother took a pen from her pocketbook and scribbled on my place mat, 'I think she just proposed.'

I said, '*Here?*'

My father said, 'People often announce upsetting news at a restaurant so that no one makes a scene.'

I said, 'This wasn't supposed to be upsetting news. This was supposed to be Laura Lee proposing and him saying yes.'

'At which point,' said my mother, 'they'd order champagne and join us, and Laura Lee could have a public triumph.'

The happy couple's table went silent. A minute later, Laura Lee was slipping into our fourth seat. My mother asked if everything was all right.

'No, it certainly is *not*.'

I looked across at the profile of Father Ralph. He had abandoned his chopsticks, switched to a fork, and was chewing like a man in shock.

'Did you two have a fight?' my father asked.

'He looks like you punched him in the stomach,' I said.

Laura Lee lifted her chin and said, 'I refuse to rain on the parade of your birthday celebration. Please ignore me. My travails will not be mentioned.'

My mother said, 'Then you know what, Laura Lee? If that's the game we're playing, if your joining us isn't meant to turn into a counseling session, and you want this to be about Frederica, then we're not sitting here rudely while Ralph sits there like a lost soul.' She turned to him and said, 'Ralph? Please join us. Pull your chair over.'

I mouthed *Wow* to my mother when she glanced my way. Her face was a telltale pink, and her lips were still moving, microscopically, with the rest of an undelivered speech.

Father Ralph said, 'If it's okay with everyone.'

I said, 'Hop on over. It's my birthday, and I say yes.' When he hesitated I said, 'Oh, c'mon. I'm used to a crowd.'

'She hates to see anyone eating alone,' said my father.

Father Ralph brought his chair with him and pushed it into the friendly territory between my mother and me.

Laura Lee said, 'You might as well bring the rest of the Amazing Chicken.'

A passing waiter made the transfer at the same moment that he arrived with our appetizers. Laura Lee took the opportunity to sing a melancholy, solo 'Happy Birthday', at the end of which I blew out the flame in the center of the pu pu platter.

'You have a lovely voice,' Father Ralph said to her.

Laura Lee harrumphed.

I said, 'Laura Lee? Your friend just paid you a compliment.'

'My *friend*?'

'Maybe this wasn't a good idea,' Father Ralph murmured.

'Look,' said my father. 'We're all adults here. The silent treatment is for children. We are a family who talks things over, so when in Rome . . .'

'Rome?' Father Ralph repeated.

'Not your Rome,' said Laura Lee. 'It's a figure of speech, which I doubt they throw around over brown rice at the monastery.'

'Whatever's going on – is this something that we can mediate?' my mother asked wearily.

Laura Lee said, 'Not unless you do marriage counseling.'

'You're *married*?' I squeaked.

'No,' said Laura Lee, 'and apparently someone is suddenly feeling ambivalent about a career change.'

'Do you *not* see that you are talking about this in public? A stone's throw from my parish?'

'Who told you to dress like that?' she answered. She turned to me and asked, 'Where's your boyfriend tonight?'

I said, 'I don't have one.'

'Who was that boy I saw you with in the beau parlor?'

'That's over,' I said.

'A not atypical dating pattern in teens,' offered my mother.

Laura Lee yanked her clip-on earrings – a floral spray in lilac and silver – off her earlobes and handed them to me. 'Happy birthday,' she said. 'I would have wrapped them, but I don't know where Grace keeps her wrapping paper.'

I said, 'That's okay. Really. You don't have to give me a present.'

'Of course I do!' She turned back to Father Ralph. 'Last year I gave her my wedding pearls, which I had appraised at eight hundred and fifty dollars. I hadn't even met her yet, so how ironic is that? Six months later she would become not only my number one ally on campus, but the daughter I never had.'

It was at that precise moment, on my seventeenth birthday, on February 1, 1978, that I saw it clearly at last. I had adopted a woman who stole, told lies, wore funny clothes, seduced college presidents, sneaked wine into the dining hall, read while she walked, and proposed to priests. I had saluted and indulged her quirks because unconventional behavior was the foremost quality I had been raised to admire. But now it seemed so undeniable and diagnosable: that Laura Lee French was, professionally speaking, nuts.

Five days later it began snowing hard enough for Brookline schools to send us home early. By late afternoon, weathermen were predicting a storm of historic proportions. My parents, of course, had to be coaxed away from their office hours, underestimating the hurricane-blizzard raging between them and me. I yelled at them when they got back to their respective dorms, their two-person human chain having taken thirty minutes to walk a quarter of a mile. The snow wouldn't stop. No boots or hats or waterproof ponchos made going outside possible. Cars were stranded in the middle of streets, then buried. No one drove, no highways were drivable, no shoveling or plowing was possible because the snow rose higher than the men who might remove it.

On campus, no one could come or go. Eventually cooks and servers stuck at Curran Hall on Monday night stayed stuck, stayed on campus, slept on infirmary beds. Backup and powdered food came out of storage. The milk went first, then eggs, then anything that would qualify as fresh or green.

From the first day of what turned into the Great Blizzard of '78, Dr Woodbury was unable to return from Providence, Rhode Island, ordinarily one hour from Dewing. Bunny went home, heeding the radio's warnings, urging the nurse to leave at the dot of three P.M. Laura Lee was in charge of Mrs Woodbury. After one hour, she called the infirmary: Mrs Woodbury needed help.

'What kind of help?' asked the nurse.

'She's hungry,' said Laura Lee.

'I hope you're joking,' said the nurse.

Laura Lee said, 'Dr Woodbury is lost somewhere in the storm. I don't even know where he is. I'm not allowed to go up to her room.'

'Why not?' asked the nurse.

'For personal reasons,' said Laura Lee.

The nurse felt entitled to hang up on Laura Lee after ordering her to pitch in and to be thankful she wasn't a one-woman skeleton crew with a half dozen infectious girls under her care.

Next Laura Lee tried Aviva at Tibbets Hall and my father and me at Griggs. 'Explain to Mrs Woodbury that it's an emergency,' my father advised. 'No, I most certainly won't send Frederica. I'm not even letting her visit her mother a stone's throw away. We're playing Scrabble.'

Laura Lee asked him if he thought Student Employment could send a girl to undertake the quasi-nursing chores.

He said, 'Laura Lee? Do you not understand that no one is at the college? The school is closed. Student Employment is closed. And even if her office were open, Mabel Fiske would never ask a student to leave her dorm in *this*.'

I could hear the tone of Laura Lee's ranting, but not the words. My father said, 'Of course she'd be agitated . . . Yes, that, too . . . But she isn't violent, is she?'

He listened to her reply, then flinched. 'Hung up,' he reported.

I asked, 'Do you think she'd let Mrs Woodbury die?'

My father said, 'No, I don't. Nor do I think a patient calling for ice cream is a genuine emergency.'

'Didn't we decide Laura Lee was a sociopath?'

'I think I'll open that new bottle of Scotch,' he said.

I waited until he had poured himself a glass before I said, 'You know, if you and I ran over there together, and wore boots and hats and carried umbrellas, and held on to a rope – we could make it easy.'

My father walked to the window. 'Look at the drifts,' he said. 'The snow must already be several feet deep.'

'So? How tall are we?'

He swirled his Scotch and sat down. 'Are we doing it for Laura Lee or for Mrs Woodbury?'

'Mrs Woodbury, I swear. I'd hate to find out tomorrow that she was lying in her own feces.'

My father said, 'We can't stay more than a few minutes. I mean it, Frederica. We'll feed Mrs Woodbury, assess the situation, and then we leave immediately. With the snow falling at this rate, and the wind, it could be a foot an hour.'

'Let's go,' I said, and dumped my unpromising Scrabble tiles back into the box.

The once shoveled paths were now only an indentation between drifts. My father wanted to turn back, but when I kept shouldering my way into the wind, he had to follow. 'She'd better appreciate this,' I heard him yell. When we passed students, he'd order them back inside, which would provoke another round of his beseeching me to stop this foolishness.

I said, 'Don't be a sissy. It's only snow. We can't drown in it. We're almost there.'

The president's manse looked to be up and running. 'Maybe Dr Woodbury made it home,' I said. We stomped up the front stairs to the door. The wind was driving needles of frozen snow against us still, despite the shelter of a porch roof. I rang the doorbell once, then a second time.

'We're going in,' said my father.

Laura Lee was halfway down the stairs, smiling a hostess's smile, dressed in a heather blue skirt and matching sweater that

I could swear belonged to Marietta. 'Hello, you two!' she called. 'How is it out there?'

'We're practically dead of exposure,' my father panted, and dropped onto the silk-upholstered bench where visitors waited to see the president.

'You really didn't have to come,' she said.

I said, 'Dad, the bench. You're going to ruin it.'

'You're dripping as much as he is,' Laura Lee chided.

'Where is she?' I asked Laura Lee.

'Do you mean Grace?'

'Yes, I mean Grace! Why do you think we came over here?'

Laura Lee leaned over the banister to state prettily, 'We're fine. In fact, we were having the *best* conversation when the doorbell rang.'

This brought my father to his feet. His face was bright red from the cold, his sleety eyebrows melting down his face. 'What did you say to her?' he asked.

I took the opportunity to dash past Laura Lee, up the stairs, and into the hallway. I passed Marietta's room, then the scarlet room assigned to the out-of-state daughters, and then I headed toward the wing that was the master suite.

Laura Lee called upstairs helpfully, 'She should be in the green guest room, Frederica.'

And she was. Grace Woodbury was on her feet, unaided and stark naked, standing before the mirror, applying lavender eye shadow to her closed lids and nose. Her hair was unkempt and two-toned; several inches of it, from the roots outward, were gray.

'Hi, Mrs Woodbury,' I said softly. 'It's Frederica. Are you okay?'

'Getting dressed,' she said, and held out a tube of lipstick as proof.

'Good,' I said, finding my mother's-helper voice. 'Getting dressed is . . . good.'

'For church.'

I said, 'But it's snowing hard. Nobody can go outside.'

'I have to,' she said. 'I'm getting married.'

There was a quilted bathrobe in a heap around her ankles. I picked it up, and said, 'This is pretty. Should we put it on?'

'Pretty,' she repeated.

'It's cold outside,' I said. 'A humungous blizzard like you wouldn't believe.' I put her arms into the sleeves and fastened the big plastic buttons from the bottom up, wondering what I'd say when I reached the top.

'Thirsty,' she said.

I said, 'I'll be right back, okay? You stay. I'm going to get another friend.'

'Eric?' she asked.

I patted her arm. I went as far as the doorway, where I stuck my head into the hall and yelled as loud as I could for my father.

27

Time and a Half

DAVID AND I COULD HAVE soldiered across the quad to Griggs but were reluctant to leave mentally diminished Grace with mentally unstable Laura Lee. The snow was already up to the first-floor windows, and – no small consideration – the president's larder was stocked to a much greater and more inviting degree than our inadequate refrigerator at home. We called Aviva and asked if she was up to braving the storm and crossing campus, with us at the other end as a reward. She said, 'How can I leave? I think you're forgetting that I'm in charge of not only my dorm but yours.'

My father said, 'If the telephone lines go down or the power goes out, and you need me for anything, sweetheart . . .' He listened, looking pained, then said into the phone, 'I don't know. Snowshoes?'

'Tell her Mrs Woodbury took her clothes off while Laura Lee was supposed to be watching her,' I prompted.

'Did you hear that?' my father asked Aviva. 'We can't trust

Laura Lee, and we sure as hell can't take Grace out in the storm to – what? I don't even know? The infirmary? Laura Lee asked them to admit her, and they said, "Fat chance."'

Mrs Woodbury was sitting with us in the front parlor, listening or not, understanding or not, and surveying the room as if pleased with these congenial strangers and their handsome antiques. Laura Lee was glued to the president's private line, harassing the state police, insisting we had a missing person to report. Earlier, my father had retreated from Mrs Woodbury's room, turning the fairly embarrassing chore of dressing her over to Laura Lee and me. Our docile patient had sat on the edge of the bed, lifting an arm when we asked for a foot and vice versa. Laura Lee was supervising rather than helping, telegraphing me looks that I interpreted to mean, *Who cuts her hair?* and *Her nurse must not believe in shaved armpits*, and, most clearly, *Is it any wonder that her husband turned to me for love?*

Poor Mrs Woodbury. I knew from the way she calmly accepted the ministrations of me the kid and Laura Lee the enemy that there were no villains in her house, that she submitted to this upkeep with the benign acceptance of a toddler whose mother habitually left her in the care of strangers. When we had dressed her in a pair of perky pajamas and a shiny Christmas-plaid robe, and had slipped Chinese slippers onto her unattractive feet, I called to my father, not wanting to trust Laura Lee as Mrs Woodbury's guide down the stairs. David answered my call; he knocked first for propriety's sake on the open doorjamb, and then boomed in a nursing-home voice, 'Don't we look nice! What a charming outfit!'

Mrs Woodbury looked down at her lap. 'Santa,' she

whispered reverently. We talked her down the steps, promising good conversation and ice cream. My father kept up the chatter: *What a pretty stair runner. What a lovely banister. Currier and Ives originals, according to my daughter, the campus guide.* When we reached the foyer, I sent him and his patter away, suggesting that he call Griggs's bell desk or Aviva – anyone – and steered the obliging Mrs Woodbury into the kitchen.

From the number of cans of Chickarina soup in the cupboard, I guessed that I'd found her favorite meal. I held up a can and asked if she'd like a bowl now. 'Soup,' she said.

I found a can opener and a saucepan. I could hear my father worrying aloud to RAs about nervous parents and unaccounted-for girls. Alone in the kitchen with Mrs Woodbury, I kept up my own nursery school patter as I stirred her soup and predicted its upcoming deliciousness. 'Have you ever seen so much snow?' I asked. 'It looks like Antarctica, don't you think?'

She shook her head, not unhappily. I said, 'Do you remember that you moved to Massachusetts from Maryland? Not much snow there, I bet. No comparison.'

'Eric did it,' she said.

I thought I should report this utterance – another mention of her husband – to a professional. I called in what I hoped was a sunny voice, 'Dad? Can you come here for a sec?'

'Dad!' Mrs Woodbury echoed in comradely fashion.

He didn't answer my first summons. When I called to him again, he yelled back, 'I'm on the phone with Russell.'

I said to Mrs Woodbury. 'He's speaking to Mr O'Rourke, the dean of students. You've met him many times.'

'Eric?' she said.

I said, 'Eric's not home. He had a meeting in Providence today. The capital of Rhode Island. It's very slowgoing on the roads during a blizzard.'

I snapped off the burner, found a ladle, found a bowl that looked cheerful and juvenile. I led her to the breakfast nook, tucked a dishtowel under her chin, and handed her the spoon.

'Feed me,' she said.

I mashed up the big pieces just to be sure a meatball didn't kill her. My father had not appeared. I asked her carefully, 'Do you know who Eric is?'

She puzzled out my question for a few seconds before answering, 'Daddy?'

I said, 'Okay. That fits. Why not?'

I could hear my father talking to Dean O'Rourke, yet another administrator stranded off-campus. *Buddy system*, I heard. *Bed check . . . I had no other choice.*

Mrs Woodbury opened her mouth wide, a big misshapen O. I said, 'This is your first course, often called the soup course. You'll have some more food with us, in the dining room. Can you say "Chickarina"?'

'Ice cream?' she answered.

I told her that ice cream was the dessert course. Later. Then I asked – employing one of my best babysitting tactics – 'Want me to tell you a story?'

Mrs Woodbury nodded. I knew she wasn't going to mind borrowed source material, so I retold 'The Three Little Pigs', always a hit with the under-five crowd because of my sound effects. Even though I told her the abridged version, approximately three minutes, she alternated intent stares at my face with ardent gazes at the refrigerator.

'Still hungry?' I asked.

'Thirsty,' she said.

'How about some milk?'

'Ovaltine.'

'Okey-dokey,' I said. 'Let me look.' I was pushing bottles around in the crowded refrigerator when Laura Lee swished into the kitchen, headed for a windowsill above the sink and its array of pills, took one from each bottle, swallowed a palmful with a few gulps of water, turned off the tap, and left without a word.

I delivered the chocolate milk with a straw, and asked Mrs Woodbury, 'Do you know who that was – the lady who just came in to take her vitamins?'

'Yes?' she said uncertainly.

'Is her name Laura Lee?'

'Eric did it,' she repeated.

'Is she a babysitter?'

'Yes,' said Mrs Woodbury.

'Is she a *nice* babysitter?'

My patient nodded.

I leaned a little closer. 'Is she a menace to society?'

Mrs Woodbury said yes.

I whispered, 'A sociopath?'

Mrs Woodbury smiled back hopefully.

I checked the doorway to make sure no one had sneaked up on us. 'A crazy woman and a homewrecker?'

Mrs Woodbury's eyes told me that something had clicked. 'Whooo, whooo – blow your house down,' she recited.

I patted her dry, ringless left hand. 'Good girl,' I said.

*

My father seated Grace at the head of the table, where she tucked her napkin into her bathrobe and passed gas, a string of staccato toots, without apology.

'Hence our attempt at a little socialization,' said my father.

'Don't blame me,' said Laura Lee. 'I was, as you know, banished from the second floor.' She had a desk phone at her elbow and was redialing the police after every few bites of the tuna fish sandwich I had fixed.

My father said, 'What if he's trying to get through to you? He's going to be getting a busy signal all night. Why don't you take a break?'

'Eric knows both numbers. Unless he's buried under an avalanche somewhere.' David and I looked to Mrs Woodbury, who was staring at her half sandwich, to see if Laura Lee's words had registered. I asked if something was wrong.

'She hates mayonnaise,' said Laura Lee.

I said, 'You could have told me.'

'I forgot. The nurse mentioned it in passing once. I've got a lot more on my mind than your friend's eating habits, Frederica. Such as: where is you-know-who and why hasn't he called?'

My father took a handful of potato chips from the cut-glass bowl I'd chosen and dropped them onto Mrs Woodbury's plate. She smiled.

'Help her,' said Laura Lee.

'Let her try,' said my father.

The phone rang, causing all of us except Mrs Woodbury to jump. Laura Lee picked it up in midring and gasped, 'Eric?' Her face sagged instantly. Without a word, she handed the phone to my father.

'Eric?' said Mrs Woodbury.

'No,' said Laura Lee bitterly. 'It's not Eric. Eric either doesn't want to call or can't call because he's stranded in his car. Or stuck in a snowbank with amnesia. It's David's wife, Aviva.'

'My mother,' I explained to Mrs Woodbury, jabbing myself in the breastbone, happy to use a noun I thought she'd understand.

My father was saying into the phone, 'Okay, we'll turn it on. Thanks, hon,' prompting Laura Lee to mimic his 'Thanks, hon' derisively.

'Everything okay?' I asked.

'I assume so. She said we should turn on the TV.'

'Why?' Laura Lee cried. 'Was there a horrible accident?'

My father said calmly, 'Traffic has come to a dead halt on 128. The cars can't move. The drivers are abandoning them.'

'Where's 128?'

'It's a big circle around the city, south to, I'm guessing, Braintree or thereabouts, and north through the western—'

'Would he have taken it?'

My father hesitated, looked at me. I said, 'It's possible. He'd get off at Route 9—'

Laura Lee ran out of the room, hand over her mouth. In a few seconds, we could hear television voices fractured by the flipping of channels.

'Eric?' said Mrs Woodbury.

My father said, 'No. Eric's not home. Those voices you hear are on television. They're anchormen.'

I said to my father, 'Do you really think she understands "anchormen"?'

'It's possible. I'm sure there's a TV in her room.'

I said, 'If Dr Woodbury's car got stuck, don't you think he could have gone to the nearest house and asked to use their phone?'

'Not every family operates like ours does,' he said. He wiped his mouth with the monogrammed napkin I'd found in the sideboard, and said, 'Please excuse me.'

Mrs Woodbury's gaze followed David's exit. 'As soon as I finish my sandwich, we'll go watch television, too,' I told her.

'*Sesame?*' she asked.

I said, 'I don't think *Sesame* is on now. They're watching the news. Because the snow is really bad. I mean – you can't see a foot in front of you.'

She watched me eat. I picked up a chip and crunched it instructively. She pinched one of hers, opened her mouth, and pushed the chip in the generally correct direction.

'Excellent!' I said.

She crushed another into her mouth and then another. 'Not so fast,' I said. 'Chew it and then you can swallow.' I demonstrated, more athletic chewing in exaggerated fashion. From two rooms away, reporters were throwing out, 'State of emergency . . . Record high tides . . . Record low barometric pressure . . . Cars marooned on Route 128,' which incited an agitated discussion between David and Laura Lee that I couldn't quite make out. Mrs Woodbury said again, '*Sesame?*'

I asked if she liked *Mister Rogers' Neighborhood* as well. She nodded enthusiastically. I said, 'Some people think he's gay, but I don't. Do you?'

My father strode into the room and headed for the phone. I asked him if anyone knew what time Dr Woodbury's meeting had been in Providence.

'It was a lunch meeting . . . maybe one-ish?'

'Where exactly?'

'Laura Lee doesn't know.'

I said, 'Bunny would know, Dad. Call her at home.'

He left with the phone and its mile-long cord, and I returned to our enculturation. 'Do you like President Carter?' I asked her. No answer. 'Do you identify with Rosalynn? I mean, as a fellow First Lady?' Mrs Woodbury smiled, missing eye contact by a few place settings. 'Are you interested in politics?'

When she didn't answer, I said, 'Did you watch the Watergate hearings?'

She said, 'Water?'

'We had a party the night Tricky Dick resigned. Chili and cornbread? Do you like chili?'

She nodded, frowning.

'Not so much?' I asked.

She did a little pantomime, pointing out the window, then hugged herself in an approximation of a shiver. 'Chilly,' she explained.

I said, 'Well, close enough. That's a homonym. "Chili" and "chilly". Very good.' This was getting less interesting, reminding me of how tedious I found babysitting. I said, 'Excuse me for a minute. I'm just going to check on those other people. You'll still be able to see me, okay? My name is Frederica. Can you say "Freddie"?'

'Freddie,' she repeated.

I walked the few steps into the foyer at the same moment Laura Lee ran past me and bounded up the stairs. My father appeared, not to follow but to scowl in her wake. 'Bad news?' I asked.

'I reached Bunny. She *did* know where Eric's meeting was.'

'Where?'

'An alum's house. It was a fundraiser. He ignored the forecast because the woman, apparently, was dangling an endowed chair in front of him.'

'What time did he leave Rhode Island?'

'He didn't. The hostess convinced Eric that he shouldn't risk the drive back home. He's there. Safe and sound. Guest of honor.'

'Did you talk to him?'

'We didn't call there. He notified Bunny, who didn't think it necessary to inform anyone else, such as . . .' He tipped his head in the direction of the stairs.

I asked, 'Do you think someone should go up there?'

'To say what? "At least we know he's safe and sound even if he's a selfish bastard"?'

'I know! Who did he think was going to take care of his wife?'

'I suspect he thought Bunny would arrange for coverage, or that the nurse would stay.'

'Did you say anything to Bunny?'

'Such as?'

'Such as: "You should be fired for desertion."'

He laughed, an exhausted paternal laugh, then added wearily, 'Bunny knows we fight hard so that the staff doesn't have to perform work outside their job description.'

I said, 'Dad! It's a state of emergency. Is babysitting the president's wife in *your* job description?'

We both, automatically, turned to peer into the dining room to check on our charge. She was again staring at her tuna fish sandwich as if it were a frog she'd been instructed to dissect. My father called, 'Grace, don't worry. You don't have to eat that. Look: Frederica will take it away.'

I asked my father, 'Do you think she can hear okay?'

We had our answer immediately, as Laura Lee shrieked from above, presumably into a telephone, causing Mrs Woodbury to flinch.

'Do you have any idea what you've put me through?' we heard.

Mrs Woodbury said, 'Mummy?'

We returned to our seats at the table. My father said, 'No, hon. That's Laura Lee, upstairs on the phone. Remember she was eating with us, and dialing the telephone?'

Mrs Woodbury said, 'Okay.'

I asked, 'Do you think she said "Mummy" because she was raised by a mother who yelled and screamed a lot?'

'Good question. My guess would be yes.'

From above we heard, 'But—' and 'but—' again after what must have been a rant at the other end, followed by the slam of the phone accompanied by the loud sobbing of someone trying to be heard in the next room.

'Maybe you should go up there, Dad,' I tried again.

David Hatch then muttered something that I'd never heard him say in my seventeen years as his daughter and as a front-row witness to his housefathering: 'Let her cry.'

We might have let her cry if the racket hadn't set Mrs Woodbury to wailing. I said, 'Someone has to tell Laura Lee to shut up or cry in private.'

'If only Aviva could be here,' my father said. 'I hate to put you in this position . . . so much responsibility. It isn't fair.'

I said, 'We can handle it. You've got a Ph.D. in psychology.' I smiled. 'And I have ice cream.'

Mrs Woodbury's crying changed to an interrogatory whimper.

'Would that make you feel better?' I asked her.

Laura Lee must have given up on the prospect of our rushing to her psychiatric aid, because we could hear her descending the stairs miserably. She joined us at the table, whipped the air with her napkin before smoothing it onto her lap, then asked, 'Does anyone want to know what that was about?'

'I think we can guess,' said my father.

Chin trembling, she said, 'I called Eric at that alum's house and told the woman who answered the phone that I was calling about Mrs Woodbury. Or maybe I said I *was* Mrs Woodbury. I forget. When he came to the phone, I said, "How dare you leave me alone with your helpless wife?" And do you know what outrageous thing he said to me?' She touched her chest with a splayed hand and coughed out a sob. 'That he would pay me time and a half for the hours I covered for the nurse!'

My father said, 'Time and a half? To a salaried employee?'

Laura Lee closed her eyes, inhaled, exhaled, opened her eyes. 'Frederica? Could you tell your father that he has, characteristically, missed the point by a mile?'

I said, 'You tell him. I promised to get Grace some ice cream.'

'She's going to get as big as a house before this is all over.'

'So what? It makes her happy. It's not like she's going to star in *The Nutcracker* next Christmas.'

Laura Lee reached over, helped herself to Mrs Woodbury's

untouched sandwich, and took a large bite. 'If it weren't for this child I'm carrying, I wouldn't want to eat anymore. Or live! I have no one. Eric said he didn't want me to be here when he got home. And you know what I said? I said, "This is the president's home, and you won't *be* the president of Dewing College when I go public."'

'Were you serious?' asked my father.

'Who doesn't already know?' I asked. 'Everyone on campus does.'

'*The Boston Globe?*' she said smartly. '*The New York Times? The Chronicle of Higher Ed?*'

'Going public would only hurt the college,' said my father.

'Good,' said Laura Lee.

'And my parents,' I added. 'Who have been unbelievably nice to you.'

'So? If the college folds, you'd get to live in a house and have a normal childhood instead of being a teenage housemother.'

My father said, 'I've had enough! You're not to speak to my daughter in that tone of voice again. Ever.'

Mrs Woodbury resumed her crying. Laura Lee joined in. The record-breaking wind howled. The lights flickered, inside and out, but recovered.

'Thanks, Dad,' I said. And meant it.

28

Cabin Fever

NO ONE HAD EVER SEEN snow like this. 'As emphatically as I can possibly state it, all people are to remain in their homes. Virtually every roadway in the state is impassable,' pleaded Governor Michael Dukakis from the TV screen. My new best friend, Gracie Woodbury, I learned, could wash dishes if there were bubbles to entertain her and if I didn't mind a little breakage. Some part of her brain remembered how to polish furniture, a make-work activity that kept her busy as long as she had a soft rag in her hand and me to point her toward another breakfront. Soon I came to recognize the crossed legs and sashay that meant she had to pee. Except for the occasional crying jag, prompted by loud noises and family photographs, she was easy, sweet, manageable.

Laura Lee was ostentatiously useless, alternately pleading morning sickness, heartbreak, relocation, and revenge. On day two, prompted by nothing more than Aviva's using the words 'cabin fever' to describe the state of her boarders, Laura Lee declared that Tibbets Hall needed her. My well-meaning mother, she informed me, didn't understand that population. They were individualists, at least by Dewing standards. They were sensitive, despite their hard outer shells. Some danced. She had to go to them.

I expected my father to argue, to block the door, to hang on to her wrist as she set forth into the storm. Instead, he swept his arm and bowed in a grand gesture of chivalry. 'Be my guest,' he said. 'Good-bye and good luck.' Laura Lee performed an about-face, marched up the stairs, then marched back down wearing her raccoon coat, high-heeled green suede boots, and a jaunty burnt orange beret that barely covered the tips of her ears. She grabbed the knob of the front door with both hands and pulled. A gust of snow blew into the house as if it had a generator behind it. 'Close it,' I yelled. 'Get back in. You can't go out in that.'

She closed the door and leaned heavily against it, breathing hard. 'I'll get an umbrella,' she panted.

Behind us, sitting and watching from the stairway, my father said, 'Don't be melodramatic, Laura Lee. If you went out in that and the wind blew you over, we wouldn't find you until spring.'

'I'll go mad if I stay here!' she cried.

I said, 'Would you let one of your girls go out in this? What if all of them were acting like this? *Let me out! Let me out!* We'd have to pad the walls.'

'This is a state of emergency,' my father said calmly. 'You have to get a grip.'

'It's too much,' she said. 'Too much.'

'What is?' asked my father. 'Too much snow? Or too many level heads?'

Laura Lee pulled off her beret with a jerk and sent it sailing into my father's chest. 'You want to know what's too much? How's this, David? I'm with child by a man who doesn't want it and has seized that as a reason to send me away. On the heels of that, I get this natural disaster, which couldn't have happened at a worse time. The real tragedy is that if Eric could be here, we'd have had this private time in this cocoon' – she swept the room with an open arm – 'in this beautiful house, fires in the fireplaces, the two of us alone to work things out. But what happens instead? This ridiculous storm with no end in sight! I can't leave. He can't get home. And what do I have for company? My lover's loony wife.'

I said, 'I don't think she's loony.'

'Where *is* Grace?' my father asked.

'In the study. *Sesame Street*'s on,' I said.

My father said, 'Laura Lee? You're not a stupid woman. Was this storm really sent for your personal inconvenience?'

'That's not fair! Wasn't I just heading out the door to help Aviva? And of course I'm aware that this storm is wreaking havoc. They keep showing that same footage over and over again: the people up to their armpits in the slushy ocean water. I've seen it a dozen times.'

My father stood up and said, 'I have calls to make and calls to return.' He stopped halfway down the hall and turned around. 'I want you to know that I'm calling Eric for reasons that are purely administrative.'

'What are you going to say?' Laura Lee asked eagerly.

'I'm going to say, "There's no relief in sight. The deans and the provost are stuck in their respective homes, which may as well be in California for all the commuting they can do. You have to name someone as acting president or acting something."'

'It had better be you,' I said.

'Or me,' said Laura Lee brightly.

'You can't be serious,' I said.

'I certainly am. He named me acting hostess to the president. It's a women's college. And it's high time there was a woman in charge.'

'And you'd be that woman?' my father asked, striding back toward us. 'With no administrative experience, no seniority, no civil defense training? It boggles the mind how highly you think of your abilities! It's inconceivable to me. It's . . . it's . . . do you have any grasp of reality to say that the president, who has relieved you of your duties as housemother, who has asked that you not be here when he returns—'

'Dad—' I said. 'Okay.'

'Let him rant,' said Laura Lee. 'Your father wants to be in charge, a promotion at last! The hero of the Blizzard of 'Seventy-eight. If he feels better calling me names, fine.'

He was so good at not rising to the bait that I expected him to respond coolly. What I heard instead was, 'You can't even look after yourself, charging like a madwoman into a life-threatening storm! We need you to calm down and to stop getting Grace agitated with your histrionics. Frederica has ten times the sense you do, and she's not even half your age!'

'I'm pregnant,' said Laura Lee, sniffling. 'It's natural that I would be frantic, with these hormones coursing around my body and the father of my baby a virtual prisoner in another state.'

My father said, 'Trust me: pregnancy does not make every woman frantic.'

'Like Aviva, you mean? That paragon? Let me remind you that she had a wedding ring on her finger and a devoted husband, who probably invented maternity leave.'

Go, I mouthed to my father.

As soon as he'd turned away from us, Laura Lee gave him the finger, energetically and with both hands. 'No offense, Frederica,' she said at the same time.

When I didn't respond, she coaxed, 'Oh, c'mon. Don't you be mad at me, too.'

I said, 'Maybe you should go take a nap. Or a nice long soak in a tub.'

She sat down next to me, elbows on the step behind her. 'Do we know anything about this woman in Providence who's playing hostess to Eric?'

'Why?'

'Is she young? Old?'

I said, 'Are you thinking that he's on a *date*?'

She leaned forward and took my chin in her hand. 'One always has to think that. And you know why, don't you? My past. What happened to me in my first marriage. You can't be too vigilant. He strayed from his wife. He'll stray again. You never know what Trojan horse an unlikely girlfriend will come riding in on.'

We were snowbound and trapped. No plows in sight and the governor begging us to stay indoors. I could bat her hand away and say, 'You need help, Laura Lee,' or I could politely excuse myself. 'I think I hear the closing theme song,' I told her. 'I'd better go check on Grace.'

'You're a wonderful girl, Frederica,' said Laura Lee, giving my chin one more squeeze. 'I hope I've told you that before. You'll make a great mother someday.'

What a lying hypocrite I had turned into: 'So will you, Laura Lee,' I said.

After her nap, and after a long soak using Grace's English soap and Swedish bath oil from better days, Laura Lee appropriated the private line for her own mischief. Assignment desks at Boston newspapers were overwhelmed. Editors covering an unnavigable city with skeleton crews did not have time to take notes on the romantic transgressions of a minor college's president. She was shocked. No takers! What kind of newspaper ignored a tip like this?

When David and I said, more or less, 'A newspaper covering news,' she appealed to Aviva, victim to sociologist. My resourceful mother said, 'I think there's only one thing you can do at this moment in time, Laura Lee, given the state of the city: write it yourself. You should close yourself in a room and write your heart out.'

'A novel?' Laura Lee breathed.

'I'd view it as a record,' said my mother. 'And if that turned into a *roman à clef*, so be it.'

'I'm not a great writer,' said Laura Lee.

'Just record the facts,' said my mother. 'This is what our complainants do before we consider going forward with a grievance. It's very helpful.'

'Just the facts?' Laura Lee asked. 'Like a list?'

'Whatever feels right,' said my mother. 'Whatever tells the story.'

'Can lists be turned into a novel? Like if I hired a ghost-writer?'

'One step at a time,' said my mother.

'But I don't have a desk. David's using Eric's day and night.'

'Where does Bunny work when she's there?' my mother asked. 'She must have a desk and a typewriter.'

'I can't type,' said Laura Lee.

'Then just pick up a pen and tell your story. It'll keep your mind off the blizzard.'

Aviva told me later that she was surprised at Laura Lee's next question, yet pleased that it manifested an unselfish impulse. 'How are my girls over there? Bored out of their wits?'

'We're coping,' said Aviva.

'Anyone over there take dictation? Or touch-type? Either would help. And of course I'd pay.'

'I'd get right on that,' said my mother, 'if I weren't a little preoccupied with the storm of the century.'

'Oh, right,' said Laura Lee. 'I keep forgetting.'

Life stood still in the dorms. All homework, all reading, all papers due, were put aside with the confidence that classes, when they resumed, would be a multidisciplinary meteorological review and teach-in. Aviva reported that the girls of Griggs and Tibbets were uncharacteristically collegial. Unable to leave or date or catch a movie, they ate canned soups and popped corn, got into their pajamas early, and had the good clean fun – charades, hootenannies, talent shows, s'mores – of an earlier time. If anyone whined, someone else reminded her: thousands of homes destroyed. Thousands of cars stranded on the highway. People dead.

After two dark days of relentless wind and snow, the sun came out. Cars, mailboxes, hydrants, parking meters, Dumpsters – everything – had disappeared under drifts. Driving was banned in the city, and would be for four more days.

Aviva, the only housemother on the faculty, got permission from the academic dean to convene Criminology and Penology in Griggs Hall, attendance voluntary, for the bored and fidgety. Fifty students showed up for a seminar that usually taught fifteen. Departing from the syllabus, my mother talked about the Boston Strangler and Harvey Hawley Crippen, the mild-mannered London dentist who filleted his wife's body after murdering her. By Friday, my mother counted eighty carpetbaggers, including me.

My father spoke to President Woodbury several times a day, and over the course of the week I could hear a change in his voice. He was dispensing advice, vetoing suggestions offered by a president who couldn't comprehend from a side street in Providence what a shut-down city and a thousand snowbound adolescents might involve.

'How's Grace?' Dr Woodbury asked, for the record, at the end of each call.

'I have a rotation,' said my father. 'I've hired – well, *you've* hired at a fair wage – a few responsible students to keep her company. Frederica's chipping in. We think Grace is getting . . . a little more aware.' He frowned as he listened to the response. 'No, not about that. Laura Lee is just another stranger at the dining room table.'

He listened, color creeping up his neck. 'Not only out of bed, but – without the tranquilizers and sleeping pills – she's joined the living,' he told Dr Woodbury.

I could hear anger crackling through the receiver. My father answered tersely, 'The prescriptions ran out, and there isn't a pharmacy open in this city. If you'll excuse me, I have a parent holding on the other line.'

He didn't. I asked when he'd finished, 'Did she really run out of pills?'

'In a manner of speaking,' said my father. He twisted his mouth one way, then the other. 'I accidentally flushed them down the toilet.'

It was just the two of us in the breakfast nook, eating the last of the eggs, boiled, with Uneeda Biscuits. Governor Dukakis was giving his first briefing of the morning, wearing a crewneck sweater, reporting from the state's emergency bunker. Grace and Laura Lee were still asleep. I said, 'Was he furious?'

My father confided that Woodbury's phone call the night before led him to believe that our president had snapped. He was near blubbering, cataloguing his woes as if he were the sole sufferer of these indignities: he'd had to wear borrowed underwear that had belonged to the recently deceased husband of his hostess. She ate only TV dinners, and those had run out after lunch on day three. They'd been eating hot cereal, prepared with water instead of milk the way he liked it, some old cheese, tuna packed in oil, and root vegetables, boiled beyond recognition. The woman was no intellectual companion. She had graduated back in the days when Dewing was a secretarial school. In fact, she was dotty. She had visited his room in the middle of the night, had sat on the boudoir chair, facing the drapes, staring. She seemed to have no memory of it by morning, but nonetheless it was disconcerting, even a little frightening. Should he call a doctor? He was so desperate to leave that he considered walking back to Brookline, but he didn't have proper boots, and the dead husband's were too small. Did a college president in exile qualify for a lift from the National Guard? Could David look into that?

'The Guard is rescuing women in labor,' my father had told him. 'Unless you have appendicitis, you're going to have to sit tight.'

'I'm moving south,' Eric had whined. 'I can't take your winters!'

'Did you tell him it was the storm of the century? That it won't happen again if he lives to be a hundred?' I asked.

My father winked above the rim of his coffee mug. 'No, I did not,' he said.

From my borrowed upstairs windows, the out-of-doors looked irresistible, a Technicolor nondenominational Christmas card, every surface, every branch, frosted and glistening. Downstairs Laura Lee pecked away at Bunny's Correcting Selectric. Sometimes Grace wandered by the breakfast nook and took a seat so she could stare at the typewriter's twirling metal ball of letters, as if she knew what Laura Lee was writing.

'We're fine,' Laura Lee would say when I stuck my head in to check on Grace. 'Why don't you go visit your mother, or get some fresh air?'

'Because I don't trust you with her,' I'd say cheerfully.

'Such devotion,' Laura Lee murmured, not looking up from the keyboard. 'You must be getting paid.'

'Time and a half. My father worked it out with you-know-who.'

'Eric Woodbury,' Laura Lee pronounced deliberately, loudly. 'The father of my child.'

'C'mon, Gracie,' I said, hustling her toward the mudroom. 'Let's leave Laura Lee to write "The Autobiography of a Very Cruel Woman."'

'Eric?' Grace whimpered.

'He's no good, either,' I said.

I dressed Grace and myself in extra layers and rubber boots and led her out the front door, down indistinguishable steps, through powder up to our thighs. No paths were plowed or shoveled, but cooped-up girls had stomped from dorm to dining hall, and we made our way in their boot prints.

'Snowman,' Grace would say, pointing happily, when we passed one of the crude ice sculptures that were springing up all over. I had promised her hot chocolate at Curran Hall, my first sampling of the modest hot-beverage-and-cookie program my father had instituted when the dorms emptied onto the quad. As we left the cafeteria, I helped myself to two trays, then led Grace back outside to one of my childhood hills.

It took a lot of smoothing and flattening to fashion a run that wouldn't swallow us. I went first, kneeling on my tray, paddling in the snow for enough traction to get me launched.

'Whee,' I yelled back to Grace instructively. 'Wheeeee.'

She put her tray down at the top of my path, kicked it, riderless, down to meet me, and clapped when I dove to stop it.

'Not the idea,' I said. 'What I'm looking for here is a little "Put me in, coach!"'

'Freddie up,' she answered.

I worked my way back up the hill. 'Your turn,' I said. 'See: like a sled. Like a half-assed mini-toboggan.' I sat her down, curled her fingers around the tray's rim, and said, 'On the count of three . . .'

Her first ride wasn't fast or clean or a straight trajectory, but she was out of jail and shrieking with joy when she reached the bottom.

'You did it!' I yelled.

'My turn!' she answered.

'Now get off your tush and hike back up here,' I said.

She rolled off her tray and ate the clumps of snow stuck to her mittens before scrambling to her feet.

'How great was that?' I asked.

'Love Freddie,' she called back to me.

Her nurse came back to work on Monday and promptly quit when she found a whole new order: a strange man in charge, hinting at her complicity in overmedicating the patient, and that same former ghost of a patient out of bed, dressed, and cheerfully Windexing kitchen appliances. I left the house at six A.M. for my first day back at school, on foot. Residential life would soon return to normal, my father said. Today the two RAs who had been sleeping in our Griggs apartment to heighten the appearance of their authority would go back to their rooms. 'What about Laura Lee?' I asked.

'I'm working on that,' he said.

'Can she go back to Tibbets?'

'Conference call at ten this morning,' he said.

'With whom?'

'Woodbury. O'Rourke. DePiero. Me.'

'Not Laura Lee?'

'I hope you're joking,' he said.

He kissed me good-bye, pulled my scarf up to my nose, and made me promise I would turn back if sidewalks weren't cleared and I had to walk on the street.

'Promise,' I said.

I called that afternoon from Patsy Leonard's house and proposed I stay there for a few nights, that school was closer and easier from her Brookline Village street than from Dewing, and I needed a change of scenery. My father, sounding preoccupied, agreed too easily.

'Is Grace okay?' I asked.

'Fine,' he said. 'The nurse quit, but Bunny's back.'

I made a second call, this one to Aviva's office, and found her in. I repeated: was it okay if I stayed at the Leonards' for a few days? I'll be so much closer to school and, really, her mom says it's no problem at all—

'I think that's a fine idea,' said my mother. 'We'll keep in touch.'

We'll keep in touch? Something wasn't right when a Hatch parent said those words in distracted fashion to her beloved and only daughter.

'I can put Mrs Leonard on if you want to talk to her.'

'Won't be necessary,' said my mother. 'I'm sure it's okay. Have fun.'

I called her back and said, 'What's going on? Did someone die?'

She answered, finally, after a sigh that nearly stopped my heart. They had wanted to tell me in person. I was not to worry. They'd fight it, of course. They had due process on their side, not to mention tenure, and there was a question of whether Woodbury even had the authority—

'What?' I pleaded. 'Just tell me. What did Woodbury do?'

'He fired your father,' she said.

29

The Little Guys

IT HAD BEEN A LOVELY INTERLUDE, lodging in a private house that wasn't a cinderblock dormitory, sleeping in a bedroom that had never known life as a utility closet. Further, I had enjoyed the new David Hatch, the one who wasn't railing against authority and had even started wearing a jacket and tie. Thirty-six hours after the axe fell, we hadn't done a thing that resembled moving back to Griggs.

'Is this a palace coup?' I asked. We were chipping away at the frozen front porch, transporting pots of steaming water from the kitchen sink to melt the treacherous stairs.

'No,' he said. 'This is me holding the rudder until he gets back. This is me going down with the ship.'

'Can he arrest us for trespassing?' I asked.

'Let him try,' said my father, waving to Grace inside, supervising us from a front window, her hair in rollers courtesy of Salon Frederica.

*

Dr Woodbury finally returned, eight days after the first flakes fell and the first minute – or so he said – that the commuting ban was lifted in Providence. I was making myself useful, spotting my father as he shoveled snow off the presidential roof, looking none too sure-footed.

The first thing Woodbury said, alighting from the passenger side of a tow truck, was, 'I fired you, Hatch. Do I have to call Security?'

'Security's busy,' my father answered between grunts and pitches. 'Security's a skeleton crew, like everything else.'

'Don't have a heart attack, Dad,' I called.

President Woodbury asked, 'Don't you ever go to school?'

I said, 'I went today. But I came right home after my last class. I have storm-related responsibilities.'

He frowned at 'home', then asked, 'Why is your father shoveling my roof?'

I said, 'Because roofs cave in when they have a ton of snow on them, and he happens to think of the house not as yours but as belonging to the People.'

'Where's my wife?'

'Grace,' I said coldly, 'is doing fine. She's in the daycare center. It's her second day, and she's very happy.'

'Whose idea was that?' he asked.

I said, 'The Hatch family's. She was bored and needed more stimulation than she was getting – asleep.'

He was, after all, a smart man, an educator, and a diplomat. He said, 'I know you must think I've made some terrible decisions—'

The tow truck driver asked, 'How's that cash comin', pal?'

Dr Woodbury said, 'Excuse me,' and squeezed himself along

the narrow path to the house. After a minute or two, the driver honked. Dr Woodbury appeared and called from the front door, 'Will you take a check? I thought I had cash on hand, but it's not where I left it.'

The man jerked his thumb skyward. 'Does your friend have cash?'

Woodbury looked up at the roof and back to the driver. 'I'm afraid that would be very awkward.'

'He fired that friend,' I announced.

The driver asked me, 'So what's he doin' up there, workin' away?'

I said, 'He's very dedicated. He didn't want the roof to cave in.' I lowered my voice to confide, 'We're sort of ignoring the dismissal due to the emergency blizzard crisis.'

The driver squinted through the front windshield, assessing the property. 'Do they have a union at a place like this? What is it? A school?'

I said, 'A college. They certainly do. In fact, the guy with the shovel is the union president.'

'Him?' asked the driver. 'On the roof?'

'That's my dad,' I said. 'And your passenger is the president.'

'What're they allegin'?'

I said, 'It wasn't for cause. It was personal. Very.' I whispered, 'He ran the college single-handedly while this guy was twiddling his thumbs in Rhode Island.'

Dr Woodbury interrupted from the top step, 'If you're worried that my check isn't good, I can assure you that it is.'

'They say the banks ran out of money,' said the driver. 'The actual green stuff. 'Cause the Federal Reserve Bank was closed, and that's where the cash comes from.'

'That's ridiculous,' said President Woodbury. 'And I'm afraid you don't have a choice, sir.'

'Is there a problem, brother?' my father called down.

'Dr Woodbury doesn't have cash to pay the driver,' I said, 'and the driver doesn't want to take a check.'

My father said wearily, 'There was cash in your top desk drawer, Eric. I moved it to the bottom drawer, under the Yellow Pages; it's in a manila envelope marked "Instruction Manuals".'

'He was protectin' your money,' said the driver. 'He could have stolen it with you out of town. You've got yourself an honest caretaker there, no matter what else he did to piss you off.'

Woodbury didn't answer. He went back inside and returned with the envelope – no thanks, no pardon. Slipping and sliding in only tasseled loafers, he made it to the truck and counted out twenties until the driver nodded.

'Receipt,' said Woodbury.

'Long gone,' said the driver. 'I'll mail ya one, in care of management.' He winked at me.

'Bye,' I said. 'Drive carefully.'

'Good luck to the little guys,' he answered, raising two fingers in a V.

'Now get the hell down from there, Hatch,' Woodbury yelled up to my father. 'And take your smart-mouth daughter back to whatever you call home when you're not squatting at someone else's.'

I said, 'Grace gets out of school at five. She's expecting me to pick her up.'

'That won't be necessary,' he snapped.

I added, 'There's nothing wrong with her. She's just a little . . . simple.'

'I don't take advice from children,' he said. 'Especially children named Hatch.'

'Where's your car?'

He was on his way back inside, but I thought I heard him say, 'Irretrievable.'

'Couldn't they just give you a charge?'

He didn't answer, but slammed the door behind him. Later my sources would tell me that he'd left the Cadillac on the street like a rookie, and it had been totaled by a plow.

That night we sat around our kitchen table, reunited in Griggs Hall because our fellow pariah, Laura Lee, had restored herself to housemother status in Tibbets. The atmosphere was nerve-racking and World-War-Two-ish with us speaking in hushed tones, waiting for the enemy's knock on the door.

'What if he just sends a moving van,' I said. 'What if some new family shows up and says, "Excuse us. We're the new houseparents. What are you still doing here?"'

'I'm teaching my classes tomorrow,' said my father. 'And holding office hours. It will be like any normal Wednesday.'

'And you'll go to school,' said my mother. 'You have to get back into your routine. The subway's running. Food's being delivered. There's nothing else that needs your exclusive attention. David and I are absolutely fine.'

'What about Grace?' I asked.

My mother said unconvincingly, 'Grace is going to be fine too. They're going to research the adult equivalent of daycare for her, and I'm sure it'll have the same activities she likes so much.'

'Who's "they"?' I asked. 'Who's been looking around for a program?'

My mother paused. 'We are.'

My father added, 'We thought if we found the right place for her, we could recommend it to Eric—'

'Who's too overwhelmed and distracted to give it his proper attention,' my mother finished.

'And incompetent,' said my father. 'Not to mention unprincipled.'

Unexpectedly, my voice choked as I tried to say, 'It's the saddest thing.'

'We know,' said my mother.

'All she wants is a friend. And she's gotten kind of . . . lovable,' I managed.

'You'll visit her, sweetie,' said my father.

'Where?' I snapped. 'At the house? I'm sure he's got armed guards at every door.'

'We'll work something out,' said my mother.

'In the manner of a custody arrangement,' said my father.

'He should be reported,' I said.

'To whom?' asked my mother.

'Someplace. Some bureau. Some state office that watches over retarded women with asshole husbands.'

My parents nodded as if I'd said something not only wise but devout.

'He shouldn't get away with any of this,' I said.

My mother said, 'I know you think we can fight every battle—'

'You can! I've seen you and Dad handle, like, ten grievances at once.'

'Not like this,' she murmured.

'This is different,' said my father. 'This is my own neck on the chopping block.'

'And you know what that means,' said my mother.

I did: Hatch solidarity. Three necks for the price of one.

David called the union's counsel, an old shop steward turned lawyer, who sounded almost gleeful at the meaty news that management had dared fire its faculty union president.

'I know,' I heard my father say to him. 'I know it gets your juices flowing, but it feels a lot different when you're the hunted.' After a series of, 'Okay . . . okay . . . right . . . will do,' he handed the phone to Aviva, and said to me – as I chewed my ragged cuticles in my bedroom doorway – 'Saul thinks everything's going to be okay.'

'Oh, sure,' I said. 'Like I don't recognize when you're sugarcoating the truth.'

'Shhh,' he answered, pointing to Aviva, who was shushing us with flaps of her wrist. I moved closer to her, listening for the true measure of the trouble we were in.

'Not yet,' she said. Then: 'If it comes to that.' I studied her face. She reacted to something Saul said by pinching the bridge of her nose. Her voice was unsteady when she replied, 'I don't know if we can accept that, Saul. But I'll never forget that you offered.' She said good-bye, hung up, left her hand on the receiver.

'What?' I asked. 'What did he say?'

'Are you okay?' my father asked. 'Aviva? Honey?'

She walked to the sink, turned on a faucet, turned it off, finally said with her back still to us, 'Saul said . . . because it was us. Because it was David . . . there wouldn't be a bill. He'd waive his fee.'

'Because he thinks Dad won't have a job?'

'No,' my father said too quickly.

'We only spoke for a minute,' said my mother. 'He was between sessions with an arbitrator.'

'But he's not worried?' I asked.

David said, 'He wants us to stay put, at least till I get something in writing.'

'From whom?' I asked.

'From the college. A termination letter.'

My mother turned around, smiling too bravely. 'Who at Dewing would sign such a thing? No administrator that I know. I don't even think Bunny would *type* such a thing. She'd quit first, after all we've done—'

I said, 'Ma! You wouldn't type such a thing, but other people aren't like you! People do what they're told. They follow orders. They name names. They don't stick up for their friends, they don't go out on strike, they don't wear black armbands. They collaborate with the enemy and then get decorated.'

'Frederica's right,' said my father. 'No one is going to stick their neck out. I've been a pain in the ass to pretty much everyone at one time or another. I have to save myself.'

'You have Saul,' I said. 'He'll yell and scream and go to the newspapers.'

My father smiled a grim smile. 'Right. With Laura Lee. We can hold a joint press conference.'

We sighed heavily at the mention of Laura Lee – another problem to be solved, another broken axle in our crisis caravan. Or so we thought.

30

Valentine's Day Night

THE KNOCK WE'D BEEN EXPECTING did come, one night later, on February 14, 1978. It wasn't Dewing Security or Mayflower Transit, but Laura Lee French – ex-wife, nuisance, and family embarrassment – wearing a sly smile that seemed, for once, more outward than inward. 'Could you come out to the quad for a minute?' she asked. 'You, too, Frederica.'

We put on our coats, our hats, our scarves, our gloves, our boots. All the while she ducked our questions – *Is anything wrong? Is it a student? Should we get coverage?*

'Nothing's wrong. Hurry up,' was all that she would say.

Did we notice that the foyer, the lounge, the living room, were empty? That no work-study student sat at the bell desk, and no roommate kept her company? 'Wasn't Claudia on duty a minute ago?' my father asked, his head swiveling left and right.

'Bathroom break,' said Laura Lee. 'Now march.'

One of us must have opened the front door. I heard my

father, in the lead, mumble, trancelike, 'Oh my lord' and 'Could this be . . . ?' I elbowed myself forward for an unobstructed view of whatever was paralyzing my parents.

Before me was a beautiful sight: a thousand Mary-Ruths holding candles in the dark. There were no banners, no signs, no chants, but their message was unmistakable: we are gathered together to protest the firing of Professor Hatch.

Aviva caught on first. I knew this because my bold, unbending, iron-willed mother put her hands over her face and began to sob.

'Who did this?' I asked Laura Lee.

'I can only take credit for the choreography,' she said, and with that fluttered one end of her fluffy pink scarf, signaling a thousand synchronized candles to rise over the allies' heads.

'Like Rockettes,' I whispered.

'Without a single rehearsal!'

'Who told them I was fired?' my father asked.

'Who cares?' said Laura Lee. 'It spread like wildfire.'

Were there faculty, staff, and fellow houseparents there, too? I can't say because the crowd has doubled in my memory. The yearbook photo of that night occupied two panoramic pages, bled across the gutter, shot with a slow f-stop that melted the stars and candles into streaks of white.

My father put his arm around my mother, who continued to cry as she murmured apologies for her atypical labile response. I ran back inside for Kleenex and returned to cries of 'Speech! Speech!'

My father walked forward, three careful paces to the edge of the stairs. 'I'm simply overwhelmed,' he said.

'Louder!' yelled a voice in the back.

'I'm overwhelmed, I'm dumbfounded, but very, very grateful,' and with that he, too – emergency president, seasoned housefather, union agitator – began to cry.

So there I was, the last Hatch standing. I stepped forward and yelled, 'Wow. This is incredible. Is this, like, the whole school?' A cheer went up. 'Any alums?' I asked. A few voices supplied graduation years. 'He's in shock,' I continued, warming up, grinning. 'So let me ask: you're all here for my dad, right?'

Another cheer and a swell of yeses.

'Because you found out that he got sacked?'

A thousand boos rolled our way.

'Even though he has tenure,' I continued. 'Even though he kept this school open and running while the so-called president disappeared—'

My father said, 'Frederica! I think that's enough. I want the floor back.'

Not quite finished, I yelled, 'Okay! Here's the man of the hour, my dad, the reason you're all here: David! Louis! Hatch!'

My father slipped off his humble knitted cap and smoothed his thinning hair. 'I don't know if this' – he swept his arm across the crowd – 'will change anything, but when I look out and see all of you, and know that the word went out – "to every Middlesex village and town and Dewing dormitory," to misquote Henry Wadsworth Longfellow – I can only believe that this is *your* shot heard round the world, whether we win or lose . . . whether I stay or go . . .'

That led to a chant of 'Stay, stay, stay,' initiated by his daughter.

My mother touched my father's arm, meaning, *Let me*.

Stepping forward in her down-filled coat of an unsightly orange, she called out in a shaky voice, 'I want to thank every single one of you. I mean, I look out there and I see freshmen who don't even know us . . . students I've argued with . . . students I've put on probation . . . students who have dropped my classes . . . students I've flunked' – laughter – 'but here you are, homework due, probably overdue, sacrificing your Valentine's Day to a cause bigger than yourself . . . I'm overwhelmed . . . and I want to thank whoever planned this, whoever found candles in a shut-down city and pulled off the biggest surprise party in Hatch family history.'

Laura Lee stepped forward. What would she say? *Don't forget that I, too, am an endangered houseparent. Did I ever tell you that I used to be married to your man of the hour? Oh, and how do you like this headline: I'm pregnant with President Woodbury's love child, just in case any one of you hasn't figured that out yet.*

But all she said was 'Thanks for coming, ladies. Thank you for your spontaneity and for not spilling the beans. Please extinguish your candles before going back inside.'

'Wait!' said a familiar voice.

'Aviva?' said my father.

There was no bullhorn in my mother's hand that night. Still the crowd fell instantly silent. 'This is only phase one!' she cried. 'This is preaching to the choir! Do we really want to waste this magnificent show of solidarity? We don't? Then follow me! And keep those candles lit.' Like a manic umpire on a close call, she threw her arm in the direction of the big white house across campus, finger pointed and eyes narrowed. A roar went up.

She turned to my father and said with her old urgency, 'You stay here. Please. This shouldn't take long . . .'

My mother was right: it didn't take long, especially when the object of one's dissent refused to show his face. Woodbury must have sensed the approaching phalanx of Dewing women bearing candles and radiating disfavor. By the time the single-file ranks of the newly zealous reached the circular driveway, the president's house was utterly dark. Chants of 'Hell no, Hatch won't go' didn't draw him outside, nor did all seven verses of 'We Shall Overcome'.

But it was cold, and some of the protesters had dates. A primitive construction-paper heart was taped to the second-floor window of Grace's room, and her puzzled face appeared next to it when the singing stopped. Even a relatively angry mob of Mary-Ruths led by an impassioned Aviva Hatch was not inclined to storm a president's house.

31

The Wages of Sin

NO HATCH WOULD HAVE GUESSED that Ada Tibbets herself, famously wealthy grande dame and suspected anti-Semite, would emerge as our champion. Not that it was a matter of justice being served or contracts being honored, because women of her disposition weren't interested in righting occupational wrongs. What got to Ada Tibbets in the end, what horrified her and made her threaten to cut Dewing out of her substantial revocable trust, was the moral turpitude of the incumbent president of the Mary-Ruth Dewing Academy – or whatever they called it nowadays.

Who filled her in, we wondered? It could have been anyone with a strait-laced soul or vindictive heart in possession of a pen, paper, a stamp. Some days I would have put my money on the perennially overlooked Bunny, a woman scorned by administrators of every stripe. Might a poison-pen letter carry a Connecticut postmark, implicating Marietta? Was it a committee of parents who had heard the rumors and felt it was their duty to squeal? Or perhaps it was a priest who felt that the wages of sin was a pink slip.

The famously imperious voice called our apartment in the late afternoon, a few days after the candlelight vigil that solved nothing.

'Ada Tibbets here,' she said. 'With whom am I speaking?'

'Frederica,' I said.

'How old are you now?' she asked.

'Seventeen,' I answered. 'Why?'

'Don't be impertinent!' she barked. 'I'm trying to paint a picture of your family.'

'Sorry,' I said. 'Did you want to speak to one of my parents?'

'Of course I do,' she said. 'Your father. In private.'

He was a few yards away at the kitchen counter, squinting at directions on a cold-remedy box.

'*The* Mrs Tibbets, for you,' I said in my most sonorous receptionist's voice.

He looked awful – he was coming down with something. His face was pale; he needed a shave and there were dark circles under his rheumy eyes. Of course I stayed at his elbow to hear why Ada Tibbets, for the first time in my life, was calling us at home.

It wasn't that she had the exclusive power to bring down a president, but she had the ear of the trustees, and a phone tree in the top drawer of a no-doubt priceless antique desk. Amazingly, none of her cronies had heard about Woodbury's affairs, administrative or sexual, or of Grace's attempted suicide, its resulting brain damage, or the expanding uterus of an innocent novice housemother. Benefactress Tibbets had been shocked, dismayed, appalled to learn that the college was collapsing under the weight of scandals so repellent that she had taken to her bed upon receiving the unsigned account that had elucidated her. The trustees, even those retired to Florida and Arizona, *did* know that a storm of historic proportions had closed down the college. They also knew – having called the president's house at all hours – that Dr David Hatch had risen to the occasion while H. Eric Woodbury was absent for a week, despite what seemed like a negligible distance separating Providence from his sacred duty.

It was a short conversation. My father was mostly silent because Ada Tibbets, apparently, was delivering an impassioned speech. Finally, he closed with 'Yes, I do' and 'I certainly shall,' which didn't calm me at all, because his eyes were red, and his handkerchief seemed poised to mop a distressed brow.

'What does she want?' I demanded the instant he'd hung up.

He walked to our one living room window. It overlooked the quad and – now that the trees were bare – the widow's walk above the president's house. 'This is something I have to tell your mother first, hon,' he said. 'I hope you'll understand.'

'Then call her, for God's sake,' I said, checking my watch. 'You can catch her in her office if you call right now!'

'Not this,' he said. 'This requires my telling her in person.'

'Is it really bad?' I asked.

He turned and faced me. 'I promise you it's not bad,' he said.

32

Home

DAVID LOUIS HATCH, PH.D., was inaugurated as the tenth president of Dewing College on March 30, 1978. We kept the ceremony low-key due to the awkward circumstances of his ascension, but still we hosted delegates from fifty-five New England colleges, and snagged Archibald MacLeish to read from his poems.

We moved into the president's house even before my father's induction, as soon as Dr Woodbury packed up his belongings and slinked back to Maryland, where he'd had the foresight to keep the family home. I personally emptied the closet and bureau drawers in the former First Daughter's room and mailed two cartons to Marietta's boarding school with an insincere note – my mother insisted – claiming that our door was always open. She wrote back, a couple of expletives on an index card alluding to snitches at Brookline High, and a postscript that said, generically, 'Hi to Mom.'

I stepped in to recommend another adjustment to the

Woodbury flow chart: that Mrs Woodbury stay. It wasn't an easy sell to anyone, especially my parents, who worried that Grace needed more supervision and stimulation than Dewing daycare could provide. I pointed out that they had lived their entire Dewing lives with a hundred girls swarming above and around them. How hard would it be, given the help that came with the office, to assimilate one simple and harmless soul into the household, who, in her own cortically impaired way, was good company? In the end, we struck a deal: Grace could stay, a foster child of sorts, until I went off to college, provided she didn't disturb the family peace and if I didn't shirk my custodial duties.

I took the green and gold room, the smallest bedroom in the manse, but the one closest to Gracie's newly pink one. It was twice as big as my Griggs Hall cell and overlooked the backyard rather than the campus, which contributed to the feeling that I no longer had to breathe the same air as a thousand undergrads.

Dr Woodbury, to save face, pretended to resist our informal guardianship of his still legal wife. But once I had converted my father to the cause, he did the rest. Grace, he asserted, needed the constancy of her room, her TV, her chums. She'd woken up from her stupor – no aspersions intended, he told the sedation-happy husband – to find Frederica at her bedside, leading her to solid food and to life's simple pleasures. 'You've heard of animal imprinting?' my father asked. 'Well, that's what we've got here, in human form. You're welcome to get a second opinion, but my advice is, don't move her one single centimeter.'

*

The dean of residential life had the nerve to suggest that it would be so very helpful, given the upheavals of the past few months, if Aviva could moonlight as housemother in Griggs or Tibbets – her choice – until the end of the year. David, now in the privacy of a big and relatively secluded house, discovered his voice. He ranted in rhetorical fashion about the ill-considered suggestion, as if he had eighteen years too many of pent-up discretion and low-decibel stewing. Aviva resigned from the union executive board, which would have placed her across the table from her own husband and also because she was confident that the new labor relations climate would not require such a high level of gumption.

Guided by the misapprehensions of Ada Tibbets, who believed that the rookie housemother had been seduced and abandoned by the previous administration, the board of trustees recommended that Laura Lee be allowed to keep her job and her health benefits through her confinement. My father, arguing before the board in executive session, failed to persuade a majority that Laura Lee was too mercurial to shepherd Ada Tibbets's namesake hall. Counsel for the college agreed with the board, and that was that: the only way to avoid a festival of lawsuits and their attendant publicity was to let Miss French stay.

The issue of child support was the last thorny subject my father took up with the outgoing president, who maintained, in the way of all dodgers and liars in the years before DNA testing, that he was not the father of Laura Lee's unborn child. Yes, he'd consider revisiting his alleged responsibility after the birth, and yes if the child's blood type was O he might be the father – but so might a million other guys.

It was a noteworthy lesson, even for someone who'd been fed a daily diet of italicized lessons: that people in high places, luminaries with advanced degrees in Classics and in possession of excellent manners, can disappoint you as profoundly as anyone else.

Laura Lee held her head up high once she received the board's vote of Victorian confidence, but those of us who knew her saw how hard she took Eric's abandonment. She believed he would come through once he'd left town in disgrace, his wife in someone else's custody, his daughters estranged. She called our private line often to ask if we were shunning her. Might it be our newfound stature and status? Or had we forgotten our roots and didn't want to be seen in the company of a lowly, out-of-wedlock houseparent? Perhaps, despite lip service to all things fair and square, we had decided to forsake our cousin? But whatever sins she had committed or whatever behaviors we found unforgivable and annoying, couldn't they be considered water under the bridge?

She called one night to report proudly that she'd finally told her mother she was pregnant. Bibi had cried tears of guarded joy, which she didn't revoke upon hearing that the boyfriend had failed to leave a forwarding address. Bibi had asked – and Laura Lee repeated gamely to my mother as they passed each other on Longfellow Lane – if David would consider claiming paternity so that the baby could have a name. My mother led Laura Lee to the nearest bench, where she lectured professionally on the dangers of rumors and gossip in a closed culture.

Still, who was a better sport than my mother? On August 7,

Laura Lee gave birth to a long, strawberry blond baby girl, blood type O, at the Boston Hospital for Women, Aviva Hatch in attendance. The new mother named her baby Juliet, and named me, aged seventeen and a half, her guardian.

Not long afterwards, Laura Lee dressed Juliet in a sunbonnet and sun suit and arranged her in a nest of blankets in a clothes basket, which she placed on our front porch along with a small, Orphan Annie suitcase. The doorbell rang and our house-keeper answered; her scream brought the entire family to the porch. We might have called 9-1-1 if we hadn't understood immediately that it was Juliet, and if Laura Lee hadn't been sitting a few yards away on the porch glider, dabbing her eyes with a cloth diaper.

My father asked calmly, 'And what is this supposed to be a metaphor for, Laura Lee?'

'For nothing! It's me saying I have no choice but to face facts. How can I take care of a baby when I have no home? There's a note to that effect in her diaper bag.'

David said, 'My understanding is that no one is asking you to leave until you're back on your feet.'

'I want to stay,' she said. 'I feel that the new regime and I will be a much better fit than the previous son of a bitch's.'

My father carried the basket to the glider and set it at Laura Lee's feet. 'So you were leaving Juliet on our stoop so we can raise her as our own? Even though we did such a questionable job with Frederica?'

'It breaks my heart, but I think it's for the best,' she said.

'Can I hold her?' I asked Laura Lee.

'You should address those questions to me from now on,'

said my mother. 'And the answer is no. Never wake a sleeping baby.'

'I haven't heard anything about my replacement,' said Laura Lee. 'I think that means that you're keeping the door open.'

My father sat down next to her on the glider. 'Laura Lee. You were a disaster. The trustees went beyond the call of duty to give you this extension.'

'I was only a disaster in terms of my private life,' Laura Lee countered. 'Can't you separate the personal from the professional, especially now that I'm a mother, and my maternal instincts are at an all-time high?'

I volunteered that the housing office had had someone lined up, an obviously ambivalent applicant, who had just gotten into medical school from the waiting list. Poof: withdrawal. Poof: a vacancy.

'Go inside, Frederica,' my father answered.

'Can I show the baby to Grace?'

My mother said, 'Laura Lee wasn't serious about leaving the baby on our doorstep, so don't start petitioning for another bedroom to be painted pink.'

Laura Lee crouched down and enfolded the laundry basket in a theatrically protective embrace, endangered-mother-lioness-style. Above her head, my parents rolled their eyes.

At the appointed time, the two oldest Woodbury daughters came back for their mother. I wanted to slip away first – no good-byes, no scene – but I was overruled. Grace would be confused, my parents said; she had to hear the facts and see for herself that the team was breaking up.

'Gracie,' I told her at breakfast. 'I'm going off to college today, a different one. It's in another state, but not ridiculously far away. You'll be going to live with actual relatives. I'll call you at your new house.'

To my relief, she didn't understand; her eyes were on the present I was holding, wrapped in purple paper, a parting gift of picture books, sequels to her favorites. 'Freddie go,' she said eagerly.

Her daughters came for her that afternoon. Marietta, they reported, was headed for her own freshman orientation at a previously all-male college, proud to serve the cause of coeducation. They had brought Grace a snapshot of Marietta in a cap and gown, standing between her sisters – scowling, they insisted, only because the sun was in her eyes. My parents swore that Grace pointed to the graduate and said, 'Baby.' They also swore that she left willingly with her first- and second-born daughters, and that her tears were tears of joy.

33

Emeriti

A SCALED-BACK LAURA LEE stayed in Tibbets Hall until Juliet started kindergarten, a juncture that coincided with her inheriting Bibi's fully-paid-for Schenectady house. I was away at college for four of Juliet's five years on campus, but I heard long-distance about the splash she was making, mascot-wise. Laura Lee wrote and sent me photos. Juliet was a beautiful child and looked so much like her mother that it was easy to forget the genetic contribution of Eric Woodbury. According to Laura Lee, Juliet loved to look through yearbooks past and could always pick out Cousin Frederica, no matter how unflattering or how crowded the photographs. The baby's undisputed favorite layout: the candlelight vigil, which she had attended in utero. Even at five, Laura Lee insisted, Juliet grasped its significance and grasped that her mother had contributed to the pageantry and, in some small way, to the advancement of Cousin David.

*

Ten years ago, Laura Lee asked my father if she might enroll Juliet a year early at Dewing. For better or for worse, she claimed, the child felt a profound attachment to the school and had always seen herself returning, despite her high grades and fabulous PSATs.

'Why now?' my father said. 'Why not let her apply when she's a senior?'

'She's ready,' said Laura Lee. 'And if she isn't, she's got you and Aviva there for backup.'

'Put Juliet on the phone,' my father said.

'Why the rush?' he asked her. 'Don't you want to graduate with your class?'

Juliet said – our first inkling that she was the most sensible child ever born – 'Yes, I do, but I also need to go away, and I can't have both.'

He and my mother translated her answer to mean, 'I need my freedom, and I need to get out of Schenectady, but my mother is listening to every word, so I'm hoping you can read between the lines.' The need, it turned out, was that Laura Lee was sick. And like a doomed parent in another century, she was putting her dearly loved child on a train.

My father recused himself from the vote that brought me back to Dewing after a series of jobs at more prestigious schools too far from home. I am here now, vice chancellor for administration, in charge of all things financial. My family and I live on a side street and in a house that I suspect is based on the Patsy Leonard model of single-family, two-car, conventional happiness. On those rare days when I feel a fleeting nostalgia for communal living and dining, I eat my lunch at Curran Hall.

My father and mother are retired and living nearby, which is to say in an apartment so close to Dewing that it may as well be a dorm. They are both in good health; they audit classes and rally on the Boston Common against wars and oppression, weather permitting. For fun they vet every contract I sign, boilerplate or not, then return it with the offending clauses circled for my reflection and repentance.

Juliet lives and teaches in New York and visits every summer. I'm not quite old enough to be her mother but will on occasion refer to her, in shorthand conversation with strangers, as my sister. My grandmother adored her and, in her time-warped view of the David Hatch marriage continuum, saw Laura Lee's child as something more than a cousin twice removed. Juliet and I have noted that there is a certain symmetry to our lives: that she returned to Dewing at sixteen, the same age I was when her mother's existence came to light.

With something like influence at my disposal, and as a gift to Juliet, I created a Laura Lee French Prize to be awarded to the senior who most embodied the qualities of the late house-mother, euphemistically synopsized as individualistic, distinctive, artistic, and passionate. The award itself is now eagerly awaited. When the winner is announced – always a famously kooky but popular pain in the ass – the crowd goes wild.

Juliet has never met her father or her Woodbury half sisters. Laura Lee raised her not quite with the photograph of a uniformed serviceman on the mantel, but with the academic fairy-tale version of the courtship: that despite his better instincts and fine character, he'd been married and in the spotlight when their fabled love combusted. To run away with Laura Lee, or even to acknowledge paternity, would have ruined his brilliant career and broken the hearts of his sacred children.

Juliet is twenty-seven. I should be able to tell her the truth about the commotion her parents caused on campus, but I am not the social science team of David and Aviva Hatch, who live their lives under oath. I let Juliet interpret what I mean when I say that Dewing was never the same after Laura Lee arrived. And I always confirm, in good conscience, what her mother raised her to believe: that every character in her story, at one time or another, loved each other deeply.

Acknowledgements

To Mameve Medwed and Stacy Schiff, ideal readers and perfect friends, always on call and always right.

To Bob Austin, who shared my bunker during the blizzard of '78.

To everyone at the William Morris Agency, especially the divine and witty Suzanne Gluck, and geniuses Alicia Gordon, Eugenie Furniss, and Erin Malone. Also to Charlotte Mendelson at Headline Review for her good humor and enthusiasm.

To Brian McLendon for ongoing good deeds.

To the good people at Houghton Mifflin, especially Janet Silver, Lori Glazer, Megan Wilson, Libby Edelson, and Jayne Yaffe Kemp.

And a paragraph unto herself for Jane Rosenman, dear editor: nothing but shining hours.